The Band of Starlit Waters

BRAD BUSSIE

DEDICATION

For Morgan and Thomas,
Two friends gone too soon
For my son Tanner,
Who has the wonder of story in his eyes

PROLOGUE

Shade cackled with glee as the tower exploded and rained down flaming rubble and what he hoped was a twitching corpse to the beach below. He no longer cared if Tyler died. He would find other ways to secure his hold on the Temple of Spero and the city of Moonlit Waters.

His footing slipped as the fighter roared past and strafed the transport with heavy weapons blazing. Most of the bridge had been destroyed, but a few charred monitors remained. The stream of information on one of the smoldering screens was grim. The ship's structure was severely compromised, and the engines were failing.

He had made his point.

The fighter hammered the transport again, and he felt the ship lurch to the side.

Shade paused for a moment.

Why did the fighter avoid targeting the bridge?

"Allen, get us out of here," he shouted over the wind.

Shade felt the ship turn slowly and braced himself as the craft accelerated. He stared at the monitor again and clucked his tongue in annoyance. They would not make it to Teka in this condition.

"Find us somewhere to set down, preferably out of the weapons range of Arral," Shade shouted as the wind became a shrieking stream of compressed air. He fought his way down the decking and entered the ship through the charred blast doors. He took a last look at the shattered bridge, wondering if any of his Immortal Guard survived, and hammered the hatch release with his fist.

With the wind and noise sealed away, he took a steadying breath.

"Master, I have identified a chain of islands suitable to land on. I must inform you, it will be an unassisted descent. We will be out of range of the coastal defenses momentarily," said Allen's mechanical voice.

"Good," Shade said, smoothing his wild, windblown hair. He could only imagine what Allen meant by unassisted descent, but he imagined it would be more crashing than landing.

There was no way Tyler could have survived the blast. Shade had witnessed and caused enough death in his millennia of existence. He had even died himself once or twice. Tyler's horrified face would forever reside in his mind, and it brought a smile to his face as he strode down the corridor, making his way to engineering.

The once neatly maintained corridor had become a minefield of shattered deck plating, ruptured power conduits, and dangling wiring that sparked and smoked. The bombardment from the Temple of Spero, as well as the Golem, had gutted much of Croyan's vessel. The image of Tyler slowly faded, and he was left with a troubling feeling. In his anger and haste, what had he really accomplished?

Judging by the empty corridors of the ship and what he had made out from the chaos on the beach, his army had not fared as well against the Acreans as he had predicted. The enemy had become far more potent with the VAST in the last several hundred years, but that wasn't what was bothering him. A lone woman on the beach, hair flying wildly, destroying everything that fell under her terrible gaze, nagged at him. The power she wielded was something else entirely.

Shade felt the ship lurch to the side, and this time, it did not right itself back to center. One of the stabilizers must have failed. He didn't want to lose this ship entirely. It would take him centuries to scavenge the parts necessary to fix other wrecks he knew about across the globe. The darkness within him was clawing at his insides, urging him on. He had the distinct impression he no longer had centuries.

The thought was terrifying.

He brushed the human emotion aside and quickened his pace to engineering. Several parts of the grated floor were missing as he walked. He could see the glittering ocean below but could not feel the wind. A thin, shimmering shield strained visibly, barely containing the atmosphere within the transport.

The ship lurched again, and he staggered, catching himself on an exposed piece of ruptured paneling. The panel was polished to a mirror sheen, and he looked at his reflection. He did so love his eyes, like chips of dark obsidian. This time he found green eyes staring back at him, and the reflection of his face twisted, and his own mouth sneered, and his voice bellowed, "You killed my best friend!"

It had been nine hundred years since the pitiful wretch within him had wrested enough control to surface and command the body. Shade felt himself about to lose a power struggle against a presence he thought long cowed. He gripped the panel in both hands and closed his eyes, concentrating. The darkness roiled within him, and he heard the man he had once been scream in agony.

Shade wasn't sure how long he stood in the corridor, hunched over a broken panel. When he did open his eyes and stand tall again, the battle was most certainly won. The pitiful wretch was locked away again.

"Master, beginning our descent," Allen's voice crackled over the badly damaged ship speakers.

"Keep us in one piece!" Shade shouted, his voice emerging from his lips with a croak. He coughed to clear his throat and hacked painfully into his palm. Green and black fluid covered his hand and dribbled down his lips.

He continued down the broken corridor and staggered again as the ship creaked and swung haphazardly from side to side. One of the thrusters must have been firing erratically. It took him far longer than he expected to reach engineering. The combination of damaged corridors, legs that felt like he was walking through a mire, and someone's less than optimal piloting further darkened his mood. When he finally tumbled into engineering and locked his gaze on Allen, he knew they were in trouble.

Appendages whirled in a frenzy as the suspended torso of Allen sloshed in a tank of foul liquid. The cylindrical, opaque housing that surrounded his body still bore signs of recent repair. The chariot that kept the engineer mobile spat smoke and sparks from various damaged sections. Battle had found everyone aboard, it seemed.

At the sound of Shade's entry, Allen turned and examined him with sightless eyes. His human eyes had long since rotted away, leaving the empty sockets bound tightly by a visor that glittered with an inner light.

"Master, you are damaged," Allen said, his voice modulator sounding like it had seen better days. "I am confused. The Master does not get damaged."

Shade snorted and waved his hand in a dismissive gesture.

"How many remain on board?" Shade asked. He couldn't be bothered to search the darkness for them himself.

Allen turned away and rapidly tapped his spidery appendages on several consoles at once.

"Five, including us, remain on board," he said.

Shade paused for a moment, accepting the news slowly.

"The survivors are Immortal Guard," Allen said. He continued his task of keeping them in the sky while Shade took the only intact chair and sat heavily with a sigh.

"Well, that's something at least," Shade said, his voice a hoarse whisper.

The ship lurched suddenly and began to lose altitude steadily. Allen was a blur of movement, tapping screens at inhuman speeds. Alarms blared, and the lights in engineering flickered and went out. Red emergency lighting clicked on just as all of the screens flickered and went dark. The hard-won core from the derelict vessel that Bulca and her brood had sacrificed themselves to obtain disappeared behind an automated blast door that slammed into place.

Shade raised an eyebrow. They really were going to land *unassisted*.

He sensed the ground approaching at an alarming rate and smoothed his dark hair with barely trembling fingers. He glanced down at his torn and dirty robes covered in stains of unknown origins. He must have looked a mess.

The ship impacted the ground in catastrophic fashion. To call what happened a landing would be like calling sudden and violent unconsciousness a lullaby. The darkness within Shade responded sluggishly as the chair he sat in shattered into shrapnel. He tumbled through the air and collided savagely with the far wall of engineering. Allen faired far worse.

Spindly appendages from Allen's chariot bent and cracked as he bounced first off the ceiling and then against several control panels. Glass, polymer, and fragments of metal swarmed through the air like angry bees. Tubes that transferred life-giving fluids tore and spurted green ichor against the crumbling deck plating. The cables suspending Allen in his cylindrical prison snapped on one side, beating him mercilessly against the glass.

The swarm of airborne debris hammered Shade as the transport rolled repeatedly. A thin shield of darkness formed against his skin and turned anything that touched it to ash. The wall behind him smoked and groaned, and one final flip of the ship forced him painfully through the wall and into the corridor beyond. He bounced and skidded against the ceiling, which had rapidly become the floor. The transport was certainly upside down, and Shade howled with mad laughter as he shot down the long corridor like a bullet exiting the barrel of a gun.

1 – HOLD FAST

Thomas groaned as the reanimation cocktail of drugs or "juice" hit his veins. Little study had been done on repeated cold sleep and waking. He figured he had repeated this same cycle hundreds of times, maybe even a thousand times. His watch seemed endless.

His eyes fluttered open, and the cryogenic lid to his chamber swung open with a slight yawn of cold mist.

"Good morning, Lieutenant," a voice said. Thomas waited patiently as the drugs did their work on his system before venturing a reply.

"Hello Morgan, status report?" he said.

The AI paused far longer than usual.

Thomas sat up and looked around. Everything was as it should be. None of the instruments showed caution levels or abnormalities. He tapped his wrist, and a virtual display pulled up. He had been asleep less than six months.

"Morgan, why did you wake me?"

The AI flickered into existence before him, having the same posture as always. Morgan stood tall with his arms behind him in what Thomas called his "philosopher's" pose.

"Sir, there has been a development," Morgan said. "Commander Tor is alive."

A flood of emotion threatened to overwhelm Thomas's fragile system. He had been watching and waiting for a moment like this for hundreds of years. To Thomas, only ten biological years had passed. At first, he had stayed awake for months at a time. He had cycled to staying awake for only a few days every year when he was sure no one was coming to the rescue. He had been naive. How could anyone have possibly come? Without the jump gate deployed, no one could.

"Have you spoken with him?" Thomas asked eagerly.

Morgan looked troubled. "I had him on the bridge of the *Valkyrie* for a moment, but his life sign vanished a short time later. Too many of our satellites have been compromised to get a good reading. There has been significant weapons fire in recent days and several large explosions."

Thomas balled his fists.

Croyan.

More accurately, the abomination that Croyan had become. By all indications and recorded conversations, the man he had been was long dead, and something else wore his skin. Something that enjoyed tormenting the living.

"What can we do, Morgan?" Thomas asked.

The AI flickered slightly as his processor assessed the situation.

"We observe, Lieutenant, as we have done for centuries, and when Commander Tor arrives, we complete the mission," Morgan said. "But we need you awake when the call comes, and if I know Commander Tor, it will be soon."

Thomas brought himself upright on his barely feeling legs and took a steadying breath. Morgan was unable to give him the access he needed to make a real difference in the people's lives on the planet below. The command codes had only been given to a select few, and with the order of succession broken with Croyan, there was little that could be done without another officer. Two keys to launch the missile as the old military adage went.

"We will be ready," Thomas said, taking a shaky step towards the rehabilitation module that connected to the officer's stasis chamber. Recovery always went faster when he forced himself to work out. A long row of workout machines faced windows displaying the yawning expanse of space and the Acrean surface below. Thomas walked stiffly and chose a machine at random. There should have been thirty others working out beside him, but he was alone as always.

The shining planet below reminded him of what was at stake. He began a slow walk on the workout machine and stared absently out the window. Debris littered space as far as his eyes could see. It rotated around the planet with the *Spero* several times a day. On increasingly rare occurrences, some of the debris would collide and hurtle away or come crashing down to the planet in a fireball. How many people were still trapped and slumbering out there?

Information on exactly what had happened was classified. Thomas was woken only after the catastrophe had taken place. Four habitation modules had made the journey with the *Spero*. One had landed safely as intended, the second broke apart and sank into the fathomless depths of the Acrean oceans, the third exploded on drop and continued to tumble aimlessly in the debris cloud around the *Spero*. The fourth and final module was still attached to the ship but cut off from Thomas by the ship's security lockdown. All the help he needed was only a few decks away.

Morgan had become, in effect, his prison warden.

The feeling gradually returned to Thomas's legs, and he broke out in a light sweat. Sweating was good. It meant he hadn't done irreparable metabolic damage through repeated suspended animation cycles. Maybe this time, he could stay awake permanently. All of his hopes were riding on Tyler Ryan Tor, Commander of the UEA *Centaur*. He continued to stare out the window and promised himself he would walk by the hangar later and enjoy the sight of the sleeping vanguard, moored within the cavernous hold of the *Spero*. A single ship had survived and brought them safely to this part of space, and it sat waiting until it was needed again.

Thomas shook his head, bringing himself back to the present. He was sweating profusely and breathing hard.

Best not overdo it, he thought.

He wandered the halls to the quarters he had claimed as his own, took a quick shower, shaved, and changed into his duty uniform. He stared at his reflection in the mirror, noticing a few more gray hairs in his self-cut brown locks. Time had slowed for him, but it was catching up. His hard hazel eyes that reminded him of his father's, who was now long dead, stared back at him. He still thought of his family often and wondered if the colony ship they had boarded had arrived where it was supposed to. If disaster had befallen the *Spero*, he could only imagine what happened to the other two ships. He wondered if he would ever hear the fate of the *Spero's* sister ships *Virtus* and *Animus*.

"Lieutenant," Morgan said, interrupting his thoughts.

He switched off the mirror light and took a deep breath. "Yes, Morgan?"

"Maintenance is required in engineering," the AI said.

Thomas sighed. This was his life. Keep the ship running, monitor the plight of the people below he could not help, and wait. He smoothed his uniform and put a smile on his face. It could be worse, right? At least the lifts still functioned, and he didn't have to crawl down endless ladders to engineering.

He left his quarters and took the long way to engineering to give his legs extra exercise. He always slept better after waking up from hibernation when he had consistent physical activity. There was nothing quite like having insomnia with a body that felt like it had pulled hard gravity for a week. He wandered aimlessly for a time, in no particular hurry towards the central lift system.

Thomas found himself approaching a darkened part of the *Spero* that was exposed to a hard vacuum. Oxygen and moisture were particularly damaging to a ship's systems, so most of the ship was kept preserved under sanctuary protocols. The passageway he was walking down ended at a blast door with a single squat window. He approached the door and leaned against it to peer through the window. A long dark corridor greeted him silently.

What was he expecting to find?

Thomas imagined smiling colonists roaming the corridor, chatting excitedly about their journey. The daydream was fleeting and the dark hallway beyond swallowed the imagined light like the snuffing of a candle. He sighed and resumed his trek to engineering, this time taking the direct route to the central lift system.

The lifts would have been packed with people twenty-four hours a day had the mission succeeded. Now, a cavernous room with hundreds of translucent tubes lay partially illuminated and silent. Morgan kept the lights and energy signatures of the *Spero* near undetectable. There was no telling who was listening out in the void.

Thomas checked the long-range sensor outposts often when he was awake. In the nine hundred years since orbital insertion, nothing more than a stray comet had registered. Should the alien race that had triggered the mass exodus from Earth ever find them here, the *Spero* and Acrea would be dust.

"One problem at a time," Thomas grumbled to himself.

He found the engineering tube with little effort and called the lift with a touch of his palm on the waiting pedestal scanner next to the tube. His stomach growled and he patted his belly like a favorite companion.

"A little work and then the commissary, I promise," he said to the empty chamber. Talking to his stomach would be considered crazy.

Morgan was always monitoring for any signs of crazy.

The lift arrived soundlessly through the tube with a flash of light and a soft chime which announced its arrival. A double door split down the middle and hissed on either side, revealing a spacious interior.

Thomas entered and chose a seat at random from the several benches that stretched around the cylindrical space. He stared sadly at the occupancy limit sign.

50 passengers maximum, the sign read.

He swept his gaze around the empty lift and then settled his sullen eyes on the floor as the doors hissed closed.

The decks fell away with the silent motion of the lift. Thomas found himself daydreaming again when Morgan flickered into existence.

"Heavy weapon detonation on the planet's surface," he said without the urgency Thomas would have expected.

"Source?" Thomas asked, springing to his feet.

Morgan paused and froze in place for a moment, processing.

"Two warheads impacting the *Valkyrie* shield," Morgan said.

Thomas felt a wave of shock and a sickening sense he had been in this situation before. The last time warheads had detonated on the planet's surface they lost thousands of people and three quarters of the surviving population were plunged into the dark ages.

"Commander Tor is on the field. I am picking up a Golem-class fighter powering up," Morgan said.

"What the hell is going on!" Thomas shouted. He began to pace the lift, clenching his fists. What he wouldn't give to actually fight something. Instead, he stared at a slightly transparent artificial intelligence that looked completely calm.

"Lieutenant Commander Croyan is aboard the attacking vessel," Morgan said.

Thomas ceased his pacing. Morgan had sounded almost smug.

"They can't kill each other," Thomas groaned. "We need them!"

Morgan paused, processing the situation.

"What can we do?" Thomas asked in a whisper.

"Hailing the UEA *Conrad*, stand by." Morgan said, flicking out of existence.

The lift continued its swift path towards engineering as if nothing was out of the ordinary. Thomas had never spoken to Conrad directly, given his power restrictions. Morgan and the other AI could have a year's worth of conversation in a fraction of a breath. All information was secondhand, and in a time like this, it made Thomas angry.

Lights continued to flash by as the lift floated smoothly through the tube. Thomas wondered about the likelihood of another officer being recovered. The debris field from the failed orbital insertion was enormous. More people potentially ringed the planet in cold sleep than lived on its surface. So many things had gone wrong.

Morgan appeared again, this time near the double door of the lift. "Conrad is unresponsive," he said.

Thomas swore softly and was about to say something when Morgan paused as if processing an event.

"Warhead impact, *Valkyrie* shield failure," Morgan said. "Commander Tor is off the grid. His life sign is negligible." Thomas noticed for the first time that the AI looked troubled.

A short time passed, with Thomas staring expectantly at Morgan's flickering image. The lift was silent, having reached engineering. Had he missed the arrival chime?

"A small group of survivors have retrieved him and are moving him swiftly to the castle," Morgan said.

Thomas held his breath.

"He is alive," Morgan said.

Thomas exhaled sharply and hung his head in his hands.

"We need to talk to someone down there. Anyone! Conrad can't be the only one listening," Thomas said. He didn't even try to keep the anguish out of his voice.

"The power requirements would exceed stealth parameters," Morgan replied smoothly.

"To hell with stealth parameters! Tyler. Needs. Our. Help. NOW!"

Thomas wasn't exactly sure when he had gotten to his feet or why he thought screaming inches from the face of the avatar of an artificial intelligence would actually do any good. He was fairly certain that if the avatar had any substance, he would be shaking it.

The image of Morgan flickered, processing.

"A narrow beam, with high power, would be within safety limits," Morgan said.

Thomas, anger fading, threw himself back into his seat with a sigh. "Who is even left with anything to hear us, Morgan?"

"Processing," Morgan said, flickering out of existence.

The lift door opened silently and bathed Thomas in the harsh light from engineering. Thomas stood, knowing it would take Morgan some time to weigh all of the options. Power consumption was always the limiting factor on the *Spero*. That and the fact that he didn't have access to most of the ship's systems.

Thomas emerged from the lift and ignored the marvel that was engineering. A sweeping cavern of glittering consoles, panels, and an enormous glowing reactor filled the space. The lift doors closed silently behind him, and he walked mechanically toward the maintenance display board. His mind wasn't really on the task at hand. He had waited centuries for a day like today.

Everything was riding on Commander Tor. Thomas had worked on the plan for weeks after the initial chaos of slamming three out of four habitation modules into a decaying Acrean orbit. Something about the atmosphere's composition had shredded the modules as they descended. One module had slammed into the expansive Acrean Ocean, the second disintegrated during the descent, and the third landed safely near what was now known as Moonlit Waters. Intense scans from state-of-the-art equipment on the *Spero* had never found what in the atmosphere had caused the cataclysm.

Thomas stared at the maintenance screen, not really seeing it. He was preoccupied with time and loss. No one should have to watch and wait for nine hundred years for anything. The wait could finally be over, but he needed to get Commander Tor the help he desperately needed. Morgan had to find a way.

He sighed and rubbed eyes that had become tired. He tapped the maintenance screen and found directions to the power conduit that needed purging. He tapped the image of the conduit and turned to see the floor lighting, blinking in the direction he was to travel. It looked like he was going to the other side of the reactor.

The reactor on the *Spero* was a marvel of engineering. The power emitted from the core within was said to have the same energy as a star. Only four reactors had been made, one for each colony ship and one for the battleship known as the *Luna*. The battleship had bought humanity the time it needed to flee the Sol system. The physics behind the reactor pointed at an endless supply of energy. There was no way to turn it off.

With the reactor's power needing to go *somewhere*, the conduits throughout the ship often needed manual purging. Had the ship been operating with all systems full, the conduits would flow freely. The *Spero* hadn't been built to hide. It was a capital ship built for war and humanity's ultimate survival.

Thomas found the panel covering the conduit and removed it with little effort. He was in a side passage that housed various engineering equipment. He leaned the panel against the wall and searched for the handle that would purge the conduit. He located the handle and pulled down on it sharply. The satisfying hum of flowing power answered his work.

"Maintenance complete," said Morgan's disembodied voice.

"How is that processing going?" Thomas asked, replacing the panel over the serviced conduit.

Morgan flickered into existence over his shoulder, standing in his classic philosopher's pose.

"Lieutenant, I have made contact with Pelagos. Conrad provided the relay," Morgan said.

Thomas raised an eyebrow. He had never heard of anyone named Pelagos. "I am unfamiliar with Pelagos. Who is that?"

Morgan quirked a simulated smile, which looked strange on his usually impassive face. "Not a who, but a where," he said.

"On the surface, I would imagine," Thomas said absently.

"Not exactly," Morgan said.

Thomas stopped and waited expectantly. Morgan stared back at him. Thomas raised an eyebrow, motioned with one of his hands, and placed a particularly annoyed look on his face.

"Pelagos is located in a system of caverns beneath the great Acrean Ocean."

Thomas's breath caught in his throat. He had just been thinking about the cataclysm and the colony modules.

"Impossible. Why wasn't I told? Did the module that crashed into the ocean survive?" Thomas demanded.

"Very possible. It wasn't relevant. Partially, yes," Morgan said.

Thomas closed his eyes, leaned his head back, and exhaled loudly. He was about to lose his temper.

Morgan seemed to recognize the pending danger and held up a hand in concession.

"There was nothing we could have done for them, Lieutenant," Morgan said.

"But I could have talked to someone. If they are able to receive you now, I could have talked to a real person, Morgan!" Thomas snapped.

"It is unlikely your mental state would have lasted as long as it has with that level of human interaction," Morgan said.

Thomas paused before he shouted the expletive that was forming on the tip of his tongue. Morgan was probably right. If he knew there were still people with technology that Shade hadn't twisted, he would have stopped at nothing to get to them.

Morgan waited.

"What exactly does contact with Pelagos mean?" Thomas asked.

2 – ALL OR NOTHING

Razmal burst through the door at the sound of voices. Tyler sat naked from the waist up on what everyone had been sure was going to be his deathbed. A rather tall woman with wet-looking black hair and glittering skin stood near the window. His eyes were obviously playing tricks on him as he couldn't seem to focus on her for more than a moment before her skin shifted its pattern and color, which deflected his gaze. She wore a peculiar lavender-colored shell mask that looked to be straight out of the ocean and a quicksilver ribbon slithered around her middle.

Razmal cleared his throat and paused in the doorway. "Uh, hi," he said, his voice cracking with emotion.

Tyler smiled. Razmal noticed that the color had returned to his face.

"Razmal, meet our guest," he said, sweeping a hand as if to present her.

"Crylona," the woman said, her accented voice muffled by the seashell mask. She stayed near the window and looked ready to bolt out of it at the slightest provocation. Razmal stepped into the room and quietly closed the door behind him.

The room looked just as he had left it, minus Crylona and Tyler. It was a sparsely furnished circular room with one window, a bed, and a washbasin set on a ledge near the door. It took him a moment to realize that the quarterstaff that Tyler was so fond of was missing. He turned an accusing stare on Crylona, noticing how the ribbon that flowed around her had the same sheen as Tyler's staff.

"This is Starmist," she said, following his eyes with her own and putting her hands on her hips at his accusing stare.

Tyler seemed to sense the contention and grinned. "All is well, Razmal. Polaris is safe."

Razmal looked from Crylona to Tyler and back again. "So, how did she get in here, and what does she want?" Razmal asked, his tone sounding more firm than he had intended.

"I think we were just getting to that," Tyler said, his voice sounding tired.

Crylona stood quietly for a moment as if gathering her thoughts. "What is important is that the Sleeper lives," she said.

"Thanks to you. Please, call me Tyler," he said.

"Tyler," she said, squinting at the unfamiliar name.

"He was Tyrant when I first met him," Razmal added, spreading his hands helplessly.

Crylona cocked her head in what appeared to be curiosity.

"A long story for another time," Tyler said. "Please, why have you come?"

Crylona squared her shoulders and tossed her hair as she stood at attention. "I, Crylona of Pelagos, come with a desperate plea. Our council seeks an audience with the Slee... err… Tyler. Our very way of life is being threatened."

Her words sounded rehearsed and uncomfortable.

"Let me guess: Shade?" Razmal interrupted.

Crylona made a strange gesture as if to ward off evil spirits.

"No, but we do know of the shadow man. Our plight has been centuries in the making. The denizens of the Deep have grown bold, and we can no longer hold them back from our cities," Crylona said.

"Just exactly where are your cities? I thought Moonlit Waters was the only major settlement on Arral?" Tyler asked.

"True," she said, staring down at the floor. "Our cities are not on Arral.

Razmal looked at her in disbelief. "So where exactly are they? In the sky?"

She locked him with a stare that chilled his bones. "The Deep," she said, motioning out the window to the ocean lit by Yalonia's muddy light.

"Impossible," Razmal whispered.

"Please, Tyler, may I show you something?" Crylona asked, creeping beside his bedside.

"It will be faster than talking," she said.

Tyler nodded and seemed to realize he wasn't wearing a shirt for the first time.

"I… err… should probably put something on," he stammered.

"No need," she said, touching his bare chest with her slender shimmering hand.

The thin silver ribbon that swirled around her middle crept down her arm and pooled around her hand. The liquid seemed to hesitate for a moment before pouring itself over his exposed chest. The four torchstones set at even intervals around the room dimmed, and a ghostly radiance began to leak from Tyler's eyes. Razmal became aware of the sound of the rhythmic motion of waves on a distant shore and felt himself being pulled towards the bed by an unseen force.

"I see it," Tyler said in awe, his eyes wide and staring.

"The balanite makes this possible," Crylona whispered.

"It is so beautiful," Tyler said. "This place you are showing me. It is familiar."

"For a Sleeper, it should be," she said.

Something seemed to occur to Tyler, and his jaw worked soundlessly for a moment.

"Habitation modules, grow lights, and domes?" Tyler asked, shaking his head as if struggling to accept the knowledge. "How long?"

"Centuries," Crylona said with a sidelong look at Razmal. Tendrils of silver crawled up her hand and back up her arm. She removed her hand from Tyler's chest, and the light in the room returned to normal.

"Many of the early records have been lost," Crylona said, taking a step back and sighing with what Razmal assumed was fatigue.

"I am the first to make the journey to the surface in recent memory. Only with Starmist is it possible to come in such haste." The silver ribbon flowing around her middle seemed to perk up at its name but then settled back into its rhythmic flow when it was obviously not needed. The weariness in her voice spoke volumes to how difficult the journey must have been.

"Why now? What has changed?" Tyler asked.

Crylona began to pace the room, never straying far from the window. "You, Sleeper. I was sent for you alone. It cannot be a coincidence that you needed me, and we needed you in turn. Our reactor can no longer support our city. The shield that we have depended on to keep the water and denizens of the Deep at bay is failing."

"How did you know to look for me?" Tyler asked.

Crylona stopped pacing and crossed her arms under her ample bosom. "You made quite the impression on Conrad."

Tyler leaned his head back and chuckled softly. "I knew I loved that ship. We didn't get to spend nearly enough time together."

"We don't hear from him often, but he has been helping to work on our power issues," Crylona said.

"So I am the solution to that problem?" Tyler asked.

Crylona looked troubled for a moment, her eyes narrowing as if searching for the right words.

"You are the key. Conrad was able to point us to a vault of lost artifacts. You can open the door."

Razmal snorted and quickly covered his mouth. Tyler was always opening doors for people.

Crylona shot him an annoyed look, her almond-brown eyes flashing.

Tyler swung his legs over the bed and stood slowly to his feet.

"First things first. Razmal, the battle… What happened?" Tyler asked.

"We won. But the cost was high. Shade got away, but not before that metal creature you awakened did massive damage to his ship," Razmal said. "You can still see the smoke trail heading out to sea."

Crylona stood respectfully silent as Tyler stretched and yawned loudly. He shook his head sadly and dropped his arms to his sides. "Shade," Tyler growled.

Crylona made a gesture to ward off evil spirits.

"More accurately, Lt. Commander Croyan, my first officer," Tyler said, a heavy sigh escaping his lips.

Razmal didn't know what a first officer was, but the fact that Shade had a name and Tyler knew it was blasphemy enough for one day.

"Tyran… err… Tyler, we need to talk to Celest," Razmal said, fixing Crylona with what he hoped was a no-nonsense look.

Tyler nodded, looked down at his bare chest, and frowned. His gaze swept the room and settled on a cloth shirt of the local style.

"I need a uniform," Tyler said, striding over to the neatly folded, rough-spun shirt in one of the small alcoves. He pulled the tan-colored shirt over his head. The fabric was barely large enough to contain his broad shoulders and heavily muscled torso. Razmal chuckled at his friend.

"My armor?" Tyler asked.

"Burned from your body, I am afraid. Very little was left when they brought you to the castle," Razmal said, trying not to grin at the ridiculous-looking shirt that strained against Tyler's thick biceps. He missed Tyler's striking and imposing figure armed with his staff, clad in metal armor and a gleaming helm with a fine cloak billowing in the breeze. Tyler in a too-small shirt was borderline blasphemous.

Tyler itched his ribs.

"I miss my sleep suit. I was really starting to get used to it," Tyler said.

Razmal wasn't sure what a sleep suit was, but he assumed it had been the blackened under skin of armor they had peeled away from his charred flesh.

"Come," Razmal said, beckoning to the chamber door. He turned his gaze on Crylona. "You can use the door this time, lady."

Tyler turned to Crylona and studied her for a moment. "I intend to help you, but first, I need to see this Celest everyone keeps talking about."

Crylona nodded and placed her hands on her hips.

Razmal shrugged at the strange gesture, motioned for them to follow him, and stepped out the door.

The milky-white stones of the tower gleamed in the steady light of torchstones set at even intervals down a short hallway. A spiraling staircase of the same white stone disappeared into the darkness below at the end of the hall. They approached the top step, and Razmal sensed hesitation from Crylona. Tyler, on the other hand, was several well-worn steps down the stairway before he turned back to see what the holdup was. Crylona stood, unmoving.

"I will wait up here," she said, her eyes staring down in the darkness below. Razmal sensed fear and tension coming off of her in waves. The silver ribbon that flowed around her middle remained unchanged. Something told Razmal she wasn't going to be coaxed into going anywhere.

"Please, rest easy. We will be back soon," Razmal said. Since meeting the woman, he allowed kindness to find its way into his voice for the first time.

"You sure?" Tyler called up the steps.

Crylona made a strange signal that looked to convey certainty. "Yes, see you soon," she said before twirling quickly around and padding silently back the way they had come.

"She is an odd one," Razmal said with a sigh.

"You don't know the half of it," Tyler said with a huge grin that touched his grey eyes. "She showed me an impossible world that I still won't believe until I see it with my own eyes."

The two continued down the staircase for a time and reached the bottom. Tyler huffed and stopped for a moment, winded from the exertion. "I never thought a set of stairs would leave me winded," he said. "Especially stairs going down."

Razmal nodded, simply happy that his friend was upright. The bottom of the stairwell was well lit with several torchstones. A single corridor led into the castle grounds. Two hulking figures stood with their backs to Razmal and Tyler. Legionnaires by the look of them. Only the elite guard of Moonlit Waters filled an entryway with both bulk and sheer height. Razmal was fairly certain even Tyler would need to look up to meet one of their steely gazes.

One of the elites became alert to their approach and turned to face them. The guard wore silver carapace armor polished to a mirror shine. A full helm obscured the man's features. He clutched a massive halberd with a bone haft and aqua-colored ax head in both hands. The halberd ax was ground to a razor's edge and looked to have seen recent use. Razmal was certain that this Legionnaire had fought off the recent siege by Shade and his forces.

"Sleeper!" a deep voice from the depths of the helm exclaimed. The second Legionnaire turned quickly and jumped in what looked to be surprise. Both hulking figures dropped to one knee and bowed.

Tyler looked embarrassed and scrubbed his dark hair with one of his hands. "Please, rise. Thank you for protecting me while I slept," he said.

"We feared it was the death sleep," said the second of the Legionnaires. They could have been mirror images of each other. They were the same size, held the same weapons, and possessed the same deep voice. Both stood and slammed giant fists against their carapace-covered chests.

Tyler nodded, and the guards moved to either side of the passageway, leaving a hair's breadth for him and Razmal to squeeze past. The Legionnaires smelled like fine, refreshing soap.

Razmal led them into the courtyard and to a sky filled with billions upon billions of glittering stars. Castle Forgotten loomed large above them, Yalonia having risen behind the grand fortress and making it look even more spectacular.

"Is Celest inside?" Tyler asked, his voice hushed.

"She is in the castle's heart below, in the crystal chamber. Come, it isn't far," Razmal said.

They passed several more Legionnaires that repeated the kneeling, bowing, and fists against chests. Tyler was gracious and accommodating on each occasion. Razmal, on the other hand, was fighting the urge to roll his eyes and grumble about time being short. Something about Crylona and the urgency in her eyes and voice had affected him. An entire race lost beneath the waves needed the Sleeper.

Razmal led them into an open mouth of a wide series of tunnels at the base of Castle Forgotten. Tyler commented that as they began a gradual descent, there was no way the tunnels were natural, but he was struggling to see how anything could have crafted them either. Intricate designs covered every available surface of the tunnel. The designs were complicated runes that glowed blue, silver, and white in the near darkness. Razmal had never given the glowing symbols a second thought. They looked the way they always did.

Tyler walked mechanically next to him, his mouth gawking, and small surprised sounds escaped his throat. He reached out and nearly touched the smooth wall before looking at Razmal as if to ask permission. Razmal shrugged his shoulders, indifferent. Tyler touched the shimmering symbols and grinned. After a time, they emerged from the rune-lined tunnels and arrived at the vestibule.

The vestibule was a cylindrical-shaped room that climbed upwards and out of sight. The ceiling was shrouded in perpetual darkness, which gave the vestibule a vastness beyond its actual size. An archway stood nearby, lined with multicolored crystals that cast a myriad of colors across the smooth, polished floor.

The two approached the archway, and Tyler stopped as several symbols appeared on the arch's surface. The symbols glowed an angry-looking crimson color, and the air around them heated painfully. He paused and inclined his head as if listening to something from far away. He closed his eyes and fully extended his right arm out to his side. A ball of quicksilver raced to fill his palm, filling from thin rivers of flowing metal that coursed across his chest and down his arm. Within moments, Polaris thumped heavily against the polished crystal floor.

"Something is barring Polaris from entering," Tyler said.

Razmal shrugged and motioned to an alcove cut into the wall next to the archway.

"A safe place then?" Razmal asked.

Tyler nodded and leaned Polaris into the alcove. The surface of the staff rippled for a moment and then hardened into smooth metal. The crimson symbols on the archway faded, and the room's temperature cooled considerably. Razmal took a steadying breath and clapped Tyler on the shoulder. They walked under the archway together and crossed into the heart of Castle Forgotten.

Razmal blinked rapidly for a moment as his equilibrium upended. His breath came in labored gasps, and he found himself bent at the waist with his hands on his knees, struggling to remain standing. He stared at the crystal floor and noted his reflection on its polished surface. He looked terrible. It took him a moment to muster the energy to stand tall and take in his surroundings.

He was back in front of the archway.

Polaris lay against the wall where Tyler had left it. The archway in front of him glowed with a myriad of symbols that danced across its surface. Razmal knew if he approached the arch again, he wouldn't be standing afterward. He sighed and backed away from the shimmering archway, swallowing hard and trying not to feel rejected.

It was painfully clear that Celest wanted to speak with Tyler alone.

3 – STRANGE NOTES

Roarc had lost track of how long he ran. The silvery potion that sang in his veins was a distant memory. He was living on pure adrenaline now. Food and water meant little when he was running for his very life.

He had turned to look behind him only once after encountering the Herald. The sight of the Gale unleashing a thunderous blast that looked to incinerate a wide swath of coastline had been the final urging his legs needed to propel him onward. Several days and nights had come and gone, but his legs carried him deeper into the untamed wilds of Arral. He was heading steadily away from the coast and keeping the mountains on his left.

When his legs finally gave out, it was a surprise. One moment he was cresting the ridge covered in wavy purple grass, and the next, he was tumbling down the far side into a shadowy depression. He landed hard on his back, and the breath blasted from his lungs. Sparks danced before his eyes, and he gasped in pain from the impact of his wall shield against his spine. His torchstone had spun away into the darkness during his fall, plunging him into near dark.

He had been running for days without rest, pursued by denizens of the hill country. He heard them growling, crashing, and howling just outside his view. Only once had he stopped to face his pursuers. Five corpses, at least one day behind, nurtured the soil. It had been enough to show them he meant business, but the large numbers pacing just outside his torchstone light had shown him how brief and fleeting his victory had been.

With his abrupt stop, he could hear the creatures surrounding him. He was fatigued beyond words, and it felt amazing to simply lay on his back. Maybe it wouldn't hurt that badly to be ripped apart by beasts. It would be quick, at least. He closed his eyes against the death that he knew would undoubtedly come.

Not today half-giant, a voice sounded in his mind.

Roarc sat up with a start. That voice had been in his head once before. He groped in the darkness and smiled when his hand closed on the haft of his maul. If he were to die, he would die fighting. Let the beasts tell hushed stories of "The Great Roarc" to scare their children for centuries to come. He shrugged his wall shield painfully off his injured shoulder and looped it securely over his heavily muscled forearm.

The stars above sparkled brilliantly as the first pungent smelling creature leaped from above, obscuring the twinkling lights with its bulk. It dropped like a stone into the depression where Roarc waited, and he met it with a fully extended maul that split its skull with a sickening crack. The creature didn't even bellow in pain like Roarc expected it would. It simply crashed to the ground unmoving.

Roarc spun his maul and banged it against his wall shield in one fluid motion.

"Where are you, wolf?" Roarc asked the darkness.

Cries of pain and surprise answered his question. Roarc pressed himself against the crumbling hill to guard his vulnerable back as two creatures dropped into the hole with him. One was trying to hold in its torn guts with a clawed paw, while the other bled profusely from a gash in its throat. A piercing howl split the night, and both creatures winced in unison at its mournful tone.

Roarc, thankful for the opportunity, swung his maul and caved in the heaving chest of the creature with the torn middle. It thumped lifeless and joined the one already facedown in the dirt. The remaining beast leaped forward and slashed viciously at Roarc. Its wicked claws screeched against his well-placed wall shield. Slash after desperate slash sparked against the shield's surface as Roarc grunted and leaned into the attacks. He looked down as one of the creature's clawed feet stepped past the shield's barrier. Roarc hammered the lip of his shield downward and grinned as bones crumpled. The beast hopped amusingly on one foot, yowling in agony. A savage chop of Roarc's maul ended its plight.

More enemies spilled over the gap into the hovel. Roarc began to worry as his shield increased in weight with each passing moment and his maul moved more sluggishly in his grip. Fatigue was taking its toll and he was making mistakes. Blood trickled from several wounds on his arms and he could feel a nasty gash bleeding freely on his left leg. He stumbled as he felled another beast and caught a painful blow to his chestplate.

He could smell the soil as he staggered back and clutched a handful of dirt in his shield hand. His wall shield tumbled heavily to the rocky ground and he leaned weakly against his maul. He pressed his hand against a great river of blood from his arm and smeared four lines across his face with his fingers. The smell of copper assaulted his nostrils, and he felt the battle rage spark and then cool. He was simply too tired.

"Anytime now, wolf," Roarc said, sweat and blood dripping into his eyes.

Beasts tumbled over each other to fill the small space in front of him. It seemed half-giant was some kind of delicacy with the effort this particular pack was putting into hunting him. What had he ever done to earn such determination from mindless beasts?

An image of dead Felions and berserker rage sank a cold feeling into his belly. The light was far too dim to verify his suspicion, but the smell that clung to the hovel around him was unmistakable. The pack that hunted him knew his scent and would soon have its revenge.

An enormous figure pushed aside several of its smaller brethren to come to an arm's width from Roarc. Yellow eyes glowed fiercely to meet his own hard golden stare. He knew those eyes would be the last thing he would ever see.

"C'mon big fella," Roarc said with a rumble. "But know this, I will make you work for it."

The pack alpha loomed large before him, standing to its full height. Starlight seemed to brighten around its shadowy form and added an ominous look to its already considerable bulk.

How strange, Roarc thought. *Was this what everyone experienced the moment just before death?*

A strange sound followed by a shower of warm copper-smelling spray gushed over Roarc's face and torso. Another burst of liquid followed by air escaping a torn throat sounded like strange notes from a broken flute. The hulking figure slumped to its knees and pitched backward.

Shield your eyes, said a familiar voice in Roarc's mind.

Roarc closed his eyes tightly and buried his head in the crook of his arm. A quorum of angry hisses and growls filled the night.

His torchstone had been found.

Roarc smelled ozone and felt a breeze tickle his arm. He heard claws ripping through thick hide from multiple directions at once. It was as if an army had come to his aid. He ventured a peek from behind the shelter of the crook of his arm and caught sight of a blurred form ripping two Felions from navel to chin. The furry forms pitched sideways, and the blur of movement winked out of existence, only to reappear and repeat the process on two more of the pack.

The blur was silver, furry, and without a doubt, an Erew.

Roarc's blind blunder into the slight depression had become a night of death and the final resting place for countless beasts. Oddly, it looked as if he would live through the encounter.

Of course you are going to live. I have need of you half-giant, said the silver wolf's voice in his mind.

"Out of my head, wolf," Roarc said, struggling to stand and only managing it because he could prop himself against the crumbling soil at his back.

It's not my fault your thoughts echo around in that massive head of yours, said the wolf's voice in his mind.

How did he do that?

A long, silver-muzzled, lupine face peeked over the edge of the depression and gave him a wolfish grin.

Hello Roarc, said the voice. *We always seem to meet in such desperate circumstances.*

"I was holding my own," Roarc said, his voice sounding weaker than he had imagined. He swept his gaze over the mass of bodies and located his torchstone, shimmering happily in the shattered rib cage of an eviscerated Felion. The walk across the corpses looked to be more than his wobbly legs were willing to provide. He slumped to his knees, feeling utterly spent.

The wolf dropped the short distance from the rim of the depression silently and landed amongst the bodies. He reached down and scooped up the torchstone and flipped the stone, which tumbled through the air. Roarc caught the stone easily and held it close, drinking in its warmth that pulsed in his palm.

A pang of loss twisted painfully in the middle of his chest. Lady Dark had made him feel that same sense of safety and warmth. The image of his lady bathed in a beam of hellish fire haunted him. Who had she become? Where was she now?

Roarc was very tired.

He felt a firm paw on his shoulder and looked up into kind, lupine eyes. He noticed that the eyes held a measure of sadness.

More will come, the wolf's voice echoed in his mind. *I can help if you will allow it.*

Roarc knew he couldn't have stopped himself from toppling over in a light breeze, let alone prevented a teleporting Erew from doing anything he wanted, but he appreciated the gesture.

"Get me out of here," Roarc said, his voice coming out in a raspy whisper. He groped for his maul and wall shield and closed his eyes in gratitude when he found them both.

The wolf slipped an arm under his own and lifted Roarc like a small child to his feet. Blood trickled from several open wounds as the Erew urged him forward with a firm shoulder to lean on. Roarc felt light-headed, and before he knew it was leaning heavily on his companion, his face buried in fur that smelled like loam. He was particularly thankful at that moment to call the wolf an ally.

Roarc half stepped and was half dragged out of the hovel that would undoubtedly have been his tomb. He raised his head briefly and breathed in the cool night air. Yalonia hung large and rust-colored in the sky, painting the grassy landscape in burnt orange light. He swooned slightly and felt the wolf lean into him to keep him from pitching forward.

Hang on, the wolf said in his mind.

The landscape disappeared entirely for a moment, and Roarc felt like he was floating. He knew that they were still moving but at what pace was a mystery. It was like they were walking but moving at a tremendous rate of speed one moment and then at a standstill the next. The light was somewhere between blinding white and complete darkness, and the land around them was featureless. The next sensation Roarc felt was like emerging through a beaded curtain into a cool room.

He leaned against the wolf in front of a massive stone door. The center of the door was engraved with a prominent symbol foreign to Roarc. The symbol looked like a jagged peak surrounded by angry storm clouds.

Rest here, my friend, I will guard you while you recover, said the wolf's voice in his mind.

Roarc collapsed immediately and rolled himself to lean against the cool stone door. His wall shield clanged to the well-packed dirt beneath him, and he laid his maul in his lap. He stared up into the sky and noticed the stars were beginning to disappear from the pre-dawn light. How long had they been traveling?

Roarc sighed and thumped his head against the stone door. His eyelids felt heavy, and he closed them after a time. He hoped no one would try and come in or go out as he had not the strength to move either way. His weariness drained away, and he felt himself twitch slightly and slip into unconsciousness.

***

Roarc opened his eyes, unable to focus on anything. The sounds of insects and rustling grass tickled his senses. Fresh earthy smells assaulted his nose. His back was painfully stiff, and both of his legs had fallen asleep. He rubbed his eyes until they would focus again and looked around.

Judging by the Acrean sun in the sky, it was well past midday. He craned his neck and tried to spot any streaks of silver in the grassland beyond.

"Wolf?" Roarc called out, his voice cracking. When was the last time he had drunk something?

I do have a name, half-giant, the voice rumbled in his mind.

"Zug? Or was it Zarg? You will have to forgive me. It has been a trying couple of days," Roarc said.

Zuh'Erg, came the expected rumble in his mind.

"Close enough," Roarc said, rubbing his face with a calloused hand.

Zuh'Erg appeared through a shifting shaft of light that filtered through long purple grass. He carried a strange-looking stone jug in one of his massive paws and had a variety of what looked to be root vegetables hung over one of his shoulders.

Food and drink for you, Roarc. You must regain your strength for what is to come, the wolf projected.

Zuh'Erg loped over and carefully placed the jug and vegetables next to Roarc's still slumbering thigh.

"Join me?" Roarc offered, poking at the bounty of leafy greens, red-scaled bulbs, and light-brown tubers. Everything looked to have been recently washed.

Zuh'Erg snatched a few of the scaled bulbs and settled back on his haunches. He bit into the scaled skin with a satisfying crunch and chewed slowly.

"I had the impression that your kind only ate meat," Roarc said.

Zuh'Erg shrugged and continued his meal without comment.

Roarc started to eat the leafy greens first, savoring the peppery flavor. He had never had the red-scaled bulbs before, and they had a sour note that he found himself not enjoying. He tossed the remaining bulbs at Zuh'Erg, who nodded in thanks. The light-brown tubers were crunchy, bitter, and just right.

The stone jug dripped with condensation. Roarc lifted it and pulled out its tight stopper of what looked to be wax. He sniffed the dark liquid inside and crinkled his nose. It smelled horrible.

That is a special mix. Better to drink than to smell, Zuh'Erg projected.

Roarc exhaled sharply and raised the jug to his lips. He poured the slightly thick liquid into his mouth and gulped down several gurgling swigs. The wolf was right, it went down better when he didn't breathe. He felt days of bone-weariness veritably melt away the more of the jug he consumed.

"Where did you get this?" Roarc asked, his voice finally sounding strong to his ears. He felt incredible.

A good friend. He owed me a favor.

"I find myself owing you more than I can put into words. I am in your debt, Zuh'Erg. I owe you my life," Roarc said.

The Erew grinned at him with very large and very sharp-looking teeth. You could even call it a wolfish grin.

A debt that you will have the opportunity to repay soon. But please, drink, Zuh'Erg projected.

Roarc didn't need additional urging to finish the jug. Zuh'Erg refused whenever Roarc asked if the wolf wanted any, stating that he was plenty strong without it. When the last of the liquid rolled down Roarc's throat, he finally felt well enough to stand. He used his maul for balance and hoisted himself to his feet.

He retrieved his wall shield, strapped it to his back, and slid his maul into its sheath smoothly. He noticed that his wounds had been tended to while he slept and were nearly mended. Zuh'Erg really did need him for something if he went to the trouble of binding his wounds. But what could he possibly provide that the Erew didn't already possess?

I need your strength, and I don't read half-giant, came the matter-of-fact voice in his mind. *I'm sorry, Roarc, you are veritably shouting your questions at me.*

Roarc cocked his head and narrowed his eyes.

"You are going to have to teach me how to not be such an open book. I don't enjoy someone being able to crawl around in my mind without permission."

That isn't exactly how it works, but I see your point. We will have plenty of time to work on that. First things first, I need you to open something for me, Zuh'Erg projected.

"Point the way," Roarc replied, rubbing his hands together eagerly.

Zuh'Erg pointed a clawed paw at him. Roarc raised an eyebrow and then realized where he was standing. He turned and looked again at the massive stone door with the elaborate rune carving. The mountain loomed large, and the clouds seemed to ebb and flow around its peak.

Roarc began his search, thinking that perhaps wolf paws would be insufficient to work a latch or hidden mechanism. Granted, his half-giant hands were large, but he had far more dexterity in his fingers that an Erew did in its paws. The door fit seamlessly against the structure around it, so much so that Roarc wasn't sure if it opened inward or perhaps even upward.

After a time, Roarc turned to Zuh'Erg and shrugged. "Do you have any hints?"

The Erew mimicked his shrug back at him and sat back on his haunches, waiting.

The Acrean sun climbed steadily through the sky as Roarc ran his hands over every inch of the door, the area around the door, and a fair distance in each direction of the hillside. He could find no visible mechanism to open the door. He found himself back where he started, this time glaring at the rune that taunted him.

He knew the light would soon fade, leaving him groping by the glow of his torchstone.

"Enough of this!" Roarc snapped, pulling his maul from its strap. With a mighty swing, he struck the door squarely in the center of the rune. His maul slammed painfully against the stone, which cracked and groaned against his blow. His hands buzzed as he crashed his maul repeatedly against the stone door, beginning to break large chunks from its previously unmarred surface.

The stone door groaned and shivered for a moment before the weight of what was above the weakened center began to crumble. Much colder air pushed outward from the inside and chilled Roarc's sweat-soaked arms. A shower of dust and debris plumed outward and upward, leaving Roarc covered in fine powder.

He felt a presence beside him and started from the proximity. Zuh'Erg stood tall and proud, without a speck of dust on his illustrious mane.

That's one way to do it, he projected, with the clap of a massive paw on Roarc's shoulder.

4 – EXPLANATION

Tyler blinked away sudden tears that filled his eyes. He had imagined a massive crystal chamber, given the size of Castle Forgotten, and was surprised to find a fairly small circular chamber with a shimmering pool of liquid at its center. He eyed the pool warily.

Crystal stalactites hung at various lengths throughout the chamber. The crystals hummed in unison and shifted the full visible light spectrum like the flowing of a river. The air was a comfortable temperature and smelled clean. He was alone in the physical sense but felt a presence so ancient and profoundly alien that his head ached.

"Hello, Tyrant," said a thousand voices at once.

Tyler cringed and held his head in his hands.

"I am Celest," the voices whispered. He knew he had *heard* the words, "I am," but in the same breath, he could have sworn the voices also said, "We are, they are, and you are." He looked to where Razmal should have been standing but instead found himself alone in the room. An archway with similar symbols to the one he had passed through stood silent at his back.

"My name is not Tyrant. It is Tyler. Tyler Ryan Tor," he said with as much conviction as he could muster.

Laughter washed over him in painful waves.

"We shall see," the voices said.

Tyler stood expectantly, watching the crystal walls, ceiling, and floor flow between colors.

"I have many questions," Tyler said. He squinted against what he was certain would follow.

"You have but to ask," a single female voice replied softly.

Tyler opened his eyes fully and found the crystals in the room had taken on a light-pink color that shimmered with soft light.

"What are you?" Tyler asked.

The chamber darkened, and the crystals flared a momentary crimson before returning to soft pink.

"Celest," the female voice said.

Tyler sighed.

"Perhaps if I showed you," Celest said.

The pool at the center of the room began to bubble, and a fine mist rose from its depths. The mist coalesced into a sphere that expanded until it hung large before Tyler. Shapes began to appear in the depths of the sphere, like specters crawling along the wall of a dimly lit room. Tyler felt his consciousness falling into the sphere's core, and a scene rapidly unfolded.

The universe in its entirety was before him. Galaxies stretched out as far as his infinite eyes could see. Glowing solar systems pulsed with heartbeats, and he felt his kindred souls swell and dominate thousands of worlds. Time accelerated, and many of the brightest of the lights dimmed and then went out until only a single dot with a rhythmic pulse remained. Acrea.

"Do not pity us as if we perished. It is we that pity you. There is so much beyond this place of beginning. But we left things undone. A great darkness rises," Celest said through a voice made of starlight. As if the galaxies themselves heard her voice, some of the solar systems that had once held strong heartbeats began to emanate dark purple poison. Tyler knew instinctively that something had replaced the absence left by Celest and her people and that something had then come for Earth.

"You see, we are connected humanity and the ones that came before. Sadly, we are merely an echo of our former selves. However, Tyrant, you hold the key to salvation."

"I seem to always be the one opening doors," Tyler said, unable to keep the sarcasm from his voice.

Laughter came again, this time pleasant and oddly refreshing.

"What happened to my wife? Did she survive?" Tyler asked the galaxy scene before him.

"She still slumbers and is not currently within our reach, but you will be reunited in time," Celest replied.

Tears filled Tyler's eyes, and he sobbed uncontrollably. The starscape dissolved, and the mist retreated back into the depths of the pool. He sat heavily on the ground and let the tears fall, cradling his face in his hands.

"Nine hundred years," Tyler whispered after a time.

Celest remained silent.

"What is that thing wearing Croyan's face?" Tyler asked, wiping his runny nose on the back of his hand.

The crystal chamber darkened considerably.

"We dare not speak its name," Celest said. "You must face him and defeat him, but not yet. He is far too powerful for you alone. A great many allies must come to your aid before an encounter with him is survivable."

Tyler nodded his head. "He nearly killed me once already. Is there anything left of my friend?"

"That remains to be seen," Celest said.

Tyler stared at the crystal floor, watching his tears beginning to dry on the mirrored surface. "What do you need me to do?"

"You must complete your mission," Celest said.

Tyler shook his head sadly. "This is the wrong planet."

Celest was silent, but Tyler was sure she was waiting for him to reason his way through the problem.

"It doesn't matter what planet," he said after a time. "You are talking about the jump gate. I assume it was never activated, or we wouldn't be having this conversation?"

"Tyrant, ever the clever one," Celest said with a giggle.

"I knew the *Spero* must still be in orbit," Tyler said. "But nine hundred years… why would the gate still matter?"

"Why indeed," Celest said.

The room began to brighten again, and Tyler sat a little taller. He felt like a child that was only being told the parts of a story that he could comprehend. Celest was playing a larger game, and it was up to him to figure out how the pieces fit together.

"What must I do?" he asked, his voice echoing slightly against the crystal walls.

"You must help Crylona and her people if you ever hope to stand a chance against the one we will not name," Celest said. "Come, this is for you."

The pool in the center of the room bubbled and hissed again. Tyler expected to be pulled into another vision and scrambled to his feet. Instead, a chunk of raw crystal pulsing with every color of the rainbow emerged steaming and dripping.

"You must drive this into the great heart of Pelagos to start it beating again," Celest said.

Tyler took a hesitant step towards the pool when the crystal shot across and paused inches from blowing a hole through his face. He reached out and grasped the crystal and felt an enormous rush of power roar through his body.

"The crystal will see you safely to the Deep and into the city beyond," Celest said, her voice sounding oddly tired.

"I assume Pelagos is the city Crylona showed me in her vision?" Tyler asked.

How a crystal chamber could nod was beyond Tyler, but having just experienced it, he was a believer.

"I have many more questions," Tyler said. He had barely scratched the surface of the things he wanted to know.

"All in good time, Tyrant," Celest said. "First, I must again show you something."

Tyler stared at the pool expectantly but felt the crystal in his hand pulse and was, in an instant, standing in a different place. He was still underground by the look and dank smell. The light from the crystal in his hand strobed and cast long shadows on rough stone walls. He had seen walls like this several times before while stationed on the lunar base on Earth's moon. A machine had cut these tunnels.

He looked down the tunnel, which appeared to go on for a good distance. Behind him, he found a wall that seemed to have been where the digging machine stopped suddenly. With no sign of the machine, Tyler could only wonder what had stopped its momentum. Tunnels normally went somewhere. He turned back to the tunnel and raised his hand with the crystal in it, which allowed light to flood down to what looked like a left turn. With little choice, he started down the tunnel.

When he came to where the way took a turn, he noticed something odd. The wall to the right of the tunnel had a symbol he was intimately familiar with. It was the UEA Eagle. The blue paint of the planet had faded with time, but the interlocking rings still glittered gold. A great eagle spread its wings in the background, looking as if it might snatch the globe in its talons.

Tyler had to search the wall several times before he found the cleverly hidden hatch release. He pulled the release lever and heard a *click* from behind the raw stone wall. A hatch separated from the wall and swung inward. The door, which shined with a metallic sheen, rattled against the rough wall inside a dark chamber.

The smell of a room long sealed assaulted his senses. He shined his crystalline light inside and found a wall of blinking cryopods. A badly warped table in the center of the room was covered in dust and debris. Tyler felt his pulse quicken at the sight of so many intact pods.

"Captain Alveroy prepared many such holds knowing that they would someday be needed," came Celest's distant voice.

A vision of Arral Alveroy came to his mind in a rush. The stoic captain standing before a large blast screen surveying the lunar shipyards had been an inspiring sight. He could still picture the captain's brown crew cut, solid frame, and piercing blue eyes. Tyler had served under the man for years and had considered him a mentor.

Tyler led the way with his light and approached the row of cryopods with anticipation. Hope swelled in his chest and faded just as quickly. The chances of finding another from the *Spero* crew seemed astronomical. With each step into the roughly cut stone room, the viewports of the cryopods became clearer. None of the pods held sleeping faces.

The pods, in fact, looked to be packed full of equipment. He held his glowing crystal high, and it brightened considerably to reveal two dust-covered storage containers partially buried in an area where the ceiling had caved in. Arral had been a pragmatic man, and Tyler had a fairly good idea of what he would find in the pods and containers. He would be able to equip a full squad of marines with what was in this room.

Tyler visited each pod in turn, scrubbing grimy viewports with his sleeve and taking stock of what was inside. He turned again to the buried container, wondering what was inside. It took him several sweaty minutes to clear the debris from the containers. He opened the first one, which was packed full of various sizes of combat armor. When he had found his size, he placed the armor on the dented and leaning table. All that was missing was a helm.

The second container held several survival rucksacks, cryosuits, and a single rolled cloak made of woven Warsteel. Tyler pulled the cloak free and whistled in appreciation. Only the elite special forces battalion commanders of the UEA had ever held Warsteel. Tyler had only worn it once before.

He stripped out of his local garb and shrugged on one of the thin and supple sleepsuits. He had become accustomed to the feel of the material against his skin. The medium-duty combat armor went on next, and he tapped the collar of the chest piece to activate the powered armor. The charge of the armor struggled for a moment to form to his body and finally gave him freedom of movement in his joints. He randomly chose one of the rucksacks and tossed it onto the table with a *thud*.

He settled the Warsteel cloak over his shoulders and felt the fabric whisper against the back of his boots. He pulled the hood of the cloak over his head and nodded in satisfaction when the face mask rippled across his cheeks, and the tactical visor dropped into place. The visor flickered and came online, sharpening his vision. The chamber, lit only by his thrumming crystal, now appeared as if it were bathed in strong daylight. The cloak was the finest of UEA engineering, and very few had been made before the fall of humanity. The Warsteel around his shoulders felt like home.

Tyler rummaged through the container again looking for a final prize, and found it magnetically held against the container bottom. He thumbed the release mechanism, which took the weapon out of storage mode. The sonic repeater emerged firmly in his grasp. The weapon had a full charge, and he found and pocketed two extra power cells.

The compact frame of the sonic repeater from barrel to grip was about as long as his forearm. The weapon was capable of a high rate of fire and excelled at providing rapid bursts of suppression. Tyler had witnessed the sheer intensity of a sonic repeater on the battlefield. He was thankful for the weapon's tactical screen that glowed with a firm red targeting reticule. He pulled a holster from the container, strapped it to his thigh, and holstered the weapon with practiced ease.

When Tyler stood from where he had been kneeling, he caught his reflection in the viewport of the cryopod. He struck an imposing figure. Hard armor draped in a glittering cloak of Warsteel. His hooded and visored eyes glowed like two small orbs of ghostly jade.

"You look ready," said Celest, her voice sounding from far away.

"I *am* ready," Tyler said, shouldering his newly acquired rucksack.

As before, he blinked and was somewhere else. The crystal chamber once again thrummed around him. The pool in the center of the room rippled as if tiny drops of water were dripping onto its surface. Tyler pulled back his hood to observe the room in its true state and breathed in the unfiltered air. His mask and visor withdrew into the Warsteel cloak with a slight hiss.

"Allies, dear Tyler, are in short supply," Celest said, her voice once again strong. "And time is a luxury we do not have."

Tyler waited.

"You will not like this, but only Crylona may accompany you beneath the ocean's surface. I have a special task for the rest of your companions and what they are to face is equally as important," Celest said.

Tyler sighed. He hadn't known his small band of heroes for very long, but the thought of going into the unknown without them was disturbing. They had been his guides on an alien world and were the only reason he still drew breath. One small solace was that he felt connected to Crylona after she had shared her visions with him. Polaris seemed to trust her and Starmist completely.

"What of Lanadari?" Tyler asked, remembering the dark lady transformed, decimating enemies at the battle of Kent's Gate.

"She will remain here with us," Celest said. The word "us" shifted oddly to his ears and sounded more like "me."

"Do not worry for her, Tyrant. This is her home, and she has much healing to do."

Tyler nodded in agreement. "I only ask as I would feel safer with her around my friends. Razmal and Samson are resourceful, but they are only two."

"Ralon will be going with them," Celest said with a strange, matter-of-fact tone to her voice. "They are to head north, and that is all you need to know right now. I know you, Tyrant, and if I tell you more, it will only distract you from your task."

"Celest, may I ask you something?" Tyler asked.

The crystal chamber waited.

"Why was Ralon held prisoner in Arabellum?"

The crystal chamber tinkled with laughter.

"Apparently, Ember took issue with the fact that he found Ralon with his daughter, Cinder."

Tyler frowned. "They put him in a conviction mask for that?"

Celest giggled. "No. It was what he did to the twenty guards that came to take him from Cinder's bedchamber that landed him in the mask."

Tyler felt himself smile despite the gravity of what Ralon had done to Arabellum while held prisoner. A thought occurred to him suddenly. "Samson had said something about Ralon using the VAST, and it felt wrong," Tyler said.

The crystal chamber remained silent.

Apparently, the VAST was not a conversation topic Celest was willing to spend time on.

Tyler watched the pool ripple for a moment, feeling somewhat satisfied with his rapid-fire question-and-answer session with Celest. Something still nagged at him. It was like he was forgetting something or, more importantly, someone. His mind felt clearer, but a few gaps remained. He was positive that one of the gaps was important, but he felt his time with Celest was at an end.

What was he really up against? Descending into an alien ocean with a strange woman in a seashell mask to restart a failing reactor? You really couldn't make something like this up.

"Stab a power core with a chunk of alien crystal. How hard could it be?" Tyler said with a wry smile.

The room flared brightly for a moment, and Tyler found himself back in the antechamber with a red-faced Razmal. His Balan companion stood facing the archway, shouting obscenities at the glowing symbols.

5 – ABOVE AND BELOW

Razmal grumbled and swore a particularly creative string of curses at the archway when he felt a looming presence beside him. He turned and found his companion changed into familiar armor but with a heavier bulk than before. A long, glittering cloak made of a material that looked both sturdy and supple brushed the top of his boots. He had a strange weapon strapped to one of his thighs that Razmal eyed suspiciously. A glowing crystal pulsed in his left hand, and Tyler smiled at him warmly. Razmal felt immediately at ease. He gave the archway a final threatening scowl before turning away.

"I am sure it's quite the story," Razmal said, trying to keep the hurt out of his voice. "One that you probably can't tell me!"

Tyler grinned and shook his head as he shrugged his shoulders. He held out his right hand, and Polaris leaped from its resting place and into his waiting grip.

"Celest has a task for both of us," Tyler said.

Razmal was sure that he was choosing his words carefully by the way he said them.

"Meaning?" Razmal asked.

Tyler sighed. "Different paths this time, my friend. Crylona and I will make the descent into the Deep. You and Samson are to join Ralon and head north. She didn't sound like there was much choice in the matter. Although, if you wanted to journey back to Tonu, I doubt anyone would blame you."

Razmal frowned. He would never go against the wishes of Celest. One name was strangely absent from the list Tyler had just given him. "What of the dark lady?" he asked.

"Lanadari will remain here in Castle Forgotten. We can only guess what she has been through, and Celest will work to heal her while we are away," Tyler said.

Razmal nodded. Few were granted entrance into the crystal chamber. But those that did enter, and came back out again, were forever changed. Given the haunted look that Lanadari often wore, the injuries to her mind were many. Physical injuries healed quickly. It was the mental injuries that would take time.

"What next?" Razmal asked.

Tyler thumped his staff against the ground, looking stoic and alien in his armor once again. "Can you take me to Lanadari?"

Razmal nodded and motioned for him to follow. They headed back up the tunnel, its walls glowing with a myriad of runes that looked slightly diminished. The temperature steadily climbed with their ascent, and Razmal mopped his sweating brow with the back of his hand. Tyler moved solidly beside him, his newly acquired cloak swishing and whispering as he walked.

The two emerged from the mouth of the tunnel into midday and squinted at the bright light since coming from near darkness. Razmal smelled the various races of Arral before he could see them. The castle grounds were bustling with activity. Brightly colored Avians strutted between hide-covered stalls stretched over large polished bone frames, calling shrilly to pedestrians that passed by. Balan, Avian, Acrean, and even a few Erew made up the thick throng of castlegoers.

Trade was in full swing, and Razmal eyed several stalls as he led Tyler towards the castle's great carved steps that ended in large stone doors. Beyond the doors, the Moonlit Waters council would be in session. Mouthwatering smells from a particularly colorful stall broke his concentration and slowed his hurried steps. He heard Tyler's stomach growl through his armor.

"A quick snack?" Razmal asked.

"We *do* need our strength," Tyler said, a sly grin on his face. "Can we walk and eat?"

Razmal eyed the stall draped in brightly colored silk and found the source of the mouthwatering smell. Chunks of sizzling fish covered in exotic spices sat in shallow stone dishes nestled between crushed warming crystals. He approached the stall and held up two fingers to the lantern-jawed Balan, who was skewering fish chunks with a long hollow reed.

"Make that three," came a smooth voice from behind.

Ralon Tigerson stepped fluidly through the crowd, his long yellow hair held back in a ponytail with a thin leather cord. He wore a red flowing vest with a cream-colored undershirt tucked into his voluminous red pantaloons. A tan short-cloak hung over one shoulder, revealing a long slender sword sheathed in stiff, tanned leather. Judging by the style, the blade was made of solid obsidian. The blade's handle was wrapped in boiled leather, and a large tiger's-eye gem pommel glittered in the midday sun.

"Well met," Ralon said, bowing slightly to Tyler. He gave Razmal a downward look and a smirk. The stall vendor juggled several delicious smelling clay bowls filled with fish, seaweed, and broth. When a bowl finally found its way into Razmal's calloused hands, his mouth was watering.

Tyler grinned at Ralon and then attacked his own steaming bowl of fish with a singular purpose. Ralon reached into a pocket to pay the vendor, but the lantern-jawed Balan refused, bowed low, and made the sign of Moonlit Water with his hands shaped like a circle in front of his head.

Razmal shrugged and gulped down his meal.

Ralon ate slowly, careful not to get his clothing soiled. They set the clay bowls on the stall's stretched hide counter when they finished the wonderfully spiced dish.

"Where to?" Ralon asked.

Razmal thought he always had a sly look on his face and shifting eyes that missed very little.

Razmal motioned towards the grand stairs with an annoyed jerk of his thumb. Ralon smiled as if not seeing him. Tyler sighed softly and motioned for Razmal to lead on.

They pushed through the crowd and found themselves at the bottom of the grand stairs. Razmal glared at the hundred of intricately carved steps. Balans' legs were not made for so many stairs.

Razmal was sweating through his tunic by the fiftieth step. By the one hundredth, his legs were on fire. He lost track of his gasping breath shortly after another hundred. Tyler offered to carry him somewhere around five hundred. His haggard breathing and fiery glare set his friend grinning widely.

When they reached the landing just before the council chambers, Razmal collapsed, dripping sweat from his bald head. He glanced down and groaned. Large sweat stains had ruined his good tunic. After a brief rest and subtle teasing from Ralon, he hauled himself to his feet.

A single centurion stood before the double doors of the council chamber. He was an Avian with azure and white feathers and a powerful silver beak. Massive wings folded around him like a cloak, and he held a bone half-lance that rested tip-down on the marble landing. Green and black feathers adorned the handle just below the wide guard of the lance, which was lacquered dark gray.

"Ralon," the Avian said, his voice sounding like he was gargling stones.

"Hello, Gryphem," Ralon said.

"Your mother is less than pleased with you," Gryphem said, his Avian eyes blinking rapidly.

Ralon raised a finger to his lips playfully. "I was never here."

Gryphem hopped on a thick, taloned foot, looking uncomfortable.

"Have you seen Lanadari?" Razmal said in a rush. Watching this game that Ralon played with others was nerve-racking.

"The sparring chambers, since before first light," the Avian said.

Tyler bowed, and Ralon scooted in front of him away from the council chamber doors. "Thank you, we will be back soon," Ralon said over his shoulder.

Gryphem shrugged as only an Avian could and leaned on his lance casually.

Ralon led them around the landing to a series of bridged walkways that appeared to defy gravity. Razmal peeked over the high railing only once. The dizzying drop caused him to swoon, and he felt Tyler's strong, reassuring grip on his shoulder.

"Beautiful, isn't it?" Tyler asked.

The sheer rock cliffs, waterfalls, and mist roiling where falling water met ocean bay was genuinely breathtaking. Small flying creatures hunted the cliffs for prey while multicolored lizards clung precariously to ledges worn into the rock. Green plants grew thickly in cracks along the cliff face, providing abundant food and cover. He squinted when a metallic shape caught his gaze, perched atop one of the cliffs. Tyler's Golem, a patient sentinel, still watched the skies.

Razmal took a deep breath of clean air and nodded to his friend. "Truly, it is beautiful," he said.

Ralon led them across several more bridges before they set foot on solid ground again. The sparring chamber was cut directly into the red and brown stone of the cliffs that sheltered the Bay of Moonlit Waters. The chamber had a stiff tan-colored hide flap for a door, and it was pulled open to allow the cool air from the bay to drift inside. Two figures faced each other in the roughly circular chamber.

Razmal raised an eyebrow when he recognized Samson standing calmly across from Lanadari. Neither of them had noticed the others approach. Both stood with eyes closed and hands clasped before them. When Razmal and his companions were near the doorway, he felt a tremendous presence. The amount of VAST in the chamber was crushing. What started as a whisper quickly became a roar, and Razmal had to fight hard to keep his footing. He noticed out of the corner of his watering eyes that Tyler had gone very still and gripped his staff tightly. Ralon yawned and looked bored.

Razmal wished he had brought the hammer and shield that had become his own after Piotr had sacrificed himself to save the band from an elemental in the Canyonlands. Ever since that fateful day when Razmal had scooped up the hammer and shield to replace his crystal ax, everything had changed. The VAST, which had always existed just outside Razmal's awareness, had returned fully and begged to be commanded. He had resisted them with all of his might, but now without his adopted weapon and armor, he was beginning to lose the battle.

Tyler must have sensed something, for he strode confidently to stand beside him. He struck the smooth marble floor with his staff between them, and a clang of metal on stone resonated clear and crisp. Razmal gasped as the VAST fled from him and remained just outside of a slightly shimmering sphere of sound. It took Razmal a moment to let out the breath he had been holding and refocus on the duo that faced off against each other in the center of the chamber.

Both Samson and Lanadari had sweat dripping from their brows in small rivers. Whatever they were doing, it was taxing for both of them. Razmal could sense a tug-of-war going on between them and imagined anything caught in the middle would have been ripped to shreds. The crystal runes that ran the length of Lanadari's exposed arms shimmered a cold blue color, while a rune at the nape of her neck sparked an angry red. As if finally sensing the other's presence, Samson held out his left hand, his palm facing Lanadari, and then closed his hand into a fist. The VAST in the chamber evaporated like mist meeting the heat of the day.

"Very good, yes very good," Samson muttered, mopping his brow with one of the sleeves of his oversized silver robe. Apparently, it was hard for Samson to find a good tailor in Moonlit Waters. More likely, he simply didn't care about how he looked.

Lanadari stood with her eyes downcast, panting with exertion. Her violet-colored hair hung in wet tangles against her face. She wore a simple, sleeveless gray-colored fighting robe that hid her toned body beneath its heavy layers. Her feet were bare, and Razmal could see for the first time that the glittering runes that adorned her skin spun all the way down around her toes. The only place that the runes failed to touch was her face, which held its characteristic look of sadness.

"Welcome, friends," Samson said, walking slowly across the chamber towards the entrance. He had been through his share of battles on the way to Moonlit Waters and still walked with pain evident in his stiff movement. His smile, however, never wavered as he approached Tyler and bowed low.

"Sleeper," Samson said with reverence.

Tyler embraced Samson briefly by the shoulder and smiled. "It is great to see you, my friend," he said.

"It is great to be seen," Samson replied.

Lanadari wandered over and stood in front of Tyler with her shoulders hunched and her eyes on the floor. "Hello," she said, her voice barely above a whisper. "They said that you had woken up."

Tyler turned to Lanadari and studied her for a moment. "Do you know of our guest as well?" Tyler asked.

"A woman from the Deep," Lanadari said, her tone casual as if discussing the weather.

Tyler nodded. "She wants me to go with her."

Lanadari raised her head and met his eyes with her own. "I can feel the crystal you carry," she said. "Take care. Its power is great."

"When do we leave?" Samson asked, seeming to sense a long pause coming as Tyler and Lanadari continued to lock eyes.

"We aren't going," Razmal said.

Samson raised an eyebrow at his gruff tone.

"Erm... Tyler has to go on this adventure alone," Razmal said. "Celest has something for each of us, equally as important, I am told."

"Indeed," Ralon said.

"What do you know?" Razmal asked.

Ralon shrugged his shoulders and stuck his hands in the pockets of his pantaloons. "You and I are going north."

Razmal frowned. He had never been north of Moonlit Waters. The coast ended sharply a few miles outside the walled city and became impassable mountains that were home to a kingdom of Avians. In hundreds of years of expeditions, very little of the north had actually been mapped by anyone.

"Don't worry, I know a shortcut to where we are going," Ralon said, obviously sensing his uneasiness.

Razmal was about to ask exactly where in the north they were going, but the sounds of a gong interrupted the conversation. The gong repeated a number of times, signaling that the council was on a short recess for rest and a meal.

"Samson, will you go with Razmal and Ralon to the north?" Tyler asked.

Samson looked quickly at Lanadari and then back to Tyler. "It depends on where the lady goes," he said.

Tyler smiled. "She is to remain here with Celest."

"Then I too shall stay," Samson said with finality.

Razmal wasn't surprised. The immense power that Lanadari had wielded at Kent's Gate was hard to believe. She had cast off the dark master's influence and in turn, had saved the band from certain death. Samson didn't want the darkness to return.

Tyler nodded as if he had expected the answer. "I know you will take good care of her."

"I am standing right here," Lanadari said quietly.

Tyler jumped in mock surprise, drawing a small smile to her full lips.

"Do you mind if Samson stays with you?" Tyler asked.

Lanadari turned silver-rimmed eyes on Samson and nodded. "I would like that," she said.

Ralon, looking to have had his fill of idle conversation and wandering out of the sparring chambers with his hands in his pockets, whistled.

"Then this is farewell for now," Tyler said, bowing slightly. "I will take good care of the crystal."

Lanadari retreated back into the center of the sparring chamber and sat down. She closed her eyes and sat motionless, breathing rhythmically and deeply.

"The healing has already begun," Samson said, embracing Razmal and clapping him strongly on the back a few times. Razmal returned the brief affection and coughed uncomfortably. Samson chuckled and retreated back to the center of the chamber and sat down across from Lanadari, closed his eyes, and began breathing deeply.

When they exited the sparring chamber, Razmal and Tyler found Ralon leaning against a tall marble pillar, flicking small stones into a puddle of rainwater. He was chewing a piece of long grass and glanced at them as they approached.

"If we hurry, we will get the council just after they eat. They are much more approachable with full bellies," Ralon said.

Tyler made a gesture to proceed, and Ralon led them back the way they had come to the great doors of the council chamber. Castle Forgotten loomed large and alien behind the doors. The sky was beginning to cloud over, and the castle towers became obscured in the gathering mist. Gryphem stood in the same position as before, leaning against his lance.

"Sleeper? A word with you," said a voice from across the landing.

A tall Acrean man with long pale-green hair approached in a hurry. He wore rich azure-colored silk robes with panel designs that stretched from hem to collar. He walked with a well-made cane of polished bone and the cane clicked against the marble stone as he walked. He waved one of his arms wildly, trying to draw attention to himself.

"Ah, Triumvir Hark," Ralon said, stepping smoothly in front of Tyler.

Hark slid slightly on the marble floor and nearly collided with Ralon.

"Ralon," Hark acknowledged, barely keeping the annoyance from his voice.

"We were just coming for an audience with the full council," Ralon said.

Hark looked troubled. "We are adjourned. Triumvir Milo had an urgent matter to attend to. Your mother, however, is still inside."

"A shame. The Sleeper also has an urgent matter that requires his immediate attention," Ralon said.

Hark clicked his tongue in annoyance. "If I could just get a moment of his time," Hark said, moving to get around Ralon.

"I apologize, but this *really* is a bad time," Ralon said, maneuvering his arm to lock around Hark's. "I do so miss our conversations, Hark! How about we go see what my mother is up to?"

Gryphem hurried to open the door as Ralon half led and half dragged Hark protesting into the bowels of Castle Forgotten.

Tyler spread his hands helplessly and looked at Razmal. "What was that all about?"

Razmal rolled his eyes and sighed. "Politics."

6 – BETTER OFF DEAD

Shade opened his eyes and felt puzzled. He was lying on his back, staring up at billions of twinkling stars. How had he gotten outside the ship? It took him a moment to get his bearings, and he sat up and observed total destruction.

His nine-hundred-year-old transport ship was now a half-mile string of smoldering wreckage. He looked down at the torn rags he wore, a far cry from the fine black robes they had been before. Yalonia loomed large and rusted-orange in the sky, highlighting the twisted metal of his fallen starship.

"Not exactly the way I envisioned this particular scenario," Shade said, his voice thin and angry to his ears. He balled his hands into fists and pushed himself to his feet. Judging by the position of the stars in the sky, they had made it to the island chain.

They.

Shade closed his eyes and called to the darkness, searching for any of the crew that remained. He felt all of them immediately. His Immortal Guard were scattered but close by. The presence that was Allen barely registered at all.

"Come," he said, his voice roaring and echoing with darkness. "Bring me my engineer."

It took entirely too long for his three Immortal Guard to emerge from the gloom, dragging a mangled fragment of Allen's chariot through the dirt. The flickering flames of debris cast dancing shadows on the glass-and-metal ruin that was his engineer. Only two of the eight spiderlike leg appendages remained attached, beyond help from the looks of them. The glass cylinder was shattered, and only jagged shards remained attached to the bottom of the chariot, looking like the jagged teeth of an old crone. Allen dangled from the chariot, hanging a few inches from the ground by his life-giving tubes.

"You have certainly seen better days," Shade said. He laughed dryly and waved his Immortal Guard to step back. The three immortals moved back in unison and waited while Shade bent over his fallen engineer.

"This is going to hurt," Shade whispered.

Shade closed his eyes and felt dark energy race down his arms at his summon. He pictured the purple and black roiling currents swirling into his waiting palms and gritted his teeth. He opened his eyes and frowned at the barely awesome flicker in his outstretched hands. What was wrong with him?

He growled and forced his rage into his waiting palms and nodded in satisfaction when the flicker became a roar. He thrust his hands against Allen's cold gray flesh and released the swirling dark nimbus into his engineer. A great sound of air being drawn into bellows could be heard. The howl that split the night would have curdled cold milk.

An angry transformation began to take shape as tubes melted away, and Allen thudded sickly to the ground. The visor that covered his long-rotted eyes exploded into molten shards, leaving behind two sockets set with blazing purple coals of dark energy. Stumps of flesh sizzled and dripped like candle wax, hardening into thin bone-like appendages, complete with fingers and toes. Grey flesh darkened to an obsidian color, and Allen spat out the mechanism that had been feeding and breathing for him, displaying two rows of razor-sharp teeth. Transformed, Allen leaped up on all fours like a beast and fixed Shade with a ghostly stare.

"Master," Allen said, his new voice sounding as if it had to pass through hell itself before emerging from snarling lips. His hunched form bowed low, touching his forehead to the blackened dirt.

"Hopefully, I didn't damage that brain of yours," Shade said with a casual wave of his hand. He felt very tired.

"I am well," Allen said, coming to stand on his newly formed bone legs. To call him an abomination before would have been kind. To call him a nightmare now would have been an understatement. He stared down at his skeletal fingers that were pointed at the ends. "It is good to have hands again."

Shade looked down at Allen's blackened bone feet and grinned as a thought occurred to him. "Well, c'mon feet, let's get walkin'," he said.

Allen stared at him blankly, his flickering eye sockets staring through him. Shade winced in mock apology and motioned for his Immortal Guard to join him at his side. The three gave Allen a wide berth and came to kneel before Shade.

"Allen, before we *landed unassisted*, did you scan the area for anything useful? We are a long way from home, and I don't relish the thought of swimming for the next year to make the shores of Teka," Shade said. "I doubt we will get what is left of the transport airborne any quicker."

Allen turned and surveyed the wreckage. "Oh, I don't know about that. There is still something to salvage here. I also picked up a power signature on the largest of the islands in the chain. I don't know exactly where we are, but I will know soon."

"You three, do whatever Allen needs of you," Shade said, shooing the three Immortal Guard away like pets. They stood in unison and came to attention at Allen's side.

Allen took a hesitant step on his new legs and cracked a horrid-looking smile at Shade. Shade shivered unconsciously at that smile. He had outdone himself once again. He never ceased to amaze himself at what he could accomplish with a bit of desperation thrown in. His engineer had become some of his finest work, that much was certain. Allen motioned for the Immortal Guard to follow, and they disappeared into the smoking wreckage.

Shade stood staring at Yalonia as it climbed large and full into the sky. The human part of him would have found the display beautiful, but that part of him wasn't currently available. He had pushed the man he had been deep into the darkness after his startling return. The image of green eyes staring back at him was haunting. It would be some time before Croyan would dare show his ugly presence.

He found himself wandering aimlessly away from the crash site, lost in thought. The island night was warm, and the sound of insects filled the air. The muddy light of Yalonia allowed his keen eyes to sharpen in complete detail, even in the dark. The island, as it turned out, was covered in sand as far as he could see.

Dunes climbed hundreds of feet into the air, and Shade scaled one of the largest with ease. When he reached the high point of the dune, he turned to survey the crash site from the way he had come. Several pieces of wreckage still sparked and burned, throwing small rivers of acrid smoke into the air.

He frowned, not really seeing the salvage potential his chief engineer apparently did. Shade sighed and turned his back on the latest failure. Even if they had made it back to Teka, it would take months to rebuild his forces. He had learned a great deal about his enemy, and without Tyler to lead them, his next attempt would succeed.

The knowledge, however, had come at a staggering cost.

He would need a tremendous force to make up for the loss of his Immortal Guard. He stared off into the night, thinking. Where could he get a large expendable force to rival that of the quick-breeding races of Arral?

A thin smile came to his lips, and a thought occurred to him. The people he had cast into the swamps so long ago had the numbers he needed. They were, sadly, as savage and ignorant as the enemy he faced. He could work with that.

His plan to call down the fury of the ship in orbit had been a good one. Time had very little meaning to him, and a few hundred years of playing with a maddening AI was negligible. Instead of massive destruction brought about by orbital bombardment, he would have to get up close and personal with the plague that infested the planet.

It was good that Shade was willing to get his hands dirty.

"Master?"

Shade jumped in surprise and swung out his hand. A lash of slithering darkness whipped across Allen's face, snapping his head back. A thin line of black ichor dribbled from his wound before it closed with a wisp of smoke. Two points of smoldering purple light within empty sockets settled upon Shade as Allen popped his newly made neck in what appeared to be annoyance.

"Announcing one's presence is prudent," Shade snapped.

Allen stared at the ground. "I called to you from afar, Lord. You have been running for hours."

Shade was about to strike him again when he realized that he was indeed no longer standing at the top of a dune. Instead, he was on a wide beach at the edge of the island. Yalonia was on the opposite side of the sky from where it should have been, and dawn was beginning to color the horizon.

How had he gotten here?

The tide kissed at his boots, and he shook his head in anger and confusion. He hated the ocean and everything in it. One moment, he had been planning world domination, and the next, he was about to put himself into the sea.

"An early morning jog to get the blood flowing," Shade said, barely sounding convincing even to his own ears. "You should yell louder next time."

"Yes, Master," Allen said with his voice sounding like tortured animals. "I bring news. I was able to find and pinpoint the location of several power signatures scattered across the island chain."

"What are they?" Shade asked.

"Please, Lord, follow me. One is close by, and we shall discover how useful it might be," Allen said.

Allen led them blissfully away from the water and back into the island's interior. They walked at a good pace as the Acrean sun crawled into the sky. Shimmering waves of heat began to appear from the many dunes of sand. He looked again to his tattered robes and smiled thinly; even if heat had been a factor, he was at least well ventilated. Shade was thankful temperature had little effect on his immortal form.

Allen crested and disappeared behind another nondescript-looking dune before reappearing halfway up another. He stopped and waved his blackened arm at Shade and pointed with jagged fingers towards the bottom of one of the dunes. Half-buried in the shadow of the sand was the telltale shape of a cryopod. Shade broke into a run, floating slightly above the shifting sand.

As he approached the pod, he could see that it was connected to several other pods by the damaged internal piece of a cargo bay. He could feel the pods' faint emanations, signaling they were still operational. In an instant, Shade dug through the shifting sand to get a clear look at one of the viewports. A sleeping colonist's face greeted him as he wiped away the last of the grime.

The colonist was a woman with strawberry-blond curls, a round face, and freckles. The cryosuit she wore clung tightly to her body, and he could see the shimmering cryo fluid flowing through various tubes. Her nameplate had been well preserved under the sand, and Shade pointedly ignored reading it. Who she had been no longer mattered. Who she would become was all that he was interested in. A sinister smile came to his lips as a plan began to take shape.

"How many power signatures?" Shade asked Allen with as much calm as he could muster.

"Judging by the cluster of pods here, I believe fifty-four others are scattered across the island chain," Allen said.

"Good," Shade said, grabbing the lid of the cryopod and tearing it off in a single motion. The abrupt termination of cryo sleep set the woman to thrashing feebly in her pod. Her light-blue eyes rolled dangerously, and she gasped against the hot sandy air.

Shade grabbed her face and forced her to calm in his iron grip. Terrified eyes met his own. He leaned over and placed his mouth near hers. A small sliver of darkness oozed from his lips and fell against her quivering tongue. He released her roughly and stepped back as her thrashing resumed, this time in earnest.

A shriek of madness ripped through the air as the woman leaped to her feet and grabbed Shade by the throat. She lifted him completely off the sand and howled. Gone were her sparkling blue eyes, instead replaced by black orbs of shining obsidian. Even the whites of her eyes had faded into blackness. Shade allowed himself to dangle for a moment longer before brushing her hand from his throat like removing lint from a clean shirt. The woman tumbled through the air and landed roughly on the sand, sobbing.

"You, my dear, are the first," Shade said without emotion. "The others will look to you for leadership. Please, do not disappoint."

The woman struggled to a kneeling position and looked up at Shade with orbs of pure darkness. She wiped bloodred tears from her face, smearing her playful freckles with crimson. Tiny flecks of red began to appear in the blackness of her eyes and in moments, coalesced to form perfect flame-colored irises.

Didn't they say that the eyes were windows to the soul?

"Master," the woman said, her voice escaping her full lips in a hiss.

"Let us wake the others, shall we?" Shade asked playfully.

Allen stood silently, but Shade felt his eyes upon him as he ripped the covers from the other six pods buried in the sand. Of the six, only five still functioned. One contained the dust of a corpse long decayed. The others amounted to three men and two women who quickly joined the freckled-faced woman kneeling in the sand.

Black eyes with crimson irises fixed him with hollow stares. Rage clung to the former colonist like a palpable aura. They now had the makings of new Immortal Guard. Their bodies would burn hotter with each passing day. Soon, they would require cryogenic intervention to slow the creeping flames.

"Can you salvage enough for the suits?" Shade asked the looming figure of Allen.

Allen was silent just long enough for Shade to have his answer.

"With my lab perhaps, but here…" His grating voice trailed off, and he helplessly held out his spindly arms with the wicked-looking claws.

Shade looked at the new guard and smoothed his tattered robes. He wasn't sure how long they had.

"I want them to help you with repairs," he said.

Allen nodded his head and bowed slightly, hunching like a predatory bird. He beckoned the kneeling guard to follow. They stood uncertainly and looked nervously from Shade to Allen.

"Go!" Shade snapped.

Six new guard hurried away and fell into step behind Allen. They rushed to keep up with his long loping strides and disappeared over a dune. Shade turned and looked out over the horizon to the vast ocean beyond.

He lost himself again in silent reflection, thinking about how luck was with him in that he was now able to replenish the ranks of his Immortal Guard. Their bodies would surely last for a few days before flames and madness overtook them. It had been centuries since he had converted the first batch of colonists. Many of them had lasted quite a long time before Allen had come up with the idea for the bone-chilling containment suits.

After the failure of his forces to achieve a foothold on Arral, he would need all the Immortal Guard he could muster. His victory must be certain. Lady luck was smiling on him by providing the bodies he needed, but she wasn't going to hand him the planet without making it interesting. With sixty new pairs of superhuman hands, Shade was confident that Allen would have them all home in time for supper.

7 – HERO OF WAR

"We are going WHERE?" Razmal asked. He was shouting and wasn't exactly sure when he had come out of his seat.

"Alya Cheyl," Ralon said, his lips quirking into an obnoxious grin.

"The Avian city?" Razmal said slowly, praying he had misheard the name of the city.

"Last time I checked," Ralon replied.

Tyler sat with them in a comfortable room in the western tower of Castle Forgotten, the tall, willowy Crylona standing at his shoulder. Razmal found himself staring at her seashell mask, following the straight lines and lavender-colored surface swirls in a mesmerizing maze of natural artistry.

He met her hard eyes and looked away, quickly feeling color rise to his cheeks. She cleared her throat and tossed her wet-looking hair in annoyance.

"Sorry," Razmal said under his breath.

Ralon had one of his booted feet resting on a chair and leaned casually over his bent knee. He held a horn that smelled of strong drink that had been refilled several times from a clay pitcher that dripped with condensation. He took a long guzzle from the horn and sighed as he stared into the apparently empty vessel.

"What reason would there be for a journey to the Avian city? Last I heard, we were on less than speaking terms," Razmal said.

The relationship with the northern kingdom had always been tenuous at best. Avians typically stuck to their own kind and stayed in the high places of Acrea. Some were found trading or employed as mercenaries in larger settlements. A small flock had even settled the Moonlit Cliffs several generations ago, and the family was well known and liked. Gryphem, in fact, was the oldest son and heir to the cliff.

"You are to make them an offer they can't refuse," Tyler said, a strange look on his face like he had just told a joke but then realized that no one understood the punch line.

"An alliance then?" Razmal asked. He hoped that the others didn't notice the doubt he heard in his own voice.

Ralon shrugged his shoulders. "Go to the place, talk to the lord, give him the gift, ask for the alliance, feast, and come home. A pretty typical day for nobility."

Razmal stared at him with suspicion. "What gift?"

Ralon remained silent.

"Well, at least the likelihood of you ending up in the lord's daughter's roost is unlikely. That is unless you are also a particularly gifted climber?" Razmal said.

Ralon stared at him over his empty horn, lowered it, and broke into hysterical laughter that lasted longer than appropriate.

"It's like you know me," Ralon said with a wink.

Razmal sighed and shook his head.

Crylona put a hand on Tyler's shoulder and bent low to whisper something in his ear. He nodded and stood from his seat.

"It is time for us to go, my friends," he said, his voice sounding heavy and slightly sad.

Razmal was worried not only for himself but for his friend. Tyler hadn't said much about how he and Crylona would descend to the ocean city, but the mysterious woman from the depths seemed unconcerned.

His journey to Alya Cheyl would take months. They would not be able to take the large insects known as Gek as the Avian people often captured and ate them. Because of this, no routes existed between the cities. Several small villages were on the way north, but none of them were well-traveled. How had he let himself be talked into this in the first place?

"Razmal, I am counting on you. We need allies, and Celest was particular about you being the one to go with Ralon," Tyler said as if sensing his troubled thoughts.

Razmal met Tyler's steel-colored gaze and nodded. While not spoken to him directly, a command from Celest was still a command. The fact that she had taken a sudden interest in him was exciting and wholly terrifying. The ancient beneath Castle Forgotten had ensured the survival of the Acrean people for nearly a thousand years.

"Will you see us off?" Tyler asked, heading for the door with Crylona in tow.

Ralon shrugged and slowly pulled his booted foot off the chair he had been using as a rest. Razmal fell in step behind the trio, his mind full of troubling thoughts. They moved quickly through the city and progressed down towards the docks. Crylona chatted with Tyler about the splendors of her ocean home, but Razmal didn't really hear any of it, and once they crossed under a large stone archway and into the open docks, his mouth hung open in awe.

The docks of Moonlit Waters were enormous. Hollow-bone tri-hulled vessels lined various naturally occurring slips made of towering coral reefs, held fast with braided fiber ropes. The bay also cradled larger merchant vessels anchored deep in the harbor. Huge billowing sails, tied neatly for storage, filtered Acrean sunlight in strange patterns on carved bone decking. A steady breeze carried voices from dock workers that loaded and unloaded ships, urged on by gruff taskmasters. The controlled chaos brought a swell of longing to Razmal's breast.

"Is that a tree?" Tyler gasped.

Razmal felt his eyes go wide at the blasphemy. "I would ask anyone but you if they kissed their own mother with such a foul mouth. Since it is you, I will assume your madness has returned."

Tyler stared at him helplessly.

The twisted figure that Tyler had slandered stood not far off on one of the naturally occurring stone walkways jutting out from the lapping waves. It was facing the ocean with long arms extended at its sides as if praying.

"That is a Deru, and it is rude to stare," Razmal said, sounding sharper than he had intended.

The Deru, as if sensing they were looking, turned and regarded them with flickering eyes of cold blue fire. Its face and body were made up of hundreds of intertwined brown and green vines. It was vaguely human-shaped but with a large cavernous maw with no discernible teeth. Atop its head was a shock of rich green foliage that looked well-groomed. The Deru wore thick, flaky armor covering its torso and was the same color as its vines. The armor gave it a bulky look despite its thin frame. The ritual hardened crook, which was apparently formed from fallen Deru, was oddly absent from the towering figure.

"I have seen only a few of this race before," Razmal said, finding his breath shallow.

"I meant no disrespect, Razmal," Tyler said quietly. "The Deru as you call them here are not sentient on my planet. I had started to wonder why there were no tre… er… forests."

Razmal patted the air in forgiveness. "They are few but also fierce friends, Tyler. Their island is far from our shores, and I have never met another that knows its location. I would never suggest making a Deru angry or calling it anything other than 'Deru.' Especially the big ones."

Tyler glanced back at the Deru and whistled low. "I thought that was a big one!"

The band moved slowly through the bustling docks, and Crylona took the lead as they approached the wide beach where many smaller fishing vessels were pulled up on the sand. Men and women holding a variety of finely woven nets looked at them curiously as they passed. The waves lapped endlessly against the shore, and Razmal found the sound of the ocean peaceful. They hugged the beach for a time and left the fishing boats just out of sight.

Crylona stopped at a spot on the beach that looked like any other and turned towards the vast ocean. Moonlit Waters's shield wall that made the sheltered cove possible was far off in the distance.

"We begin our descent here," she said, her voice slightly muffled by her seashell mask.

Tyler nodded and scanned the sky for a moment. He seemed to pause as if concentrating on something the others could not see and then waited. A rumble from the sky shook the ground and sent Razmal stumbling for cover before realizing what was happening. Tyler had summoned the golem.

The large metallic figure descended on roaring jets of flame, which instantly turned the sand where they touched to glass. When the golem touched down with a crunch and shower of hot glass, Razmal grumbled all the more. The least Tyler could have done was tell them his sentinel was making an appearance.

"Hello, old friend," Tyler said softly, running his hand over one of the golem's massive arm cannons.

"Commander," the golem rumbled.

Tyler walked around the golem and patted it like a pet before coming back to its front. He laid his palm on the chest of the mechanical creature. "Mission," Tyler said softly before closing his eyes.

The golem went perfectly still, and its glowing central eye color changed from red to solid blue. The two stood there for a moment, apparently exchanging some form of information. Razmal had watched Tyler open long-sealed doors with a touch of his hand on several occasions. After a time, the golem's eye flickered back to a bright red color and stood tall. Tyler removed his hand and stepped back.

"Execute," Tyler said calmly to the golem.

"Acknowledged," the golem said, its deep hollow voice loud and menacing. It leaped into the sky, both engines burning bright, and disappeared.

Tyler nodded in satisfaction and turned to regard the others. "The city is under his protection until we return. I would suggest the guard stop any uninvited guests before they are in sight of the city gates."

Razmal raised his hand and started to say something but shut his mouth instead. It was not worth the effort as he knew Tyler would do his best to explain, but most of what his friend said was beyond his understanding. Technology was, after all, alien and heretical.

Everyone stood uncomfortably for a few moments before Ralon stepped forward, his mouth leading.

"So… how exactly does this work? I mean, maybe you have gills, but Tyler, the last time I looked, they're not the water-breathing kind," he said, stating the obvious.

Tyler looked as if he were about to say something when Crylona produced something from her satchel and tossed it to Ralon. He caught what looked to be a very similar mask to the one she herself wore.

"Keep it doubtful one. I have many," Crylona said.

Ralon grinned and stashed the mask in one of his many pockets.

Tyler stripped off his cloak and shrugged off a backpack that had been hidden under its folds. He reverently placed the cloak and his angry-looking pistol in the pack and shrugged it again on his back. Crylona produced another mask from her satchel and handed it to him. The shell was a glittering silver color on one side and had thick tan flesh on the other side. Tyler looked at it suspiciously.

"It will do you no harm, but the first time you put it on is…" Crylona said, her voice trailing off as she shrugged.

Tyler regarded her for a moment, sighed, and placed the mask over his face. The mask adhered with a slight sucking sound. He grabbed at his throat and doubled over, looking like he was trying to gag. His eyes watered, and his face turned bright red. Razmal took a step forward to help his companion, but Tyler held up a hand. A few moments passed with his hands on his knees before he stood tall and exhaled deeply.

"I have a word for that, but there is a lady present," Tyler said, his voice sounding muffled. He shook his head, and his shoulders shivered slightly.

"I am told I will be able to send word through to the temple of our success," he said. "Who knows, this might take us no time at all, and I will catch up to you in Alya Cheyl," Tyler said.

"Race you," Ralon said with a grin.

Tyler looked at Razmal and bowed. "Farewell my friend."

Razmal slammed his fist to his chest and turned away, hoping no one would see him wiping tears from his eyes. He looked back just in time to see Tyler and Crylona wade into the deep water. Tyler kept himself steady with Polaris while Crylona treaded water next to him effortlessly. The two looked at each other and nodded, and then slipped beneath the waves.

***

Razmal stood on a small hill outside of Moonlit Waters, weighed down by a large pack of equipment. He had his obsidian hammer in one hand and his dented shield strapped to his other arm. Both items had been acquired from Piotr what seemed like years ago. However, it had only been a few short weeks. The VAST whispered louder to him anytime he touched the hammer and shield. Today, it was like he was sitting in a crowded tavern with how loud they were in his mind. He gritted his teeth as Ralon approached with a far smaller pack and a belted sword.

A winged shape approached from the castle and looked to be heading for the hill on which they stood.

"Table for three?" Razmal asked.

"Gryphem," Ralon said, his voice sounding sour.

"Mommy is worried about you," Razmal said before he could stop himself.

The Avian, which indeed turned out to be Gryphem, landed heavily next to Ralon. Razmal had never heard an Avian pant, but today seemed to be full of surprises.

"Heavy," was all Gryphem could say. He was wearing a strange harness that hugged a bulging pack against the front of his body. It made sense, given the large wings on his back.

"Ready?" Ralon asked as if to no one at all.

"It's a shame we couldn't bring gek. I am not looking forward to walking for a month," Razmal said.

Ralon produced an egg-shaped crystal from a deep pocket within his vest.

"Who said anything about walking?" Ralon asked.

The crystal vibrated and flickered with an inner light. A small steel-gray storm cloud spun within the egg, rumbling and crackling with miniature thunder and lightning. Ralon took a few steps into the field and drew his thin blade from its hard leather sheath. An angry red glow lit the edge of the sword, and Ralon stabbed its point into the Acrean soil, the tiger's-eye pommel glittering. He took a few steps back and held the crystalline egg high over his head.

Ralon whispered softly, and the egg shattered, releasing the small storm cloud. The cloud boomed with thunder and began to rip itself into tendrils of gray mist. The tendrils descended and wrapped thickly around Ralon's raised arm. His eyes flashed with inner lightning, and he lowered his arm and pointed a slender finger at his sword. A powerful buildup of static danced his long yellow hair from its leather cord. Blue and orange lightning leaped from his finger and struck the pommel of his blade with a crash.

The tiger's eye of his sword drank in the energy and funneled it violently into the ground. The slender black eye of the gem glittered and opened widely. The misty tendrils pulled dangerously at Ralon, and he slid a few inches towards the sword. He leaned back against the pull and allowed the tendrils to spiral down his arm in a twisting tunnel of compressed vapor. The whirling clouds hammered into the sword and spun upward into the sky, expanding rapidly. VAST crashed into the maelstrom hungrily and consumed the energy like ravenous beasts.

"We will only have a moment when the portal appears," Ralon shouted over the raging whirlwind that rotated above his sword.

A great ripping sound followed by a sonic boom knocked the three companions back on their heels. The VAST were funneling into a small area beyond the sword and danced around an absence of space. The portal was impossible to see from the side, and even when looking directly where it appeared, the area looked more like shifting air on a hot day.

"Go!" Ralon shouted, his voice sounding strained.

Gryphem was the first through the portal, keeping his wings as close to his armored body as possible. His lance was tucked under one arm and trailed behind him like an angry, barbed tail. One moment he was dashing through the air, and the next moment he was simply gone.

Razmal mustered up as much courage as he could and started down the hill in an overburdened run. He felt like the VAST were cheering for him now instead of using their usual whisper, and his legs pumped faster with tingling energy. It was a strange sensation. He had not called to the VAST. They had instead come to him and were ushering him through the portal. In a flash, he passed by Ralon, and the tall Acrean, his face worn, gaped at him in shock. Time seemed to slow down as Razmal gave him a wink and plunged headlong into the portal.

The sensation past the threshold was like being stretched far beyond one's physical limit and then being twisted and wrung out like a rag. One moment, Razmal was tingling with warm portal energy, and the next, he was rocketing through a tall drift of northern snow. He spun end over end on the ice-covered ground before coming to a rest, facing the flickering rip in the air. Razmal scrambled to his feet, looking around for Gryphem, and found him facing the other direction looking upward. He followed his gaze up to a giant jagged mountain peak to an enormous settlement tucked into its vast crevices.

Razmal felt Ralon appear before he heard his feet touch the snow-covered ground. The VAST that the man currently commanded was painful to be around. It took him a few deep, steadying breaths and what Razmal assumed was a stubborn will to live before he released the VAST back to the wind.

"Alya Cheyl," Ralon said, pride brimming in his voice.

"My hero," Razmal said weakly before doubling over and retching loudly and wetly into the snow.

8 – FOOLISH DAY

The tunnel darkness yawned empty and chill before them. Small bits of stone and dust continued to tumble from the newly opened doorway. Roarc glanced at Zuh'Erg, hoping to gauge his next move. The Erew stood with his muscular arms crossed, gazing into the haze.

"So now what?" Roarc asked.

I told an old friend where to find us. Wait a short time longer half-giant, came the expected mental barrage. Roarc squeezed the grip on his maul, forcing back the bubbling annoyance that gripped his chest.

The Acrean sun was just beginning to crest the horizon as dawn's light spilled behind the shadowy figure, revealing an unexpected sight. As if on queue, the tall azure-colored grass rustled and bent and a tall shape pushed through. Roarc craned his neck and almost went up on his toes to see the figure as it passed through the shifting vegetation. He heard a familiar clacking and rattling sound of bone and beads as a spear-wielding Sogra appeared.

Mazoris.

"Impossible!" Roarc said, his surprise causing his voice to come out in a bellow.

Mazoris grinned wickedly and thumped the butt of his spear against the ground. The Sogra chieftain looked well enough considering how long he must have been alone in the wilderness. The last time Roarc had traded words with Mazoris was when he had faded into the grasslands looking for "weapons."

The reed and bone armor the Sogra clan chief wore was cracked and broken in several places. His necklaces and bracelets looked to have expanded to include a variety of new fetishes, and he wore a bulging pack over his shoulders. He was missing more scales than usual, and Roarc noticed an absent fang from his grinning maw.

The spear he carried was of a foreign design. The shaft was made of a segmented material that looked like long hollow grass. The tip gleamed dully in the Acrean sunlight and appeared to have been salvaged from one of the many wrecks scarring the surface of Arral. Tightly woven green cordage secured the jagged metal tip to the haft, and several feathers from an unknown bird adorned the spear.

Mazoris studied him with a predatory gaze and tilted his head as his inner eyelids blinked horizontally.

"A weapon, small giant. At last," Mazoris said, his voice a rasping hiss.

Small giant?

"Take a wrong turn?" Roarc asked, attempting a casual tone.

"Something like that," Mazoris said, rubbing his jaw. "An entire clan would not have been enough for the Tekian."

He is not *a Tekian.*

Roarc flinched in surprise at the wolf's mental barrage. Mazoris hissed in anger, which could have been fear, and he brandished his spear threateningly. The Sogra must have heard Zuh'Erg in his thoughts as well.

"Many days has this Erew been crawling around in here," Mazoris said, pointing a taloned finger to his ridged brow.

Roarc paused and considered the silver-furred Erew carefully. It would seem that both he and Mazoris had been saved by the wolf. But why? They were enemies that had arrived from Teka together, and the denizens of Arral had nearly killed them both. Why was the Erew helping them? Did the Erew also help the dark lady?

I already told you half-giant, I need someone that can read your written language, said Zuh'Erg in his mind.

Half-giant writing was more lewd pictures and scratches than a formal language, but it did have its own distinct set of dialects that would be hard for anyone not born into one of the tribes to understand.

"What of the Sogra?" Roarc asked aloud, his eyes fixed on Mazoris.

"Yesss, what of Mazoris, clan chief of the blue throat clutch?" the Sogra asked.

Did all Sogra refer to themselves in the third person?

His cunning will come in handy, trust me, came Zuh'Erg's expected mental echo.

A gust of wind bent the grass around them suddenly, and the gaping hole left by Roarc's hammer in the hillside moaned. Mazoris hissed and produced an object from his belt. The object was a primitive fetish that looked to be a dry plant with many pods packed tightly together. He shook the fetish at the dark portal, and the pods clacked and rattled.

"Cursed place," Mazoris said and continued to shake the fetish.

Roarc crossed his arms and stared into the darkness, unimpressed.

The fetish began to flow the more vigorously Mazoris shook it. A thin tendril of acrid-smelling smoke drifted from its center and began to haze the air around him. He hissed and clicked in the Sogra language and tossed the now flaming fetish into the mouth of the tunnel. He swept his spear in an arc with a kick from his scaled foot and thrust his empty palm towards the doorway. A blast of compressed air ripped through the grasslands from behind and snaked its way around his outstretched arm. The air howled around his fingers and then leaped into the waiting darkness. The flickering fetish became a blazing brand and shot wildly down the tunnel, disappearing from sight.

"Spirit catcher," Mazoris said with a shrug of his shoulders, returning to his usual stance of leaning back slightly and resting on his thick tail with his arms crossed around his spear.

Roarc had heard of how Sogra shaman commanded the elements but had never seen it firsthand. He hoped that his jaw had not been hanging wide open the entire time. He snapped his mouth closed and swallowed hard. Where had this power been when the Felions had attacked them shortly after arriving in this cursed land? Perhaps surprise was the enemy of the Sogra magic.

Focus Roarc, we have a long road ahead and need to get moving, said Zuh'Erg in his mind.

In response, Roarc grabbed his wall shield and maul and strapped them carefully to his back. He kept the loop slightly loose around his maul, keeping it ready to pull free with minimal effort. Something told him the hammer would get an extraordinary amount of use in the coming days. He glanced around and noticed that only Mazoris wore a pack that looked to be bulging with provisions and several water bladders.

Zuh'Erg sat back on his haunches facing the dark opening in the hillside. His yellow eyes had a faraway look to them. He seemed to be struggling with a decision and, after a time, closed his eyes, nodded, and settled lower on his haunches.

"What lies within?" Roarc asked, wondering just how long they would stare at the tunnel.

A way home for my two new friends, Zuh'Erg projected.

Roarc frowned. Given the vast Acrean Ocean that separated Arral from Teka, a journey on foot could not be made. Even if it could be done, it would take years. In fact, a journey by ship would have an equal chance of success. The great ocean had a foul temperament. Roarc crossed his arms, feeling his own temperament becoming that of the ocean.

Did Roarc even want to go home?

The only person he cared about had sent him away. He knew, however, that she had done it for his protection. Lady Dark had undergone some kind of transformation, and Roarc didn't know exactly what that meant. He knew that he could no longer feel her presence, but somehow, he knew she was still alive.

"Home," Roarc said, his voice sounding harsh and cutting to his own ears.

Zuh'Erg stood and held up a clawed paw, stopping Roarc from launching into a tirade.

We each find our own home half-giant. The way forward is a difficult one, and you will, in the end, have a choice. You may not value the life of your Sogra companion nearly as much as your own, but we must at least see him safely back to Teka, Zuh'Erg said in his mind.

Roarc glanced over his shoulder at the Sogra, who was sunning himself, both eyes closed, humming.

"Let's get on with it then," Roarc said with a sigh that rumbled.

Zuh'Erg gave a wolfish nod and strode into the waiting darkness.

***

They descended into finely crafted tunnels and lost the light of the sky behind them within moments. Roarc wasn't sure if Erew could see in the dark as well as a Sogra could, but half-giants were utterly dependent on illumination. His night vision was nonexistent, and he felt a moment of panic when they rounded a short bend and he stumbled into complete darkness. He pulled his torchstone from his belt and sighed in relief when it flared to life and pushed back the gloom.

The tunnel was tall and wide, with a floor made of interlocking cobbles that were worn smooth. The air temperature felt constant and comfortable and had a slightly damp smell. A slight breeze came from the way they had come and carried slightly warmer air with it.

"What is this place?" Roarc asked, raising his torchstone to see if its light would touch the ceiling.

This is the first place. The ancient road that leads to another of the great cities, Zuh'Erg answered.

"Another of the great cities?" Roarc wondered aloud.

It is said to rival the beauty of Moonlit Waters. I have never heard its name, but I am told the city sits under an endless ocean of starlight, Zuh'Erg projected.

"I didn't realize there were more ancient cities," Roarc said. He hated feeling uneducated. His people were constantly ridiculed for having basic or even childlike intellect. It hadn't always been that way. In the beginning, when there were still giants, they had been a highly intelligent race. That was, until Shade.

Brighter thoughts, half-giant, you are proof that intelligence is still possible for your kind, Zuh'Erg said in his mind. The words had a rounded and kind tone to them.

Very few know three ancient cities have escaped the ravages of time.

"Where is the third?" Roarc asked.

Silence answered him. Zuh'Erg had stopped walking and held up a hand for them to stop. The sound of Mazoris sniffing the air and then hissing in warning was all the prompting Roarc needed. His maul sang from its sheath, and he held it in one hand and closed his other around his torchstone, dimming its light.

They stood in the darkness and silence for what felt like hours. Zuh'Erg stayed utterly still, both ears switching and rotating to catch the slightest sound from farther down the tunnel. Mazoris continued to sniff the air but otherwise remained quiet. Roarc, as usual, felt useless. He couldn't hear anything other than his pounding heart, and all he could smell was swampy Sogra.

We must proceed with caution and keep words to a minimum, Zuh'Erg finally said in their minds after a time.

Roarc breathed a quiet sigh of relief and stared down at his palm with the torchstone. He needed both hands free if a battle did come. As they started walking again, he holstered his maul against his back and shield and began picking at a torn thread of his jerkin. By the time they stopped again to rest, eat, and hydrate, he had a long piece of thick leather thread that he used to tie the torchstone securely. He hung the stone around his neck and felt better when its warmth sank into his chest.

They continued on, and the floor slanted ever so slightly downward. It was impossible to tell how long they had traveled without the Acrean sun to guide them. The walls of the tunnel looked exactly the same, and they had not yet come to a junction or split to take a different way. The tunnel kept going on endlessly in a single direction. Roarc began to feel like the walls were narrowing, and the weight of the world above was crushing down on him. He shook his head vigorously, dismissing the disturbing feeling.

The only break in the monotony of the tunnels came in regular intervals as alcoves on either side of the tunnel. The alcoves went back only a short way and contained a single hole in the floor that dropped an unknown distance. Roarc had asked to explore one and was standing rubbing his face, wondering what it could be, when Mazoris jostled by and began to relieve himself in the hole. Roarc palmed his face with his hand, backed his way out of the alcove, and continued down the tunnel, shaking his head and grumbling.

When his legs felt like another step would tear them clean off, Zuh'Erg signaled for a halt. Roarc sank thankfully against the nearest wall and slumped into a seated position. He didn't care that his shield dug painfully into his back or that his maul had him propped too far to one side. He wasn't moving, and that was all that mattered. A waterskin found its way into his hands, and he drank eagerly.

We will rest here for a while. I will stand the first watch, Zuh'Erg projected before slipping out of the torchstone light farther down the tunnel.

Roarc closed his eyes for what felt like a moment. A gentle shaking against his shoulder came far too soon. He opened his eyes and met a reptilian backside. Roarc cringed and crinkled his nose. No one wanted to wake up with that kind of a view, not even another Sogra, he suspected.

After several failed attempts to stand, Roarc finally clawed his way to his feet by turning on his side and heaving himself up, using the wall as leverage. His legs and feet were not happy. The days of running and burning the foul liquid Colin had given him had not been kind to his body. His endurance was nearly limitless as a half-giant, but the foul silver liquid had pushed him past what nature had intended. Now he felt nearly crippled as he stooped painfully against the wall.

Mazoris watched him with his predatory gaze and nodded as if coming to a decision. He produced a small gourd bowl from his pack and a carefully wrapped oiled leather pouch. He opened the pouch and shook a dense-looking root into his waiting palm. He squeezed the root and several drops of liquid dribbled into the bowl. An overwhelming citrus smell assaulted Roarc's nostrils. Mazoris grabbed the waterskin that had apparently tumbled to the tunnel floor when Roarc had lost consciousness and poured water into the bowl.

Mazoris stirred the liquid with one of his long talons and then offered Roarc the bowl. He stared at the offering and then looked at the Sogra's filthy talon and took the bowl with a grimace. The liquid bubbled and hissed in the bowl. He forced a polite smile before downing the contents in a single gulp. A chill tore through his middle as the liquid moved its way down to his belly. What started as pain in his core quickly spread through his muscles and extremities as cold relaxation.

Roarc sighed and stood straight again. It seemed like he was the only one he knew without a magic healing potion or a bag of enchanted crystals. He stretched his back and raised his arms high in the air, eliciting a satisfying series of cracks and pops down his spine. Today was going to be a good day.

Zuh'Erg emerged from the shadows, his lupine eyes studying. He nodded and grinned his wolfish grin, apparently satisfied with what he saw. They shared a quick meal of dried meat and washed it down with water from their waterskins. It felt strange to eat at such regular intervals again. Roarc had barely eaten since sharing a last meal with Lady Dark. The thought of his lady sent a pang of loss through his chest. He missed her.

Once the provisions were stowed away and Mazoris had shouldered his pack, they proceeded down the tunnel once more. Roarc found himself daydreaming as he watched the swaying and predatory gait of Zuh'Erg loping a few feet in front of him. He had never met an Erew before as none lived on Teka. He wondered if they were all like his silver companion.

Zuh'Erg seemed to know a great many things and shared only what was necessary. What did he actually know about where they were going, and what were the chances that their paths had crossed again? Roarc doubted very much it was a coincidence.

You think too loudly, half-giant, Zuh'Erg projected with a mental chuckle.

Roarc shrugged at him, feeling foolish.

They continued for a time when a constant noise began to murmur through the tunnel. Roarc recognized it at once as running water. The farther they traveled, the louder the sound became. By the time they emerged from the tunnel into a large circular chamber, the sound of water was a dull roar. He spotted the source of the sound high above, where four waterfalls emptied into a fathomless depth that plunged into darkness below. They had emerged on a wide bridge that spanned across the massive chamber. His torchstone light barely illuminated the chamber, and thick shadows clung heavily to unknown objects.

Mazoris stopped at his side and surveyed the chamber without comment. It was difficult to read the Sogra by appearance. So much of his communication was verbal, and his face always looked like he was ready to eat something. Zuh'Erg was several paces in front of them, looking over one side of the bridge and then the other.

Roarc let his eyes adjust as much as possible to the expansive chamber and began to make out enormous stone sculptures where the waters emerged. The sculptures were faces of strange beasts with open mouths that gushed water into the depths. The faces looked like a cross between a Sogra and something powerful and muscular. He had never laid eyes upon anything alive that resembled the horrific visages and hoped he never would.

Roarc squinted at one of the sculptures, wishing that his torchstone would quit flickering and obscuring the full view of the stone masterpiece in shadows. He started when one of the shadows detached itself from the darkness and slithered down below the bridge. His maul was in his hands before the shout of warning passed his lips. Roarc's loud bellow was wholly lost in the roar of the waterfalls.

Another shadow had moved.

9 – DO YOU FEEL IT?

"Samson, do you feel it?" Lanadari asked quietly.

Samson, in fact, could feel little else. The sheer power raging around them was terrifying. The sparring chamber they stood in was crackling with more energy than he had ever experienced, and Lanadari didn't even seem to be breaking a sweat. The young woman stood in the chamber's center, arms at her sides with palms up. Samson had lost the exact moment that she had floated several inches off the stone floor and when the shimmering white light had begun its pulsing dance upward in lashing currents.

"I feel that all of Moonlit Waters can," Samson said through gritted teeth. She was making his old bones ache.

With all the power in the room, he realized that he couldn't hear the VAST anymore. The sweet song he spent so much of his life listening to was silent. Or perhaps, the music was so loud that he could no longer make sense of it. Either way, had he needed to defend himself against Lanadari's growing power, he could have done nothing short of trying to knock her upside the head with his walking staff.

Where had he put that walking staff anyways…?

Lanadari levitated for a few moments more when she closed her hands, and the light around her faded away. She settled back on her bare feet and closed her eyes, drawing in deep breaths. It looked like she was trying to calm herself. Was the power she felt addictive? Samson had battled the sweet lure of the VAST on several occasions, wanting to give it more and take more in return. Sadly, it didn't work that way. Many young students had given too much of themselves and were left empty shells.

Samson refused to let Lanadari become like them. Even with traces of the dark lady still clinging to her like a disease, he would bring this frightened young woman through whatever was happening to her.

"They were calling to me again," she said, barely above a whisper.

Samson nodded and grabbed her heavy robe from where she had tossed it in a heap hours before. An object tumbled out and clanged on the ground. Blue sparks of energy snarled and leaped from the object, nearly scorching his booted foot. Lanadari was next to him instantly, scooping the object from the floor with a look of horror on her face. She held one of the batons that had been the hallmark of Lady Dark.

Her face twisted and contorted as she fought some kind of internal battle. Samson stood motionless, holding her robes. The VAST whispered to him again, but he dared not reach out to them. No, he had to choose his next move very carefully.

"Lanadari," he said with as much calm as he could muster.

She looked him in the eye, and he watched her white irises rimmed in silver cloud and darken.

"Lanadari!" he said with more force.

She blinked rapidly and her irises drained of the darkness and became milky white once more.

"Teacher," she breathed before falling to her knees.

Samson draped the warm robes over her shoulders as sobs wracked her body. She had a white-knuckled grip on the baton that had fallen from the robe, but lightning no longer snarled along its length. He had felt the other baton in the robe as he had put it on her. Why did she keep them so close?

"I believe that is enough for one day," Samson said, patting her on the shoulder. He turned and nearly stumbled as a voice hammered into him.

"Samson," said the voice, sounding like many male and female voices as one. If he thought his bones hurt before, what he felt now made his training with Lanadari akin to a tickle fight.

"Bring her," the voice commanded.

Lanadari looked up at him with big, tear-filled eyes.

"Celest," Samson gasped, staggering a step and looking for his walking staff in earnest.

A whisper of VAST brought his staff floating into his waiting grasp, and he clung to it in thanks. The women in his life, it seemed, didn't realize what they were doing to an old Balan.

"Apologies, young one, but it appears our day is not yet finished," he said. "Celest summons us to the crystal chamber."

Lanadari stood quickly, looking like a young girl in her oversized gray-colored acolyte robes. Samson wore fine silver robes edged in crimson, which signified his status with the Temple of Spero. There had been only one Balan in history with a command of the VAST so strong that he had held the title of oracle. It had been two hundred years since the time of Gresh the Oracle, and his legend grew larger with each passing decade.

The irony of the gray acolyte robes was not lost on Samson as he regarded her. She could match any elder practitioner or priest he had ever encountered. He reached out and took her rune-covered hand for a moment, fighting the visions that touching her skin produced.

This girl was special.

He urged her out of the sparring hut and across the many bridges that led to the grand steps outside the council chamber. Gryphem was strangely absent from his usual place of honor, and in his place was a mountain of a man in gray chitin plate armor. He wore a flowing gold-colored cloak and leaned on an enormous milky-white two-handed blade. Ramos gave them a nod as they passed and returned to attention when they began to descend the steps.

Samson led Lanadari through the crowds of people in the central square and to the tunnel lined with glowing runes. The light from the runes on the wall that touched Lanadari's exposed skin caused her own runes to flicker and take on the same ghostly blue or shining silver.

When they reached the antechamber with its large archway, Samson called for a halt and removed his robes. He wore a plain, sleeveless jerkin underneath, made of a soft cloth. He leaned his walking staff against the wall of the alcove next to the archway and stuffed his robes into a small cutout in the wall. He motioned for Lanadari to follow his example, and she nodded.

It took her only a moment to shrug her way out of her robes, fold them neatly, and place them on an empty shelf in the alcove. The muffled clang of her batons against stone gave Samson a sense of relief that she knew well enough to leave them behind. She stood slender and glittering in a sleeveless tunic that hugged her too tightly at mid-thigh.

Samson cleared his throat, tearing his gaze from her snaking and shimmering runes that covered her arms and legs. He steered her before the archway with a hand at the small of her back and waited. The runes on the archway flared brightly, and Samson felt like he was drowning in bright light. A moment later, he stood side by side with Lanadari in the crystal chamber of Celest.

The sound of his thundering heart throbbed in his ears.

The chamber itself was totally silent, with many colored lights threatening to overwhelm the rest of his senses. He turned, feeling sluggish, as Lanadari took a staggering step into the chamber. A pool in the chamber's center sparkled and echoed the light show from the crystal walls. Her gaze was locked on the water's surface, and she took another step.

Samson couldn't bring himself to move or even speak, for that matter. He felt like he had become part of the chamber, rooted in place.

"Lanadari," the voice that had summoned them said. "Come and bathe in the pool."

Lanadari seemed to move easier after the voice subsided and quickly reached the pool's edge. Samson was still locked in place, unable to make a sound or move more than his head.

"Patience, shaman. Your time will come," said the voice.

Samson relaxed as much as he could with most of his body frozen and waited. He looked on as Lanadari stripped off her garments and slipped naked into the pool. He did his best to avert his gaze, but he couldn't help noticing that every inch of her body was indeed covered in glittering runes.

When she entered the water, the light in the chamber ceased its strobing of rainbow colors and instead locked into a soft blue tone that brightened and darkened every few moments.

"Welcome home, lost one. I am Celest." The voice sounded like so many people talking at once that it was hard to focus.

"Home," Lanadari said in a whisper. She floated to the top of the pool on her back and stared up at the crystal ceiling.

"Your affinity with the crystals was no accident. We arranged for the bag you carried until recently to find its way to you. We tried for years to call you back to this very place," Celest said.

"But why?" Lanadari asked, her voice a harsh whisper.

"The one you call Shade must be stopped," Celest said, her voice coming so loud that Samson was sure the crystal walls around him would crack.

"He has toyed with me for nearly my entire life. I have watched him kill entire tribes with his bare hands. I couldn't stop him, even if I wanted to," Lanadari said.

"Perhaps as Lady Dark, but in time, training here, your spark may trigger a conflagration even he will be unable to stand against," Celest said.

Lanadari remained silent, floating naked and vulnerable looking in the pool.

"I am afraid," Lanadari said after a time. "As much as I try to forget being the dark lady, she still clings to me like a disease."

Samson had felt the dark presence slithering just out of reach on several occasions when training with Lanadari. The batons she kept seemed to trigger who she had once been. Perhaps if she destroyed the weapons, she would be free of any dark influence.

"She cannot hide from who she is," said Celest. "But, the water here in this pool will help cleanse away some of the darkness and lingering demons that may have had hooks in her." Somehow, Samson knew her voice was for him alone.

"Only when Lanadari accepts all parts of her will she be ready to face HIM," Celest said, her last word full of venomous anger.

"Go now and rest. Your teacher and I have much to discuss," Celest said. "You will come here daily and soak in the healing waters. There is much you must learn, and time grows increasingly short."

Samson swelled with pride at being called her teacher. While Lanadari was far more skilled with the VAST, she still needed control, which he knew well. Lanadari continued to float in the pool for a few more moments before her runes flickered, and she faded from sight in a sizzle of steam.

"Now, shaman, it is time to prepare you for what is to come," Celest said.

"I am ready," Samson said with as much conviction as possible.

"There is a Deru that recently arrived here in Moonlit Waters. I want you to go and speak to it," Celest said.

Samson stared at the far wall of the chamber. He hoped his mouth wasn't hanging open.

"But a Deru? They can't…" Samson stammered.

"Speak? I know," Celest said. "They do indeed communicate, but not in any way you would understand."

"Will it even understand my words?" Samson asked, spreading his arms helplessly.

"You should only be concerned with how you will understand it," Celest said, a tinkle of laughter in her voice.

"What do you want me to say?" Samson asked, secretly thinking about the various ways he could possibly offend one of the ancient Deru.

Little was known about the arboreal race. Few of the Deru had ever set foot on the great continent of Arral, and no one knew where they came from. The only common factor was they always emerged on the docks of Moonlit Waters as if they had simply been overlooked a moment before and were a natural part of the bustling seaport.

"Tell it that you are happily taking on additional students," Celest said.

Samson laughed. He couldn't help himself. His laughter came from deep in his belly, and he wiped a tear from his eye.

"Did I say something funny, shaman?" Celest asked.

"You can't be serious. Training a wildly gifted girl is one thing, but to invite an ancient Deru to sit in with us… I don't know what to say." Samson said.

"Say yes," Celest said.

Samson looked around the chamber and shook his head in disbelief. He would do as he was told, but it seemed like an impossible task. Could the Deru even hear the VAST? Their whispers had never hinted that such a thing was even possible. He hadn't ever asked directly. The Deru hadn't come up in regular conversation.

Here in the crystal chamber, the VAST was silent.

"I will do as you ask," Samson said after thinking it over a bit longer.

"Good," Celest said. "I have had a place prepared for the Deru in the gardens. One of the attendants will show you the way."

Samson felt a slight breeze on his face like a gentle wave from a hand fan and found himself standing outside the crystal chamber facing the archway. The runes carved along the edge of the archway were dark.

"A pleasant day to you as well, mistress," Samson grumbled under his breath.

He collected his possessions, dressed, and made his way up the tunnel. The only sound to be heard was his staff clacking on the floor and his labored breath in his ears. Faint smells from the market drifted down the tunnel, but he ignored his complaining belly. Samson wasn't entirely sure how long a Deru would wait. He nodded to the guards as he emerged from the tunnel and headed mechanically towards the docks, lost in thought.

The crowds in the market were a blur of voices, colors, and smells. Samson kept his way as straight as he could to the docks between the tightly packed bodies. He preferred the quiet of his village of Tonu to the hustle and bustle of the big city. The only refuge from the sights and sounds of Moonlit Waters was the Temple of Spero, but since the battle, only essential members were allowed anywhere near it. Sure, he could use his status as a hero and companion of the Sleeper, but what was the point? Everything had turned upside down since Tyler, then known as Tyrant, had walked into his village.

When he reached the walkway down to the docks, the traffic had thinned considerably. The docks were organized chaos, but there were far fewer people than at the market. He spotted the Deru almost immediately after setting foot on the central floating platform. A large group of curious dock workers had formed a semicircle around the Deru.

The Deru stood unmoving, arms crossed over its thick wooden chest. Samson could see the flickering blue eyes from where he was standing. They seemed to be looking right at him. Every other Deru that Samson had ever laid eyes on carried with it a long crook. As strange as it was to actually see a Deru, one without its staff was odd. Samson called to the VAST with a silent prayer and projected his voice for only the Deru to hear.

"You are welcome, Deru. I have been sent here on behalf of the ancient Celest."
The Deru stood unmoving.

Samson regarded it from across the docks and sighed. Perhaps he would need to get closer. He worked his way across the docks and then through the crowd to come and stand before the Deru. He had to crane his neck and look up as the Deru towered over him, easily three times his height.

"You are welcome, Deru—" Samson began again but was interrupted when the Deru knelt down and offered him its massive hand made of tightly woven vines. He could manage only to take one of the oversized fingerlike appendages in his own hand and squeeze.

"You are welcome here, friend," Samson whispered with the awe he felt creeping into his voice.

A flood of feeling, heavy and alien, flowed from the Deru into Samson. The smell of loam and dirt assaulted his senses, and he felt buried alive. He released the Deru's finger and gasped for breath. The Deru remained kneeling for a moment, its cool flickering eyes intense and staring into Samson. When it stood, the vines that made up its body creaked and groaned.

"I know how you feel," Samson said, having heard the same sounds from his own body the more years he put behind him.

"Come, I will show you to the gardens," Samson said.

The Deru stood unmoving once again.

"Please? Come this way," Samson said, trying to change tactics by miming the direction they needed to travel and walking a few paces away before turning and beckoning.

The Deru stood, its eyes watching him.

Samson sighed. When the Deru had offered him its hand, he felt at that moment a sense of connection. Maybe…

Samson walked with his staff thumping on the dock back to the Deru and put his palm on one of its twisted hand-shaped appendages.

"Come, I will show you to the gardens," Samson said softly.

The Deru took a large step forward, sending Samson nearly reeling into the water. The Deru shambled down the docks in the direction Samson had initially indicated while dock workers scattered in all directions. The hulking figure strolled down the rickety path leading up into the city and the gardens beyond. It turned and regarded Samson with its flickering blue stare as if to say, Are you coming?

Samson closed his eyes, drew in a deep breath, and let it hiss out through his teeth, praying for patience.

10 – ACREAN DAY DREAM

Thomas wandered the ship's halls as he often did when he was awake, not exactly sure what he was looking for. There were hundreds of decks on the *Spero*, but he didn't have access to all of them. The central corridors that ran the ship's length had been sealed during the cataclysm, and Morgan didn't have, or more likely wouldn't share, the status of the remaining habitation module with Thomas.

Thomas had only been able to account for three out of the four modules during the doomed landing attempt. The first had crash-landed on Arral, and the second had slammed into the atmosphere at the wrong angle and sheered off into countless fragments, many of which still circled the planet. The third module had careened into the ocean and was lost.

Pelagos.

Thomas shook his head, trying to stay focused. The fourth colony module was still a mystery, and after repeated attempts, he had given up pestering Morgan for a satisfactory answer. If his nearly one thousand years of life had taught him anything after this experience, it was that security was good in theory when everything was working as it should, but horribly bad when the unimaginable happened. If only Thomas could send down the *Centaur*, cannons blazing, to end whatever Croyan had become and topple his tyrannical cult. Why couldn't Morgan see the big picture and unlock both hangar and weapons control?

There was barely anything human left on the planet because of Croyan.

He came to a corridor he hadn't been to before as the wall was missing his customary chalk T that he left on panels when visiting a new section of the ship. It would have been far easier for Morgan to just tell him what was in each room, but privacy restrictions limited the AI's ability to tell him much of anything. He would often mark doors with an X if he could not open them, or various other symbols depending on what he found inside.

Thomas sighed heavily and wandered for a time before stopping and swiping his palm over a door for what felt like the millionth time. The door chimed, groaned, and refused to open. Repeated venting of the decks was taking its toll on the ship. When Thomas went back into cold sleep, the *Spero* internals would once again return to vacuum. He prayed that he wouldn't have to go back to sleep this time.

He pulled a door kit out of the engineering pack he always carried on his strolls and began to work on the door. It took nearly an hour, but the door finally screeched open. He felt immediate satisfaction when he recognized the room as one of the hundreds of workshops scattered across the ship. Most of the habitation and work areas were to the aft of the vessel and completely inaccessible to him. This was the first workshop he had found intact in all of his decades of exploring.

A half-finished Sapien-class communications drone was on a table in the center of the room. Sapien-class drones were the most human-looking drones in a wide array of robotics that the UEA had employed. He shook his head sadly. Should he keep thinking about the UEA in the past tense? Maybe one or both of the *Spero's* sister ships had made it. But if they had, why had they not tried to communicate? A better question was, how would they even communicate with the *Spero* without an operational jump gate?

More questions above his pay grade, he thought with an audible sigh.

He walked around the room, taking inventory of the parts bins and wall screens displaying a wide array of drone blueprints. He stopped and stood over the table, assessing the drone. Various parts lay strewn across the table's matte finish. A small slate with a dark screen waited silently for input. A tool kit lay on the floor next to an open container spilling over with additional parts.

He had always been good with anything having to do with machines. The thought of losing himself in a project like finishing the assembly of a drone was intriguing. Until Commander Tor made contact, he was sentenced to ship maintenance. Even his leisure time had become mundane. The ship's library had long ago run dry of anything new for him to watch or listen to. Or at least anything he found interesting or enjoyed.

Thomas tapped the slate, and the completed drone's wireframe flickered to life on the screen. He swiped the slate with his fingers a few times, and the image changed with each touch. He stopped once the image changed to an accurate depiction of where the drone assembly before him looked to be. The schematic had an estimated time to complete in the bottom right corner.

Twelve hours.

He squared his shoulders, cracked his neck, and bent over to retrieve the fallen tool kit he had noticed when he came in—time to get to work.

***

Thomas looked up at the wall display to note the date and time. It had been twenty-seven hours, but the Sapien was complete. Twelve hours must have been an estimate for a master drone engineer. He had struggled significantly assembling some of the more intricate parts and had to start over several times. He held a small pulsing power core in his hand and blinked his bleary, sleep-deprived eyes that refused to focus on the core housing in the drone's V-shaped torso.

Let's see if this was worth it. Maybe even someone else to talk to, Thomas thought.

The power core slipped seamlessly into the core housing. The core pulsed brightly, and a small shielded door snapped into place, hiding the shimmering fist-sized core. The Sapien was sitting on the table, bent backward at an odd angle. Its thin, armor-plated arms dangled behind it, and its featureless oval head stared out one of the room's portholes into space. For several minutes, nothing happened.

What had he done wrong? He had triple-checked his work, and all of the diagnostic checks showed green. Perhaps he had missed a critical power junction? He grabbed one of the power scanners from the recovered tool kit and moved to troubleshoot when the blank faceplate of the Sapien flickered, and a large blue dot appeared.

"Sapien, online," the drone said, its voice a pleasant, even tone of a woman hailing from Old England of Earth.

The Sapien moved its arms forward first and then sat up with its head coming last to perfect posture. The drone folded its humanlike synthetic hands, complete with fingers in its lap, and fixed Thomas with a blue-orbed stare.

"Designation?" the Sapien asked.

"Uhh," Thomas stammered, completely unprepared for such a long time for dialog with anyone other than Morgan.

"Error, the name Uhh is already taken by another," the drone replied.

Did he detect a hint of laughter in its voice?

"I apologize. I am unprepared. I don't know what to call you, shall we come back to that? Perhaps we can skip to directives?" Thomas asked.

The blue orb of the drone studied him for a moment.

"Directive," Thomas said slowly.

The drone sat impassively.

Thomas sighed and scrubbed his face with his hands.

"Well, what do you want to be called?" he asked.

The drone didn't move, and the blue orb on its faceplate stared at him. He looked around at the various empty parts crates, wracking his brain. He was terrible with remembering names, let alone being asked to *give* something a name. His eyes settled on a reoccurring pattern in the serial numbers printed on the drone assembly boxes.

SH646-AL37-E60

"How about SH-AL-E?" Thomas asked.

The drone nodded. "Shale accepted."

"Directive?" Shale asked.

Now it was Thomas who stared, unmoving. He had wanted to build something to pass the time, and now that it was finished, he didn't know what to do. Maybe it was his sleep-deprived brain or the profound sense of loneliness he felt, but either way, he now had a companion, and he wanted time to think about it.

"Directive," Shale asked again, this time with more firmness.

Thomas pinched the bridge of his nose with his index finger and thumb, closed his eyes, and thought hard. What was it that he wanted more than anything else? Companionship was an obvious choice. Off the ship, definitely. He gasped audibly and opened his eyes, meeting Shale's blue orb.

"I want you to find Commander Tyler Ryan Tor and take him to the nearest communication relay with enough power to hail the UEA *Spero*," he said in a rush.

"Current location of Commander Tor?" Shale asked him, the female voice with the English accent calm.

"The planet's surface, known locally as Acrea," Thomas said.

"Current location of Shale?" the drone asked.

"Orbiting the planet aboard the UEA *Spero*," Thomas said.

Shale quickly scanned the room with a scattered beam of flashing light that touched the ceiling and trailed down to the floor. The drone walked noiselessly over to one of the wall panels with a hardline data port typically used for maintenance. A data spike emerged from a hidden compartment in Shale's wrist that fit neatly into the maintenance port. The central blue orb on the drone's faceplate took on an orange hue. The entire head of the drone rotated to face Thomas, and the blue light flickered and turned yellow.

"Rest, EDO Lieutenant Thomas Caledon. This will take some time," Shale said, turning its head back to face the wall of screens.

She learned fast.

Did a drone have gender? he thought.

Thomas wasn't sure, but the fact that the voice from the drone was feminine put him at ease. He also hadn't heard his full rank and name spoken aloud in several centuries. He had urged Morgan to stop using it and instead had instructed him to call him Lieutenant. It felt different when Shale said it. Almost reverent. He had been, after all, the only engineering duty officer aboard the *Spero*.

Thomas thought about the long walk back to his quarters and shook his head. He would be asleep the moment he sat in one of the lifts. He instead eyed the now spotless table and shrugged. He had slept in worse places. He crawled onto the table and stretched out, not caring that his feet hung off the edge. Sleep took him like an avalanche when his head rested on the flat surface and he sighed.

***

"Warning, escape pod D47 on deck 11 launch detected," Morgan said over the ship's loudspeakers.

Thomas snapped his eyes open and sat up quickly, looking around the now empty workshop. How long had he been asleep? Where had Shale gone? Had he dreamed the whole thing?

Morgan flicked into existence beside the table where Thomas sat. "Lieutenant, a communications drone gained access to the ship's systems. I am still processing exactly what it was looking for in my databases, but it apparently learned enough to bypass security lockdowns and was able to cross a large section of the ship still under hard vacuum. It appears it has jettisoned an escape pod."

"Was the drone inside the pod?" Thomas asked, trying to keep the excitement out of his voice.

"One synthetic life sign detected aboard the escape pod," Morgan replied. The AI paused for a moment as if to realize where he was.

"You didn't happen to have anything to do with the drone, did you?" Morgan asked.

Thomas pushed himself up off the table and headed towards the door.

"Did you?" Morgan called, his voice sounding almost pleading as Thomas exited the workshop.

11 – UNDERCOVER

Razmal had never been so cold in his life. They had been wandering the foothills for days when a particularly blustery snowstorm had moved in, and he and Ralon had taken shelter in a cave within sight of the Avian capital city. The storm still raged outside, blowing snow in thick waves across the countryside. They sat around a cluster of torchstones that barely kept the chill out of their refuge. Their steaming breath was a sharp reminder of the miserable temperatures just outside the meager warmth of the stones.

Razmal could see his breath, and he hugged his ribs to try and keep his warmth. His carapace breastplate had seemed like a great idea when packing for the journey, but it acted like an icebox and now lay discarded near the entrance to the cave. The armor had collected a fine layer of snow.

Ralon, on the other hand, seemed blissfully unaffected by the cold in his voluminous robes and thick fur-lined cloak. He sat hunched like a predator over the torchstones, rubbing his gloved hands near the warmth.

Gryphem was somewhere out in the storm gathering information from the locals. As an Avian, he was uniquely suited for such a task. His noble heritage would serve him well as few commoners roosting in the surrounding countryside would question where exactly his nobility hailed from. Even if a commoner did recognize his colored plumage as that of a southern Avian, he would be viewed with mild suspicion, but an alarm to Alya Cheyl was unlikely.

Razmal reached for the open jug of water sitting near the stones and sputtered when he tipped the jug and brought it to his lips. The liquid had become slush from the cold. He wiped his face with his woolen shirt sleeve, then ran his hand over his bald scalp and sighed.

"How long will this last?" he asked, his voice hoarse from the dry air and lack of use.

"Cold?" Ralon asked, raising an eyebrow.

"Frozen to the bone," Razmal replied, his teeth chattering.

"You of all people can do something about that," Ralon said, steepling his fingers under his chin and staring at Razmal.

Razmal scooted closer to the torchstones and rubbed his shoulders back and forth with his hands.

"What are you going on about, Acrean?" Razmal grumbled.

Ralon crooked one of his fingers, and the torchstone flared brightly, throwing off a burst of heavenly warmth. It lasted for only a moment, and when the blissful heat faded to its meager output, the cold crashed in like an avalanche.

Razmal sensed the VAST had been at work. He gritted his teeth and shook his head. Just because he could still hear them didn't mean he would be able to control them.

"You wouldn't understand," Razmal said, staring into the flickering torchstones at his feet.

"Try me," Ralon said. It sounded like compassion had slipped unexpectedly into his normally mocking tone.

Razmal didn't often talk about the horrors of the day he had lost control. The VAST had come early to him. He was still just a boy when the first whispers interrupted his dreams. His village elders had looked at it as a blessing but little did anyone know it would be a curse that would burn them all.

"I hurt people. Lots of them. People I loved," Razmal said, feeling the pain in his chest.

"On purpose?" Ralon asked, his voice barely above a whisper.

"Of course not," Razmal said with anger in his voice.

"I know what it means to hurt people. To be out of control," Ralon said. He clenched his fists and exhaled sharply. "But you must forgive yourself and move on."

The image of Ralon imprisoned in a conviction mask, destroying a city, flickered in Razmal's mind. So they were not so different after all, except that Razmal had never called to the VAST again. In fact, up until his adventures with Tyler, he had all but silenced the voices.

Piotr had changed everything.

Razmal eyed his adopted shield and hammer leaning against the frozen cave wall. He swore he could see a nimbus of VAST radiating from the pair.

"Bring us warmth, my Balan companion. I know you can," Ralon said softly.

Razmal grimaced. He could rip down the mountain around them in the process. Just because he could call to them didn't mean that he should. It was almost as if the VAST were listening to the conversation. The air around them hummed with energy. He took a deep breath, wondering if he should grab his hammer. He always felt like Piotr was with him when he did.

"Just reach out," Ralon said. He was leaning forward and, despite the frigid air, had sweat beading on his brow. It was then that Razmal noticed just how much VAST Ralon was holding around him. It was a veritable fortress of power shielding his body from harm.

How could Razmal blame him? Sure, he wanted to see if another brother of the VAST could return to the fold, but he wasn't taking any chances with his own safety.

Razmal let out the breath he had been holding in a long, slow exhale. The VAST swirled around his misty breath, drinking it in. He closed his eyes and searched for the small part of himself that he had walled up decades earlier. It was easy to find.

He tore at the mental barriers, and they crumbled with ease. In moments, a small crack exposed the bright light within.

The VAST sang in victory.

"Am I interrupting anything important?" Gryphem said from the mouth of the cave.

His sudden appearance startled Razmal, and the barriers slammed back into place. The VAST hissed and scattered like fireflies in the wind.

Ralon groaned and threw his hands in the air.

"Incredible power! Gryphem, your timing, as usual, is impeccable!"

Gryphem loomed in the mouth of the cave and cocked his Avian head as if listening to something the others couldn't hear.

"So I didn't interrupt anything important," he said slowly. "The storm has some life in it yet. I will wait outside and enjoy the snow. Sorry to interrupt."

Before Razmal could say anything, the large Avian noble turned and stepped back into the white swirling cold. Ralon looked at Razmal expectantly, but they both knew that the magical moment had passed. His decades of mental barriers thrust upwards once again, impenetrable.

Ralon sighed and coaxed the torchstones to chase away the cold that seemed to emanate from the very bones of the mountain. This time, Razmal didn't hear the song of the VAST.

They shared a quick meal of dried meat, half a wheel of cheese, and a loaf of dark-colored bread. The meal was sustaining but otherwise not enjoyed by either companion.

"I miss hot food," Ralon said, swallowing his last piece of cold, dense bread.

Razmal nodded, lost in thought. He scoffed suddenly, remembering something, and could not keep himself from saying, "Get in, get the thing, and get out, right? At this rate, we are far off from any kind of hot meal."

Ralon gave him a sour look.

"The weather obviously complicates matters," he said with sharpness at the edges of his voice.

"Obviously," Razmal said, doing his best impersonation of Ralon's voice and accent.

Ralon stared at him with a blank expression on his face. He dusted his hands together, stood, and grabbed his pack and scabbarded sword.

"Looks clear enough," he said with a grin and disappeared into the still falling snow.

Razmal closed his eyes and sighed. What was it about the Acrean that brought out the worst in him? He would never talk to others like that, but something about Ralon grated on his nerves. He was pompous, sly, and completely self-absorbed, all traits that spoiled Razmal's mood.

The torchstones began to flicker, and the warmth faded. Razmal shivered and hugged his body. As much as he didn't care for Ralon, he needed him for this adventure. Celest commanded his obedience, and he would not disappoint his lady. It took him a moment to gather his equipment and place the cooled torchstone in his pack. With the reassuring weight of his shield strapped to his arm and his hammer belted to his side, he took one last look around the cave and strode out into the snow.

The blast of cold hit him all at once and stole his breath away. White flakes fell straight down in a steady stream, and swirling eddies of air blew through the mountain valley. Razmal could only see a short distance in any direction, and if he hadn't viewed the mountain peaks from before, he would have thought the landscape simply an uneven hillside. Gryphem perched above the cave and wore a heavily oiled leather cloak to keep his feathers dry.

Where had Ralon gone?

"He isn't far," Gryphem called from above. "I can still make him out up the trail a ways."

"What makes you think I care where he has gone," Razmal said.

Gryphem made a noise that he assumed was laughter.

"Peace my Balan friend. I know that Ralon can be challenging but deep down, he is a good person."

"I can't wait to meet THAT person," Razmal said under his breath.

"The storm has broken up enough for us to head out. I have secured us lodgings for the night as being caught exposed out here is a death sentence," Gryphem said, having sufficiently changed the subject away from Ralon.

"How safe are the roads here in the north?" Razmal asked.

Gryphem locked him with his unblinking black eyes and tilted his head. He made a sound deep in his throat. It was a sound of warning.

"Not safe," he said matter-of-factly. "Elkin mostly."

Razmal shivered, perhaps because of the frigid cold or the mention of the Elkin. He had heard the legends and studied crudely drawn likenesses of the northern herds. Few that crossed into Elkin territory lived to tell the tale. Herds ranged from the teens to the hundreds, always led by the strongest male in the herd, the bull Elkin.

Elkin were tall, hoofed beasts that walked on two legs or four, depending on what they were hunting. They had thick hide, long muzzles, and blunt teeth for breaking down plants for food. They hunted anything sentient that wandered into their territory. No one knew what they did with the bodies of their victims, as Elkin supposedly didn't eat meat.

"Are we venturing through their territory?" Razmal asked, a bit breathless and not entirely from the thin air.

Gryphem shrugged.

"Have you ever seen an Elkin?" Razmal asked. "You don't seem very concerned."

Gryphem made that sound in his throat again, the one that reminded Razmal of laughter.

"I have not, but my great grandfather often spoke of how delicious Elkin meat is," Gryphem said.

Razmal felt his stomach lurch.

"We are certain to encounter them before nightfall. This road is not well traveled, and Elkin expand their dominion rapidly. I scouted signs up ahead," Gryphem said.

Razmal tightened the strap on his shield and made sure his pack fit equally snug on his back.

"Let's seek out the lodgings you spoke of. Perhaps luck will be with us, and we will avoid the Elkin altogether," Razmal said, knowing the words sounded as hopeless as he felt.

When would he learn that luck was always turning its back on him and his companions?

Gryphem nodded and leaped from his perch, landing lightly beside Razmal. They walked down what appeared to be a seldom-used supply road. Avians, while able to fly long distances, were unable to do so carrying any significant weight. As the northern kingdom grew, more Avians migrated to Alya Cheyl, and supplies in the local area became scarce. Like any other large city, imports and trade became a necessity. According to Gryphem, the shelter they sought for the night was a well-known caravan staging area. It was the last stop on the journey to the city and generally well supplied.

The two walked for a time before stopping short of Ralon, who was standing in the middle of the road with his sword drawn. He had his eyes closed and his hair whipped across his face like it was angry.

"We are not alone," Ralon hissed.

A high-pitched bugle split the air. The sound changed pitch to a deep tone at its end and then repeated three times, louder each time. Razmal had never heard a sound like it.

A tall, powerfully built creature descended from the storm-clouded mountainside. It repeated the same bugling sound and snorted, dropping down on all fours. Mist poured from its long muzzle and nostrils in quick bursts with its breathing. Large black antlers with multiple tines spread out to either side of its head. It was blocking the road with its bulk.

Gryphem took a step forward and swung his cloak out with both arms. The cloak billowed and settled down the middle of his back between his beautiful silver wings. His half-lance, the bone polished to a mirror shine, adorned his right arm up to his elbow. The tip of the lance was wrapped in leather that held a sharpened shard of obsidian. The tip hovered only a few inches from the ground.

The creature bugled again, and Gryphem spread his massive wings, taking on a defiant stance with his lance pointed toward the creature. Six more creatures, smaller and without antlers, thundered down the mountainside to crowd next to what Razmal assumed was the lead male.

"If you have come looking for trouble, you have found it!" Gryphem shouted, his voice rocking the air around them like a shock wave.

The male creature stood up on two of its powerful hind legs, stamped its hoofed feet, and roared. Its bugle was a distant memory.

"Elkin," Ralon whispered, his voice cold and controlled. Razmal noticed the sword he wielded shimmered with VAST.

"I guess it's a fight then," Razmal said, pulling his hammer from its loop at his side.

The VAST sang to him as if they had never left. Something about battle brought them just within his grasp. All he would need to do was reach out and…

A hoof slammed into his shield, sending him reeling backward. It felt like his shoulder might have dislocated under such a heavy blow. The Elkin, what he assumed was a female, lashed out at him with another wicked swipe of its hoofed foreleg. He parried the attack with an upward swing of his shield and a downward chop of his hammer. Bones snapped and the Elkin bugled in pain.

Razmal stepped back and thumped the innards of his shield against his chest. The muscles in his shield arm corded, and he rushed forward with a mighty bash. He caught the Elkin in the torso and heard a satisfying crack as something broke in its sternum. The Elkin crashed to the snow and lay still, crimson leaking from its long maw.

Razmal looked around and found Ralon holding his own against three of the Elkin. One was spinning rapidly inside of a violent vortex of air, snow, and debris. The second of the three Elkin looked to be bleeding from multiple stabs and cuts across its thick hide. The third had Ralon parrying savage hoof strikes with the flat of his blade. His hood had fallen off his head and had settled around his shoulders. His yellow hair hung wet and was plastered to his face in ragged chunks.

The snow was still falling heavily, and the battle that raged around Razmal was chaotic with all the bugling and clashing of weapons against hoofs and hide. He quickly realized that Ralon had dispatched his latest foe and the flurry of activity was from his Avian companion.

Gryphem was a terror to behold in battle. Three Elkin lay crumpled and still on the snowy ground, the white slush beginning to darken with crimson leaking from lance wounds to each creature's middle. Only the bull Elkin was putting up any kind of defense against the hopping and swooping Avian. Each wing was itself a weapon. The feathered appendages struck with such force that the Elkin had lost several blunt teeth and one of its eyes was closed and bleeding. The real threat, however, was Gryphem's half-lance.

The obsidian-tipped weapon smashed through any defense the Elkin could muster. Razmal could see the defiance the bull Elkin once had evaporate into desperation as the deadly lance buried itself deeply into its meaty shoulder. The Elkin thrashed, and its bulk rolled enough to spin Gryphem awkwardly to the snow. The Elkin thrashed until it was back on all fours, its smoldering gaze focused on Gryphem. With a deep bugle, the bull Elkin charged and barreled into the Avian.

Gryphem and the Elkin wrestled and thrashed in the snow like fighting dogs. Razmal rushed to his feathered friend's aid, thinking a well-timed hammer strike would end the conflict. He was three steps away when the frantic thrashing came to an abrupt halt. The Elkin began to rise, and Razmal raised his hammer to strike. The creature pitched over to the side, guided by Gryphem's yellow-taloned feet. A long crystal dagger stuck out of the side of the Elkin's throat.

The bull Elkin would bugle no more.

12 – TOO MANY

The darkness swirled around them, packed with unseen shapes. Roarc smelled a mixture of amphibian slime and decaying plants. The swarming shadows skittered down walls and boiled up from under the bridge. There were far too many shapes to count.

Mazoris stepped forward, hissed something in the Sogra language, and raised his clawed hand. The brand he had cast into the darkness at the start of their descent roared upward from the depths of the waterfall. The brand was burning so bright that Roarc had to squint and look away when Mazoris closed his hand around its base. The burning brand flared even brighter, chasing away the cloaking shadows clinging to the swarm, revealing the slime-covered truth: Croakers.

The nearest Croaker leaped from under the bridge and landed wetly on oversized webbed feet. It wore a ragged black garment covering it from neck to ankle in loose fabric. In one of its webbed hands, the creature clutched a blade made of flaked stone with a handle wrapped in leather cordage. The Croaker leered at them with large eyes that shined in the light from the burning brand, and its wide bulbous head that connected to a pulsing colored throat made a thrumming sound. The Croaker's exposed skin was an earthen tone, smooth and slick with dripping slime.

The Croaker made a deep rasping sound in its throat that was then answered by countless others from all over the chamber. Several Croakers appeared from under the bridge to stand beside the first, and many more filled in behind them. Before long, the bridge was lined with a great many dank-smelling amphibians. Most of them were armed with simple stone knives, but a few bore bone spears or bone clubs.

Roarc stood tall and approached the lead Croaker. At nearly three times their size, he had to hang back a step and look down just to keep everything in view. The lead Croaker shook its blade at him and followed up with a rapid series of croaks and clicks from its mouth. Roarc stood with his wall shield at his side and maul over his shoulder, trying to look casual. The Croakers became more agitated as Roarc simply stood and stared down at them.

A spear whistled from the crowd and clanged uselessly off of Roarc's breastplate.

"That was a mistake," he said with a growl. If he waited, more might become emboldened. The half-giant stood to his full height and inhaled deeply. He heard his weapons master's voice vividly in his mind.

A stunning offense was always the best defense.

The lead Croaker's eyes widened even larger as Roarc sprang into action. He shrugged his maul off his shoulder and, in the same motion, fully extended the heavy hammer into the Croaker blockade. Croaker bodies and slime exploded outward on either side of the bridge like Roarc was parting a sea. While this particular sea was made of Croaker instead of water, it was still red.

The bridge became a chaotic scene of Croakers climbing, dropping, or simply appearing at various sections to surround Roarc and his party. Roarc caught Mazoris out of the corner of his eye, skewering two Croakers with one thrust of his spear and sending a gout of fire from his brand to scorch half a dozen more. Zuh'Erg stood calmly, featureless in the depths of his cloak and hood. He had yet to be challenged and had an almost bored-looking stance.

Roarc, with his maul and shield, waded into the crushing mass of amphibians. He found that the jagged stones they wielded didn't have a fine cutting edge, and the blows' strength could not break through his thick hide. He kept most of the crude weapons at bay, but with so many hands wielding slashing and crushing weapons, he winced at a particularly painful impact every once in a while. He felt almost bad for the Croakers that met his savage shield strikes and his sweeping maul.

There must have been hundreds, maybe even thousands of Croakers lurking in the shadows of the waterfalls. Roarc found himself hoping that he wouldn't have to kill them all. He just wanted to get where they were going and would treat any obstacle the same way. He glanced again behind him as another painful bone club hit his kneecap. Mazoris had the same effect on the army of Croakers. Countless charred amphibians lay strewn across the bridge.

Zuh'Erg stood unmoving. Several Croakers had encircled him and swung primitive weapons with croaking battle cries. He didn't seem to move, but each weapon meant for the Erew met only empty air. Spears, jagged blades, and bone clubs whistled past his seemingly stationary form.

"Are you going to just stand there, or are you going to help us?" Roarc shouted over his shoulder.

You two are doing just fine. The fight will be out of them soon enough, you will see, Zuh'Erg projected. The Croakers continued their futile assault, and Roarc was sure he caught sight of the wolf's toothy grin.

Roarc grunted and kicked a Croaker over the side of the bridge for good measure. Movement caught his eye up ahead, where the bridge ended, and a new tunnel began. Inside stood a larger and much fatter Croaker adorned in beads and wearing a headdress of feathers. The Croaker was waving a fetish that looked similar to the one Mazoris had constructed and was chanting rhythmically.

"Do not let that one live!" Mazoris shouted over the clashing of weapons and cries of pain.

The Croaker in the tunnel abruptly stopped chanting, and a blast of buzzing insects leaped from its gaping mouth. A huge cloud of biting insects broke through the din of battle and swarmed over Roarc. His skin burned with pain like he had been thrown into a blazing inferno. Roarc felt the berserker rage building, and he knew that if he didn't maintain control now, he would be lost.

He dropped his maul and grabbed the closest Croaker by its bulbous head, using it like a giant sponge to soak up the stinging and biting insects. He waded through the crowd and repeated the process several times with different Croakers, discarding them once they were more stingers and welts than amphibians. He could see that the Croaker with the headdress was beginning to wave the fetish and chant again.

Roarc hated bugs.

He snatched another Croaker, which croaked in surprise. He hefted the creature and then heaved it overhanded towards the one chanting. The Croaker he had thrown met the full impact of whatever power the fetish wielder had unleashed. Blue forks of lightning hammered into the flying Croaker, altering its trajectory and sending it sizzling back into the crowd. Both Roarc and the fetish-wielding Croaker looked surprised.

Roarc didn't let the moment spoil and reached down to scoop up a small Croaker spear. It felt like a child's toy in his massive grip, but he threw it with as much force as he could muster all the same. The spear streaked across the chasm, and the Croaker in the headdress jerked. The spear clattered against the far cavern wall, and Roarc cursed loudly. How had he missed?

The Croaker with the fetish stood for a moment glaring at him before it fell to its knees and collapsed forward into a quickly spreading pool of crimson. The spear had passed through the Croaker like it had been made of linen.

Maybe he should get a throwing weapon for the future? Roarc chuckled to himself, kicked another Croaker off the bridge, and retrieved his heavy maul.

With what Roarc assumed was the leader of the Croakers dead, the rest seemed to lose their interest in continuing the fight. They began to disappear as they had arrived. Some slipped over the side of the bridge while others leaped into the blackness above. Zuh'Erg still stood where he had started the battle, arms crossed over his chest.

Well in hand, Zuh'Erg projected as he strode across the bridge, dodging charred remains of Croaker.

Mazoris still panted from the effort and shook his head with what looked like disbelief. Roarc always had trouble with Sogra expressions.

"We are trespassers here," Mazoris said. "Others will challenge us as we go deeper. Ones that will not be so easily overcome."

Roarc nodded and motioned to follow Zuh'Erg, who had disappeared into the tunnel beyond. They quickly caught up with their Erew companion and settled into a steady pace behind him. After a long march they came to the first branch in the tunnel that went off in three different directions. The tunnel was beginning to narrow but maintained its height the deeper they descended. A large stone signpost that stretched from floor to ceiling had runes carved into its surface. Zuh'Erg motioned him closer.

The runes were written in the old language of the giants. Roarc stared at the runes for some time, thinking back to when he had learned the forms as a youth. These runes were very formal, lacking the lewd pictures and bloody handprints of the now standard half-giant writing. The letters were beautifully crafted and ancient.

"What does it say?" Mazoris asked from behind him.

"Three destinations," Roarc said absently, tracing the runes with one of his fingers. "Straight ahead, a place called Starlit Waters. To the left, the Bones of the World, and to the right, Giant's Crossing."

"A big sign with many words for three places?" Mazoris asked.

Roarc snorted and shook his head. The Sogra, however, was correct. The rest of the sign was a warning, but he struggled with the exact meaning of the words. It looked almost like a poem or song.

Ridiculous.

"The destinations are all that matter," Roarc said.

He turned to look at Zuh'Erg, who was staring down the tunnel towards Starlit Waters. His hood had slipped down off of his lupine face, and his eyes were closed. His head was inclined like he was listening for something. A moment passed, and he nodded.

To Starlit Waters.

The tunnel began to slope sharply downward, and the air grew warmer with each step. The tunnel widened again, allowing the three companions to walk side by side. The walls became finely cut and fitted stone blocks that interlocked without the use of glue or cement. Whoever had crafted this section of the tunnel had cut the stones perfectly and allowed time and pressure to bond them better than any cement.

They came to an antechamber of sorts with two massive statues standing on either side of the tunnel. One of the statues was a male giant with a long beard. He was dressed in heavy armor and had been given broad shoulders and a muscular build. His hair was long and touched his armored shoulder pads. He leaned forward on a massive stone sword, and his eyes seemed fixed on the tunnel that they had just passed through. The sword had countless runes crawling up its blade and a single shining emerald set between the guard. The statue radiated an aura of strength.

The female giant at his side was modeled after a beautiful woman. She had thin features and a willowy frame as opposed to the heavily muscled male statue. The sculptor had been sure to give her a bosom that defied nature, and it made Roarc blush. It took him a long moment to avert his gaze. She wore furs that barely covered her chest and a sweeping cloak. A long pendant with a heavy-looking gem of topaz hung around her neck, and she leaned against an enormous kite shield. Roarc felt peace and tranquility emanating from the woman.

"Beautiful," Roarc said, his voice hushed and reverent.

"Those are the biggest—" Mazoris started to say before Zuh'Erg rapped him hard against his ridged skull with the back of one of his claws.

This is a sacred place. Have some dignity! Zuh'Erg projected.

Mazoris hissed something in Sogra that didn't sound very pious.

"May we pass?" Roarc asked the statues. It was strange talking to such large inanimate objects, but something told him they were listening.

Roarc looked up at the male giant, thinking an answer would come. It was, however, the woman that gave him his answer. The heavy topaz around her neck flickered briefly. The tunnel that she guarded shimmered for a moment, and a translucent barrier that none of them had noticed faded away. The tunnel appeared to breathe in a great breath of air before settling back into silence.

"A yes then?" Mazoris asked, leaning carefully forward and staring up at the female giant. He whistled and clicked something and scooted out of the way of a swipe from Zuh'Erg's large paw aimed at his head.

They left the statues behind and walked for a while longer before the tunnel took a final bend and ended in a dramatic fashion. The transition from claustrophobic tunnels to wide open space had Roarc teetering for balance. The cavern was so expansive that the other end of it looked like the edge of the horizon.

Roarc stood frozen in awe, staring up into what appeared to be a sky filled with billions of glittering stars. Galaxies unfolded and familiar constellations burned brightly. The light from the stars gave the entire cavern a ghostly radiance enough to see by. It took him a few moments to pull his gaze from the sky, pocket his torchstone, and behold the splendor of the cavern floor.

The ancient city of Starlit Waters.

Tall towers made of dark stone rose from the mist-shrouded cavern floor. The source of the mist was a shimmering lake at the center of the city that looked to be fed by a waterfall. The lake echoed an image of the stars above, glittering and roiling with the current. Roarc followed the water upward with his eyes and failed to find its source. The water seemed to stretch endlessly into the depths of the starlit sky.

Stone buildings of various configurations, each topped with shining glass domes, surrounded the lake, and the buildings spun out in a gradually widening spiral. A cobbled road of silver stones matched the spiral design of the buildings and led to the outer edge of the city. A thick wall of gray granite surrounded the perimeter, and two gatehouses guarded the only entrances to the city, one to the east and the other to the west. Both gates looked to be made of a strong rust-colored stone. Both gates were closed.

The north end of the city inclined sharply, and at the top of the rise sat a squat fortress with thick black walls that appeared to be cut from a single block of stone. The fortress was ancient-looking and oddly familiar. Roarc had beheld something similar, but only from a great distance, when he had gazed upon the Moonlit Waters fortress, Castle Forgotten. Even from afar, the image had burned itself into his memory. While this fortress was indeed familiar, there were many differences from its surface cousin.

Instead of an open gate leading into a grand courtyard, a closed gate of twisted black metal blocked entry to the sparse courtyard beyond. The great staircase was also missing, as were the council chambers. The sky bridges and open markets were absent and, in their place, stood a single black-pearl-colored tower. The tower jutted out from the large fortress courtyard and climbed high into the air. The dark stone shined like marble and, from a distance, looked to be carved from a single pillar. A globe of blue fire suspended high above the tower throbbed with energy. Roarc felt the flames calling to him.

Something was waiting for him in the tower.

"We need to find a way inside," Roarc said suddenly.

Zuh'Erg turned and looked at him, a single bushy eyebrow raised in surprise.

Was it not me *leading the two of* you? Zuh'Erg said in his mind.

"Perhaps," Roarc said absently, staring at the single spire of the keep.

Roarc didn't see it, but Zuh'Erg grinned wolfishly and nodded as if confirming a suspicion.

The platform overlooking Starlit Waters was large enough for the three companions to spread out to the right of the tunnel mouth. Roarc felt weary from the brief battle with the Croakers. He assumed the swarm of insects had been venomous. His half-giant constitution shielded him from the most harmful effects, but the weeks of hardship on the road had worn him down. He leaned heavily against the wall and stared up into the twinkling sky.

Was he really looking at the sky?

More likely a cavern roof, but it looked so much like the Acrean sky at night. The only missing piece that betrayed it as a false sky was the missing, always-present twin to Acrea, Yalonia. Why had anyone gone to such lengths to replicate the sky this far underground? Would the constellations and stars he stared at now change with the season as the true sky did?

Mazoris clattering nearby broke him from his stargazing. The Sogra was crouched down with his spear across his knees. He was staring down at the city far below.

Rest for a moment. I will scout ahead, Zuh'Erg projected.

His cloaked form slipped silently down a wide staircase that plunged a dizzying distance to the cavern floor below.

Roarc had felt the compulsion clearly when he laid eyes upon the city. Now that he had stopped and listened to the weariness in his body, he knew that a few hours wouldn't make a big enough difference to push himself past his limits. Half-giants had legendary strength, but even that strength had its limits. He slid down the wall and sat heavily on the ground. His hammer clanged next to him, and his wall shield thumped against the stones.

Mazoris retreated from the edge of the platform and picked his own place against the wall. He tossed his large pack to the ground, circled around several times, and laid down. It took a few short breaths before he was whistling and snoring soundly. Roarc knew he should stay awake for a short time longer until Zuh'Erg returned.

He was asleep before the thought finished forming in his mind.

13 - ALL THE WAY DOWN

The transition from air to water was jarring at best. The armor Tyler wore detected the environmental shift and tightened appropriately where needed, and also left plated sections hollow or flooded depending on the depth.

Crylona hovered next to him, her wet suit glittering in the light filtering through the waves above. She touched him on the shoulder, and they sank quickly over a shelf of the ocean floor and began to descend into darkness.

Tyler felt his throat tighten in momentary fear until he felt a reassuring squeeze on his arm and a kind hand brush against his ear. The water was getting colder on his exposed face, and his eyes ached in earnest. When he thought he could take no more, Polaris pulsed and the water around him bubbled intensely. The bubbles coalesced and thickened into a single shining dome that slid over his head with an audible pop.

The cold was gone in an instant.

He looked to Crylona again and found a similar bubble had attached itself to her head. Apparently, Polaris had learned something from Starmist during their brief joining.

"I doubt anyone would believe this if I told them," Tyler said, his voice sounding strange from under the mask and inside the bubble.

"I believe you," Crylona said, her voice sounding like it came from the end of a long hallway.

"How long will it take us to descend?" Tyler asked.

Crylona paused, and he could tell she was thinking. "The first outpost is only a half cycle away."

"A half cycle?" Tyler asked.

"I believe surface dwellers split a cycle by day and night. Oddly, they call the passage of both together a day. A cycle is one rotation of our world. We can feel the ebb and flow of the ocean in the Deep as Yalonia pulls and pushes its sister."

"So, half a day?" Tyler asked, trying to keep his tone from sounding teasing.

Crylona sighed. "Would it not be an entire day?"

"Oh no, that would be a full cycle," Tyler said, his voice cracking as he suppressed laughter. If the sound of an eye roll could be heard beneath the waves, the expression Crylona gave him would have been deafening.

"We will pass two outposts before we enter the Deep. It should take us several cycles depending if we move through the Barrens unmolested," she said.

Tyler raised a finger to keep his teasing going, but the look she gave him clamped his mouth shut. He waited expectantly. He had no idea what the Barrens were.

"Gale and Rider territory," she said.

Tyler winced. His first encounter with a Gale had been nearly fatal for his entire party. Only Lanadari had proved a match for the sheer ferocity of the giant creature, its Herald, and its Riders.

"We will avoid them, and it may take some additional time," she said. Her face was hidden by her mask, and the bubble that surrounded her head distorted her features. Only her voice, with its slight quaver, let him know that she was afraid.

"I have faced them before and lived to tell the tale. I will follow your lead, but know that if it comes to a fight, Polaris and I will be ready," Tyler said.

Polaris vibrated in response. Tyler hoped that he sounded braver than he felt. A Gale in its native element was an unknown variable he hoped to avoid.

"Down we go," Crylona said abruptly. She raised her hands in the clear water as if ready to dive straight up. Starmist rippled and flowed from her waist, up her arms, and encircled both of her wrists. The balanite spread out, forming a small sphere. The sphere looked to harden and began to reflect the dull surface light that remained. The sphere flickered and sank, pulling Crylona down into the abyss.

Polaris made a snorting sound in Tyler's mind, refusing to be outdone. Balanite sprang out in all directions around him like the fingers of a giant hand. The fingers closed around him, and he sank like a stone. The rush of water by his bubbled head was dizzying. Without Polaris, the pressure alone would have crushed the life from his body, even in his armor. He quickly descended to where the Acrean sunlight had never shined and was alone in total darkness.

Polaris must have anticipated his fear of the dark. The bubble around his head took on a new silvery sheen. The bubble shimmered blue for a moment, and then the blackness melted away. With his new sight, an underwater alien world unfolded before him.

An ocean teeming with life stretched out in all directions. Multicolored creatures, many resembling fish, swam in large glittering schools. A jellyfish, the size of a starship, drifted slowly from the depths and cruised up to shallower water.

The ocean floor was a labyrinth of crevices, coral spires, and seagrass. Several hard-shelled creatures that looked like human-sized lobsters tended small flocks of plump-looking sea slugs. One of the lobster creatures was staring right at him, and he felt its hostility boil through the water. Polaris tugged at him gently, which sent him skimming above the ocean floor that sloped ever downward.

Tyler felt the sense of urgency flowing from his companion. The urgency only began to fade once Crylona came back into view. The sloped ocean floor became a blur as Starmist increased speed and Polaris surged forward to keep pace. Tyler closed his eyes for a time, finding the rushing water sound almost tranquil. The passage of time was hard to gauge and he snoozed for what felt like moments, but what could have been hours. When he opened his eyes again their speed had slowed considerably and they floated in water that stretched endlessly in all directions. It reminded Tyler of the vastness of space, but without the ever-present twinkling stars. Blackness was the only constant here.

After a time and what felt like a long descent, a metal object flicked into view below. The enhanced vision granted by the bubble that encircled his head was the only way he could have noticed the object in total darkness. As they continued to descend, the object became much larger and familiar. Resting on a jagged outcropping of a massive undersea shelf sat a partially buried UEA interceptor.

Interceptors in the UEA were generally docked inside much larger ships. They were built for short range skirmish missions and finding one crashed and alone was disturbing. What had happened to its mother ship? The thought of raising a cruiser, or even better, a destroyer, from the depths made Tyler's heart race.

What he wouldn't give to be back on the bridge of the *Centaur* again. He hoped his ship was still in one piece and not locked in a watery grave somewhere. His memory of where exactly his ship had ended up was still fuzzy. He was, however, confident it had made the journey with the *Spero.*

Starmist and Crylona settled gracefully onto the ocean shelf with a puff of organic matter where her feet touched. Tyler and Polaris hit the shelf like a speeding train, sending Tyler staggering against the side of the interceptor. The hollow bang of armor against the ship hull reverberated through the ocean.

"Graceful," Crylona said. Now it was her turn to tease him.

"Still getting my sea legs," Tyler said, rubbing flaking metal that had stuck to his armored shoulder. The interceptor had decayed rapidly while exposed to the salty brine of the Acrean ocean.

Crylona made a snickering sound and walked with a slight bounce along the length of the interceptor. Tyler followed her and stopped when she did as they passed under one of the wings. A sealed air lock stood silent guard against the crushing waters. Tyler studied the exterior, looking for a palm screen or optical scanner. Crylona ran her hand along the door frame and her slim hand disappeared behind a well-hidden compartment.

A manual release?

The air lock hissed and a compressed stream of bubbles leaped from the frame of the door. The door ground painfully short of opening fully and Tyler frowned. The metal had only moved about a third of the way from where it had started. It was going to be a tight squeeze.

Crylona slid into the opening like she was walking through a cavern. Tyler stared at the stuck door with doubt and shrugged. It took him a moment to wedge his head and shoulders through the opening. He braced his back against the frame and pushed on the door with both hands. He grunted and strained with little success.

"A little help," he whispered to Polaris.

A surge of strength wrapped its way down his arms and into his fingers. He pushed again and this time the door squealed in protest before banging fully open. He only hoped that he hadn't damaged the mechanism and could still close the portal to unseal the inner door. He floated into the air lock and Crylona yanked hard on a lever on the opposite side of the chamber.

The outer door slammed shut like it had been on well-oiled hinges the entire time.

"Guess it just needed a little elbow grease," Tyler said.

Crylona stared at him with a look of horror on her face. "Gross," she said.

Tyler winced and shook his head as she hit the pressurization button and the water began to drain from the air lock. It took several minutes for the chamber to complete the draining cycle but after a time the inner air lock door opened into the flickering interior of the interceptor.

The name placard that adorned the ship had corroded away long ago. In fact, the bronze had rotted away and left only a black stain where it had once proudly stood vigil over the air lock.

"We will need to leave our masks on, the air here is unsafe," Crylona said. The bubble around her head dissolved as she stepped across the threshold of the air lock onto the rusted and pitted deck.

Tyler looked at the decking, unsure if it would even hold his weight. The bubble around his own head dissolved away and he felt Polaris thrum down his arm and into his hand in Warquarter form.

Was his balanite friend expecting trouble?

The salt water had been kept at bay for nearly a thousand years by the ship's hard seals. Interceptors lacked sanctuary protocols like larger UEA vessels so the salty air over the centuries had taken its toll where the outside water had failed. Either way, the inside of the ship had decayed to a state unrecognizable by Tyler.

"Such a shame," he said more to himself than anyone else.

"I have often imagined what it must have looked like brand new," Crylona said.

"Functional," Tyler said, peering through one of the countless holes in the few walls left standing.

"I use this place as a safe haven when I am ranging far from Pelagos," Crylona said, running her fingertips along the pitted and etched inner hull of the ship.

Tyler stepped into the central corridor of the interceptor and peered down the flickering passage to what would have been the cockpit.

"I sleep down there," Crylona said at his side. She could move quietly when she wanted to.

They walked a short distance down the crumbling deck and pushed through a rickety flight door. Four seats, cushions long since rotted away, sat empty. The controls and view screens were blackened and dark. Everything had a weathered and rotted look. He was glad the seashell mask over his face dulled his ability to smell anything.

Only one of the six canopy lights still functioned and its illumination was barely enough to see by. It was amazing that the interceptor still had power. That small feat was a testament to UEA reactor technology. The rest of the ship would surely dissolve completely into the ocean before the reactor core ceased to glow.

In one of the corners of the cockpit was a stack of netting that looked like a makeshift mattress. A small indent in the hull that once held a medical kit was now home to various shells and baubles that glittered in the dim light.

"Small pieces of home," Crylona said. She sounded embarrassed.

Home.

Tyler felt a pang in his chest. What had become of his home? Nearly a thousand years. He could only imagine what had become of Earth. If the visions that Celest had shown him could be believed, Earth was now a dark and barren world. But what did it matter? Everyone he had known would be dead by now anyway.

Almost everyone.

An image of Croyan, his face twisted in hatred and his eyes those of someone else, would be burned in his memory until his last breath. His thoughts drifted to Kako and having to bury his blade deep into her evil body. Only at the moment of death had she been herself again. No, the ones that were still alive, if you wanted to call it that, were no longer anyone he knew.

"Home," Tyler said, closing his eyes and shaking his head sadly.

"You come from Earth, yes?" Crylona asked. She brushed past him and nestled down on the mattress of nets, pulling her knees to her chin and resting her hands on her shins.

"You know of Earth?" Tyler asked.

"As I was telling your Balan friend, our knowledge was not lost with time as it was for those on the surface. We kept our technology well preserved." Crylona said.

"I still don't understand how, with all of the technology available to your people, you remain below," Tyler said.

Crylona's eyes smiled at him coyly. "If you had everything that you needed, why would you leave?"

Tyler scoffed and grinned at her behind his mask. "So I take it from your wandering that you don't have everything that you need."

"I have Starmist, and that is enough. Pelagos is…" she trailed off and looked lost in thought for a moment.

"Not really for us," she finished.

"Then why keep the tiny things there on the shelf?" Tyler asked. "Do those not remind you of Pelagos?"

Crylona's eyes grinned at him. "I believe I said they remind me of home. Yes, I was born in Pelagos. But that is not home to me now," she said.

"This," she said, spreading her arms wide. "All of this is home. The Deep and the outposts are the only life Starmist and I need."

The thin ribbon of balanite around her middle surged quickly around her as if excited.

Tyler leaned Polaris against one of the chairs and sat down across from Crylona with a sigh. A thought occurred to him as he looked around the cockpit again.

"Crylona, why am I not hungry? Or, for that matter, even the least bit thirsty?"

She stared back at him and shrugged. "The mask provides everything you need when you are in the water. It filters out plant and animal matter for sustenance and desalinizes the water that passes through, providing a constant trickle for thirst. It even processes harmful gases like we are breathing now and turns them into oxygen."

Tyler was about to ask how she had discovered the seashells when Crylona abruptly stretched her arms above her and yawned behind her mask. She laid back and shooed him with one of her thin hands. "Enough talk. Sleep. It is a long journey tomorrow. You can share the bedding with me if you like."

Tyler looked down at her skintight wet suit that hugged her athletic body in a distracting sort of way. He looked away quickly.

"I erm, want to look at the rest of the ship before I turn in," he said quickly.

Crylona shrugged and turned away from him.

Tyler pushed himself to his feet and held out his hand. Polaris clanged into his grasp, and he walked down the central corridor into the flickering light of the ancient interceptor. He unzipped the pocket where he kept the crystal that Celest had given him and used its bright light to guide his way to the rear of the ship, where the overhead lamps had failed completely.

There were four compartments that made up the interior of the interceptor. The first was the cockpit while the second contained the air lock and passenger seating. The third section was made for cargo, and the fourth was a small engineering bay. He passed through the second section of the ship again and noted that all of the seats had decayed to black mounds of rubble.

The third section was void of cargo. Anything that he might have found useful had long since been removed or rotted away. He looked down at the decking and noticed several scrapes and smudges. Something heavy had either walked or been dragged this way. Based on the coloring, it had been recent.

What would Crylona be hiding from him?

He came to an unexpected stop in front of the engineering bay. The hatch was pitted with rust but remained strong and solid. Tyler reached for the manual hatch release and gave it three sharp pulls. Nothing happened. He listened carefully as he pulled on the handle again and noted how the mechanism sounded.

The door was sealed from the inside.

14 - I HATE MYSELF

"How many more days must I endure this pathetic menagerie of talent attempting to fix my ship?" Shade shouted, throwing a table on its side and against the wall with an errant swing of his hand.

Allen stood dark and menacing, doing his best to cower before his master. Shade appreciated the gesture but was in no mood for a suck-up.

"I want it fixed. I want it fixed today," Shade said. He hoped the venom in his words struck fear into the new Immortal Guard kneeling behind Allen. All eyes were on the sand, and no one made a sound. Shade was about to launch into a full-blown tirade when a strange thing happened. Instead of staring at the tops of everyone's heads, he locked eyes with the woman he had liberated first. She was still kneeling, but she was looking right at him. Her obsidian orbs flecked with crimson burned with hatred. He was almost at a loss.

Almost.

He closed the distance between them in the blink of an eye. Several Immortal Guard were tossed aside in his wake like rag dolls. Shade held the redheaded woman off the ground with a choking grip around her neck with one hand. His other hand was balled in a fist that leaked angry purple fire.

The woman struggled feebly in his grasp, kicking at his chest and clawing at his iron grip with fingers until they bled. Shade waited until her legs kicked weakly and her eyes rolled back in her head before slamming her to the ground. She stopped moving and lay quiet.

It would take more than that to kill a fledgling guard, but she would hurt for long enough to learn her lesson. It would be interesting to see just how long she stayed unconscious. He toed her out of the way with his tattered, booted foot and cleared his throat.

"Now, where was I? Oh, yes. Fix. My. Damn. Ship!" Shade finished with an unearthly roar that heated the air and turned floating sand bits into jagged glass shards.

Allen scuttled beside him, bobbing his powerful upper body, trying to show submission.

"We have lost nearly half of the ship's mass, which should be enough for the core and remaining engine to lift us and provide thrust," Allen said.

"And?" Shade asked with a wave of his hand. Why was everyone so annoying?

"Even with everything going perfectly, we are going to have to swim," Allen said.

Shade fixed him with a stare that would have melted a normal man's flesh.

"The core is fractured," Allen said in a rush, backing away and bowing. "Landing thrusters are gone. If we crash on land, the core will detonate."

Shade paused and raised a thin index finger to his bloodless lips. The small part of him he kept locked away also knew the truth. The resulting explosion would render the island of Teka uninhabitable and very probably crack the tectonic plate, causing a volcanic event that would finish the job that the radiation would take too long to accomplish.

Would even he survive such a cataclysm?

Of course he would. But he needed a force to return to Arral. He also needed a ship and the idea of ditching his in the ocean didn't sit well. Clearly, losing both in a crash landing was a poor choice.

A cruel smile found its way to his lips, and Allen shook his head, anticipating his master's devious mind.

"The shields are gone. One hit from the Moonlit Waters defenses would destroy us over deep ocean. The fallout wouldn't even register."

Shade growled and balled his fists.

"One more day at most to seal up the hull, and we can be underway," Allen said.

"I will hold you to the second," Shade said through clenched teeth. "Out of my sight! All of you!"

The remainder of the kneeling guard leaped to their feet and scattered. Two had enough sense to grab the redheaded woman and drag her away from any additional wrath Shade might devise. Allen loped quickly back to the ship to continue repairs, leaving Shade alone on the small dune.

The Acrean sun was high in the sky, and its rays baked the sand like an oven. Shade couldn't feel the heat, but he knew it was there by the way the air shimmered. He wanted to go back to his island shrouded in mist and not destroy it in the process. The image of shimmering heat blasting away the mist tickled the edges of his humanity.

Why was this bothering him so much?

"Because you still have a human heart," a voice said.

Shade lashed out with purple and black fire that surged down his arms and fanned out in a roaring circle around him. He glanced fervently around him but remained alone on the dune.

"When you took my body, it gave you more than you bargained for, did it not?" the same voice said. Shade stood perfectly still, trying to find where the voice had originated.

"You are a virus," the voice said.

It took Shade a moment to find the origin of the voice. It was his own mouth speaking the words.

"You have made me hate myself—the things you have done with my hands. The horrors I have witnessed with my own eyes. But killing my best friend and really the only hope I would ever have at true freedom. No. I will not sit quietly anymore," his voice said.

A flicker of movement caught his eye, and standing just out of his direct vision was an exact reflection of himself. No, it was not exactly himself. Hard green eyes stared at him, and the normally wild black hair that hung to his shoulders was pulled back in a neat ponytail. He stood tall with squared shoulders, which looked strange considering Shade always looked predatory when he saw himself in the mirror.

It was Pistos Croyan standing before him.

"You are only a shadow," Croyan said, his lips curling with anger as he spoke.

Shade chuckled, closed his eyes, and inhaled deeply. When he opened his eyes again, Croyan had a look of uncertainty on his face.

"I think you forgot how this works," Shade said. He concentrated a moment and began bending the darkness that surged in his chest inward. The apparition of Croyan burst into purple and black flames. He howled in agony as the flames consumed him.

Shade could feel what Croyan was feeling but gritted his teeth and drank in more of the darkness. He had kept Croyan in check for nearly a thousand years, and he wasn't about to let him have any kind of control again. Croyan vanished abruptly, and a thin outline of flames where he had stood guttered and went out. Shade stood on the dune for a very long time, breathing hard.

He paused for a moment and smoothed his ragged hair. This was proving to be a most challenging day. He needed to get back to his fortress. All of the means that he required to train his new guard as well as pull more from the local population into his army were there. His withdrawal from Moonlit Waters had been costly, but in the grand scheme of things, he had only used a portion of the fighting force he could conscript for the next attempt.

He swore long and loud when a thought occurred to him. After he ditched his ship in the ocean, his ability to communicate with the *Spero* would be compromised. It would take time to salvage the necessary parts to establish the satellite connection. He only knew of a couple of wrecks that his Avians could reach, and their condition was unknown. Maybe Allen would have an idea of how to pull what he needed from the transport in advance of losing it in the ocean.

He left the dune and the angry echo of Croyan behind and walked the short distance back to the ship. Allen and the new guard had done a poor job patching up the transport after the crash landing. Nearly all of the debris that had been torn from the ship and thrown for a half-mile had been gathered, mended, and patched back to the hull. The bridge of the ship and a fair part of the forward decks were gone and beyond repair. The port side of the ship had been flayed open like a fish, and it took a great deal of what remained of the forward section to patch. All in all, the vessel that sat partially buried in the sand now looked like it was held together by faith alone.

Shade had very little faith left today.

He walked around the ship to the rear section to visibly inspect the main engines. They seemed like they were in decent shape, given the circumstances. He was told that the port and starboard engines had been sheered off during the crash and had ended up somewhere in the ocean. One engine was going to have to do.

The big question that Shade had while standing at the rear of the ship rubbing his chin was how they were going to generate enough lift without thrusters. He leaned from where he was standing to look at the dunes beyond and closed his eyes. He knew that Allen was crazy, especially after living most of his life in a bottle. He had, however, underestimated just how crazy he actually was.

Shade hurried to the only working hatch on the side of the ship and stepped through the opening. It was much cooler inside the ship. He stopped for a moment and centered himself. He shouldn't be feeling anything. It had taken hundreds of years to shed the humanity he had inherited. He refused to let it come back now.

It was a short walk to engineering, which now also served as the bridge. Only Allen was in the room, given the immense radiation spilling from the cracked core housing. His chief engineer appeared to almost bask in the greenish glow.

"You are going to use the dunes, aren't you?" Shade asked. He kept his voice thin and even, not wanting to tip Allen off that he was displeased.

Allen looked up from one of the control consoles and fixed Shade with his smoldering stare.

"It won't be enjoyable, but it will get us airborne," he said.

"You do realize I want to recover this ship when we have the means to do so?" Shade said.

Allen laughed lowly and menacingly. His laughter was like nails on a burning chalkboard.

"I will barely scuff the paint," he replied.

Shade was taken aback. Was that sarcasm he had just heard? Maybe he should have broken him out of his bottle a long time ago. He considered Allen for a moment. He was large, lethal, and utterly changed.

On second thought, no. He actually liked Allen more docile and obedient.

"See that you don't," Shade said. "I want you to remove all of the comms equipment before we ditch into the ocean."

"Ah. The torment of the AI continues," Allen said.

"Until I get weapons control of the ship," Shade replied. "But even then, I will relish in taking that smug look off of his face."

A noise in the hallway caught Shade's attention, and he turned to find a surprising redheaded woman standing with her eyes staring at the deck.

"Master," she said quietly.

"I am not even sure what to call you," Shade said, tapping his lips with his index finger.

"My name is Jennifer," she said.

"Was Jennifer," Shade said, correcting her with his sharp tone. "No, I believe you have earned a name most fitting for your new station."

The new Immortal Guard kept her eyes on the deck, but he could tell he had piqued her interest. The new guard wanted first and foremost to please their master, and if he told her she needed a new name, she would never be Jennifer again.

"I will call you Kushora for your lively demeanor," Shade said.

"What does it mean?" she asked.

"I believe it translates to difficult puppy or some such," Shade said with a dull wave of his hand.

Kushora squared her shoulders and stood a little taller.

"Now, what is it?" Shade asked.

"The three cold ones have finished repairing the last power conduit. They said we are ready to test the engine," she said.

Shade turned to Allen and mouthed, *Cold ones?*

Allen shrugged.

"Splendid!" Shade said, clapping his hands together. He waited for a moment, and when Kushora didn't move, he leaned forward.

"Why are you still here?"

Kushora jumped as if she had been struck and scurried down the corridor.

"I think she meant the three surviving Immortal Guard," Allen offered.

Shade rolled his eyes. "I know what she meant."

Allen returned to his station and started tapping in commands with his wicked-looking claws. Shade was impressed that he was able to type so quickly with implements that looked to be designed for rending flesh versus fine keystrokes.

"Power flow is good. I am ready to test main engine burn," Allen said as if to a room full of people.

Shade looked around for the rest of the audience and rested his head in his palm.

"Proceed," he said in a pained whisper.

The entire ship lurched and shuddered as the engines came to life. Allen let them burn for only a few moments and then brought them back down. He nodded, apparently happy with the readings he had obtained.

"A few more holes to plug, and we are off," Allen said, brushing by Shade, who was still holding his head, now in both hands.

When Shade was alone in engineering, he walked over to his favorite place on the ship: the communications terminal. He looked around for his chair before realizing it must have been obliterated in the crash. He looked towards the far wall that he had been thrown through and could see where the hull had been mended. He clicked his tongue in annoyance and turned to the terminal.

The familiar logo of the UEA *Spero* lit the screen, and a short time later, the face of Morgan appeared.

"Still alive, I see," the AI said.

"Still as pleasant as ever," Shade said.

Morgan waited.

"Statistically speaking, I have very little chance of guessing the override code today, but I feel like talking, so here we are," Shade said.

If an AI could look surprised, Morgan would be the poster child.

"I don't have anything to say to you," Morgan said.

"Oh, I didn't plan on you talking. I just wanted you to listen." Shade said. He leaned on the console table and came closer to the screen. "I will take Moonlit Waters and its Temple. Rest assured that when I do, you and I will be spending a great deal of time together."

Klaxons and an alarm sounded behind Morgan. Shade raised an eyebrow. He had always assumed the background when he spoke to Morgan was simulated. The screen flickered for a moment, and Shade heard an automated voice, sounding exactly like the AI, say, "Warning, escape pod D47 on deck 11 launch detected."

"Interesting. Who might be coming down here to join me?" Shade asked. "I didn't think anyone was still alive up there."

Morgan severed the connection, leaving Shade cackling in front of a dark screen.

Shade pulled up the link to his satellite network and located the escape pod entering orbit. He watched the wireframe representation of the object screaming through the atmosphere for nearly half an hour. All he really wanted to know was where the pod was going to land.

He banged his fists on the console table, careful not to have any real strength behind his frustration. The pod had crashed into the deep ocean and sunk out of his scanning range.

What a waste. Maybe the ship was starting to break down from the centuries in space? Escape pods didn't typically just fall from the sky. He would have to keep a close eye on the viability of the *Spero*. All of his plans hinged on the capital ship.

Shade heard Allen's heavy gait coming down the corridor as he stared at the splashdown point on the screen.

"We are ready," said Allen.

"Is everyone strapped in?" Shade asked more out of habit than actually caring.

"All tucked in. Do you want me to have a chair brought in for you?" Allen said.

"Just go," Shade said.

Allen shrugged and moved to the main engineering console and fired up the engine once more. The ship shook violently and crawled forward like a labored animal.

"Hang on!" Allen shouted. He tapped the console again, and the ship lurched forward with massive acceleration. Normal men would have been crushed against the wall from the sheer g-forces. Shade and Allen stood unaffected.

Shade pulled up an exterior view of the ship as it barreled towards the dunes. He was no math wizard, even after nine hundred years, but the angle still looked wrong.

"Allen, I am sure you have this figured out, but—" Shade said and was thrown off his feet when the ship slammed into one of the small dunes and hopped over it like a skier on a mogul. Up and down, the ship slammed, repeatedly crashing over and through sand dunes. The largest dune loomed straight ahead, and Shade got to his feet, bracing himself on the console.

"Here we go!" Allen shouted over the rattling and protesting sound of the ship impacting sand.

A strong smell of ozone permeated engineering, and Shade could have sworn he saw a chunk of the core fall out of the housing. They hit the dune at a ludicrous rate of speed, slid up its bank, and roared like a rocket into the sky.

"Next stop, Teka!" Allen shouted, with more than an edge of insanity in his voice.

15 – WITHOUT WARNING

"I am not eating that!" Razmal shouted.

Ralon held a steaming hunk of elkin meat skewered on the end of a charred bone-roasting spit.

"It really is delicious. You should try it," Gryphem said between massive bites of meat. He held an entire leg of elkin in his large talons, and grease dripped down his beak.

"Hot food," Ralon said with a grin and took a bite out of the offered skewer.

Razmal felt his stomach lurch and held up a hand to refuse the offering. He would stick to the dried meat and cold cheese they had brought with them. Something about eating an enemy, no matter how delicious, just didn't sit right with him.

"Ah c'mon Raz, it's not like they can talk or anything. They are barely one step above livestock," Ralon said between bites.

Raz?

Gryphem nodded vigorously in agreement with what Ralon had said.

"I will pass, thank you," Razmal said. He returned to his pack and rummaged for his own meal. Once he found what he was looking for, he settled down, using his pack as a backstop, and stared up into the gloomy reaches of the main caravan tent they had settled down under for the night.

They had walked for most of the day and, just after dark, had found the caravan staging area. Four muddy and rutted roads converged on a wide meadow that was covered in snow. A great many tents, some massive and others small enough for a single person, dotted the somewhat flat area of the meadow. Most of the smaller tents were made of tanned hide, while the larger ones were made of tightly woven fibers.

Gryphem had bought them a night in one of the larger travelers' lodges. The sign hanging above the tent flap had been impossible to see in the dark. The lodge was the closest thing to a tavern for a hundred miles, and Razmal was anxious to finish his meal and find some strong drink. A small covered wagon had been wheeled into the tent, and a white-haired Acrean man served foaming mugs of what looked like ale from the back.

Razmal ate his cold rations mechanically, not really tasting them. Something about the battle with the Elkin still bothered him. They had, after all, wandered into territory that the beasts had claimed. Most fights seemed to start the same way. Someone decided that they owned a place, and when others threatened said ownership, bloodshed ensued.

He thought back to the battles in the recent past. He hadn't always felt like this. In fact, his battle-ax had seen a great deal more use than the hammer and shield he now carried. He really did miss that ax. He sighed heavily and looked around the caravan tent, deciding if he wanted to grab a tall foamy cup of forgetfulness.

There were six other groups under the tent. Two of the groups were comprised of Avians with dark and dull-colored feathers. They had given Gryphem a wide berth with his vibrant and noble plumage. Three of the other groups were a mixed rabble of rough-looking northern

Acreans. They hadn't even looked in Razmal's direction all night as most were rolling dice and drinking. The last group under the tent were robed and hooded, and it was difficult to make out what race they were.

Razmal pushed himself to his feet and cracked his back with a long stretch. Time for a drink. He glanced at Ralon and Gryphem as he walked by. They looked to have started on another round of meat and were talking with both their beaks and mouths full. He tried hard not to roll his eyes and instead fixed his gaze on the drink wagon.

Up close, he could see that the wagon was weathered and had a broken axle. It looked to have been in the same location for a very long time. The Acrean man greeted him with a nod after pouring a beverage for another patron.

"What will it be?" he asked.

"That drink with the frothy top looks great," Razmal said.

The bartender grunted in acknowledgment and poured the foaming liquid from a clay jug into a waiting hollow gourd. Razmal found it strange there was nowhere to set his drink but shrugged and accepted the beverage.

"How much?" Razmal asked, fishing in his pocket for payment.

"Your Avian friend took care of it in advance," the bartender said, turning to help another customer.

Razmal didn't feel particularly noticeable, so the fact that the bartender, who hadn't even looked his way, knew what he looked like was strange.

He took a long foamy sip of his drink and sighed with relief. It was a hearty dark ale with a smokey flavor. He stood at the wagon for a time, observing other patrons as they drank. Few paid him any heed. It wasn't until one of the robed and hooded figures came up for a drink that he felt eyes upon him.

The robed figure, this one wearing dark brown robes with a matching hood, looked right at him and approached the wagon. Razmal took another sip of his ale and noticed that the bartender had disappeared. The blow that struck Razmal on the side of the head was a surprise. He had been so distracted by the figure approaching that he had failed to notice one coming from around the other side of the wagon.

***

"No move," a rough voice said. Its words were heavily accented and sounded like they were difficult to pronounce.

Razmal couldn't have moved if he wanted. His hands were bound, as were his feet, and a rope behind him connected the two bindings. He could tell that he was on a floor that smelled like oiled leather and he was most likely in a wagon judging by the feeling of movement.

His head hurt, and his vision swam with tiny points of light. Each time the wagon struck a pothole, his head ached even worse. He had confirmed he was indeed in a wagon by looking around and seeing daylight through the back flap. He also noticed the unconscious form of Ralon laying crumpled next to a large Avian with black feathers. The Avian held a solid-looking bone club that had fresh blood on it.

They had been taken without warning. Razmal assumed Gryphem was also in the wagon, perhaps behind him, but he was unable to get a good look.

"Where are we?" Razmal asked. His voice was dry and hoarse. How long had he been in the wagon?

"Take to high place," the same rough voice answered.

Razmal closed his eyes and swallowed a few times to wet his throat enough for it to cease being painful. He craned his neck to get a quick look at the rest of the wagon and received a sharp blow to the ribs from the Avian with the club. He had accomplished what he wanted either way. Gryphem was not in the wagon. It was two dark-feathered Avians, himself, and Ralon.

It was a strange feeling of helplessness he felt, lying bound on the floor. He found himself thinking of how he had treated Tyler after first meeting him, and he was thankful his friend had forgiven him. The fact that he had not sensed or heard the approach of whoever had knocked him unconscious was suspicious. The only explanation he could come up with was that the bartender had put something in his drink. Perhaps that smokey flavor he had enjoyed was designed to dull his senses. Either way, being caught by surprise was foreign to Razmal.

"What have we done? Why have we been taken?" Razmal asked, trying to keep the way he was asking as a question instead of a demand.

"Skylord," the rough voice replied.

This was certainly not the way Razmal had imagined meeting the king of Alya Cheyl. The thought of being dragged before the Skylord bound at the wrists and stripped of his dignity didn't sit well with him.

Razmal heard a groan from where Ralon lay and craned his neck just enough to see his companion. The Avian with the club slammed it hard into the side of Ralon's head. The Acrean noble lay quiet again. From what Razmal could see, his companion still drew breath, but the blow had been savage enough to bloody the side of his head. The Avians apparently had been informed of the threat an awake and angry Ralon would pose.

Razmal tested the strength of his bonds around his wrists and found them secure. The same test of his ankles brought another painful strike to his ribs with the bone club.

"No move," the rough voice said again, but angrily this time.

Razmal lay the side of his head on the floor and winced at the pain of his burning ribs. The two Avians in the wagon had better hope he didn't find them in an alley someday. He closed his eyes and listened to the creak and the bang of the wagon moving across a rough road. They suddenly stopped, and he realized that he must have fallen asleep. The wagon flap no longer spilled bright daylight into the interior but instead cast the muddy rust color of Yalonia onto the floor.

"High place," the rough voice said. A taloned foot scooped Razmal under the back, and a heavy kick sent him spinning out of the wagon. He crashed unceremoniously to a hard stone surface covered in snow. He slid a short distance and did his best to change direction enough to end his slide sitting up facing the wagon. Ralon emerged unconscious from the wagon flap propelled by the same taloned foot. He was still bleeding and flopped uncontrollably facedown in the snow.

Razmal almost felt bad for him. Almost.

He couldn't see what pulled the wagon, but after a moment's pause and the dumping of their equipment out the back, the wagon creaked and groaned down a small side path and disappeared. He sat shivering in the snow for a few moments and looked around to see if he could get his bearings. The mighty Avian city of Alya Cheyl towered before him.

They were sitting just before a large stone archway that looked cut from a single piece of rock. Behind the archway was a path that snaked its way across various cliff faces that looked like the jagged teeth of an ancient beast. The city spanned four of the teeth connected together by a massive network of rope bridges. There were thousands of caves at various elevations across the cliff face. Some of the caves were covered with curtains made of leather, while others looked deep and unoccupied. A haze of mist clung to the top of the peaks, and deep white snow covered every exposed outcropping.

A single Avian stooped with age toddled out from under the archway. The Avian had a curved yellow beak that was white and chipped along the edges. Most of the silver feathers around its neck were missing, giving it an almost vulture-like appearance. It walked with a limp and carried a thin walking staff made of weathered bone.

Razmal looked at the Avian with doubt. How was he going to carry Razmal and Ralon when he could barely walk? Perhaps there were more Avians that would emerge from behind the archway or descend from the sky.

A hard band of VAST clamped down on Razmal's chest, and he felt himself lifted off his feet.

Impossible.

Only Acreans and the occasional Balan were able to command the VAST. Razmal concentrated as he rotated in midair, barely able to hear the VAST whispering. While he was able to generally understand what they said, now the language was completely different. It was like trying to make out a single conversation in a crowded tavern full of voices.

"What do you want with us?" Razmal gasped as the VAST tightened around his torso.

The wizened Avian clucked softly, and with a flick of his feathered and taloned hand, he set Razmal standing upright on the ground. The VAST, however, remained snugly against his chest.

"We don't get many travelers that simply appear in the middle of our country. You didn't pass any of our outposts, and yet there you were, a stone's throw from Alya Cheyl," the old Avian said. "What do you think our Skylord thinks of an Acrean, Balan, and southern Avian invading his lands?"

"I am sure there is a joke in there somewhere about how we all walked into a bar," Ralon said softly.

Razmal was able to move his head just enough to see his Acrean companion sitting and pressing a torn piece of clothing against the oozing gash on the side of his head.

"Lady Tigerson of Moonlit Waters sends her regards," Ralon said.

The old Avian tilted his head and blinked his eyes rapidly. He tapped his staff on the snow and made a shrill noise in his throat.

"Word should have been sent in advance of your arrival," the Avian said. "How am I to confirm what you say is true?"

Ralon winced and pulled the bloody rag from his face. "It's in the bag," he said, pointing at their discarded equipment.

Two mottled-colored Avians landed heavily beside the old one. Each was broad-chested and carried wicked-looking bone cudgels.

"Bring their packs to me," the old Avian said.

The two thuggish-looking Avians hopped over and scooped up the three packs, belted sword, hammer, and shield. The sight of Gryphem's harness had Razmal wondering. Where was their Avian companion? The old Avian opened and upturned each pack one by one, spilling out all of their equipment onto the snow. A soft-looking pouch of oiled leather caught his eye. The pouch radiated a strong essence.

The old Avian cooed and whistled and bent reverently to scoop up the pouch. "Is this what I think it is?"

Ralon nodded. "Do you mind if I get up?"

The old Avian waved his hand, never taking his eyes off the pouch that he cradled in the crook of his arm.

"Don't open it out here in the cold," Ralon warned after struggling to his feet.

"I know that, Tigerson," the old Avian said, clacking his staff sharply against the stone with his free hand.

Razmal felt the VAST around his chest release, and he exhaled sharply.

"Bring your sla… I mean Balan, and we will seek audience with the Skylord," the old Avian said. He turned and motioned for the two thugs to gather the equipment they had dumped. Razmal watched them haphazardly stuff things in the wrong packs and closed his eyes. He was bothered by what the old Avian had almost said. He had the distinct impression he was going to say 'slave'.

Razmal had never traveled to the northlands, and to his knowledge, Balan didn't live this far north. The Balan people had a strong dislike of cold climates. The lack of body hair probably had a lot to do with it. They did, however, trade with the northern kingdom, so maybe some of them had put on warm furs and settled.

The old Avian moved slowly and leaned heavily on his staff. They followed a short way behind him, and the two rough looking Avians brought up the rear. The base of Alya Cheyl was void of steps. A variety of rope ladders led to higher overhangs, and the path they followed looked to span from the first tooth across the others and then looped back to the main arch.

When they reached the base of the first craggy peak, the old Avian unfurled well-cared-for wings and turned back to look at them. "You two, take this rope ladder, and I will meet you up above. My friends here will leave your equipment," he said and leaped upwards. He caught an ever-present updraft and disappeared into the mist.

"I don't suppose you would let me bring my sword?" Ralon asked no one in particular. He caught a painful crack to the ribs from one of the Avian cudgels and doubled over. He laughed off the pain and straightened up and gazed at the rickety-looking rope ladder lying against the cliff face.

"After you," Ralon said and then coughed wetly into his hand.

Razmal glanced at the towering Avians and forced a smile before grabbing one of the brittle-feeling rungs and hoisting himself upwards to the waiting master of Alya Cheyl.

16 – BACK TO THE OCEAN

"Ship?" Tyler asked aloud.

The ancient interceptor did not reply.

"This is Tyler Ryan Tor of the UEA. Is anyone in there?" Tyler said.

He placed his ear against the door and heard a faint clatter from the other side. The sound of the locking mechanism rotating sounded from within. Tyler stepped back. The door slid and creaked slightly and only opened halfway. A synthetic head stuck its way through the opening, and an intense blue orb in the center of its face fixed its gaze on him.

"Scanning," a slightly metallic-sounding female voice said.

Tyler felt the gentle wash of the drone's scan touch his skin and heard the confirmation tone chime loudly.

"Tyler Ryan Tor confirmed. I am SH646-AL37-E60," the drone said. "But Lieutenant Thomas Caledon gave me the designation of… Shale."

Tyler felt hot and cold at the same time and fought back a rush of emotion.

"When did he send you?" Tyler asked in a rush.

"Fourteen standard days, eleven hours, and thirty-seven minutes ago," Shale said.

Tyler leaned heavily against the decayed wall of the interceptor and scrubbed his face with his hand.

"Where?" Tyler asked. It was the only thing he could think to say.

"The *Spero*, in asynchronous orbit above what is locally known as Acrea," Shale said.

A thousand questions hit Tyler at once. If someone was alive on the ship then why had there not been a rescue hundreds of years ago? They must know the calamity that had befallen the original colonists. The abomination that was wearing Croyan's skin was reason enough to send down a full special forces contingent with a squadron of fighters.

"He is alone," Shale said.

Tyler shook his head, not understanding. "It has been hundreds of years. How is he still alive?"

Shale stared back at him. "The ship's archives did not contain that information," Shale said.

Tyler waited expectantly.

Shale squeezed through the doorway, and it clanged shut.

"Mission?" Tyler asked, followed by a sigh.

"Locate Commander Tor," Shale said.

Tyler spread his hands and cocked his head in wonder. Drones were always so literal.

"Once located, SH646-AL37-E60 is to escort you to the closest communications terminal to make contact with the *Spero*."

Hope swelled within Tyler's chest.

"How did you know to find me here? Where is the closest terminal?" Tyler asked.

Shale paused for a moment, and the blue orb on the drone's face flickered.

"Pelagos indicated three crafts such as this one. Based on your last known location, this was the logical choice," Shale said.

"You have been in contact with Pelagos?"

Tyler turned at Crylona's voice.

Shale's central eye glowed red, and the drone leaped forward.

"Peace," Crylona said, her voice perfectly calm. The fact that Starmist crackled an inch from Shale's chest argued against the word's meaning.

Shale's head rotated 180 degrees to stare at Tyler.

"She is with me," he said. "Did Pelagos not also tell you I was traveling with a woman?"

Shale's orb flickered back to blue. "Humans all look alike."

"Who did you speak with?" Crylona asked.

The drone's head rotated back to face Crylona. "The central computer didn't give its name."

Shale stepped away from Crylona and back near the doorway leading to the cramped engineering bay. Tyler marveled at how fluidly the drone moved. He knew that communication drones came with all manner of offensive and defensive systems. Sapien-class drones were still somewhat of a mystery as the UEA had only commissioned a small number before the fall of humanity.

"Shale, is the AI on the *Spero* still active?" Tyler asked.

The blue orb that was Shale's face flickered yellow for a moment.

"Yes," Shale said.

Tyler raised an eyebrow. That was an odd reaction from a drone.

"You aren't supposed to be here, are you?" Tyler asked, crossing his arms in front of his chest. Crylona touched his shoulder and moved to stand beside him.

"How do you know?" Crylona asked.

"The only explanation as to why the *Spero* is still in orbit and unable to send aid is that the ship is either in low power mode or heavily damaged," Tyler said, giving Shale a critical examination with his gaze. "My money is on low power mode. We didn't want to attract any attention should something go wrong during the voyage. With the lack of a command crew, the ship's AI would have defaulted to as close to zero power as possible to minimize potential detection."

Tyler groaned and shook his head.

"What?" Crylona asked.

"Thomas wasn't part of the bridge crew. He is an engineer. That means he is for all intents and purposes a prisoner aboard the *Spero*," Tyler said.

"And lonely," Shale said suddenly.

"Can you show me his face?" Tyler asked.

Shale nodded in an oddly human gesture, and the blue face orb flickered and projected a misty hologram of a tired-looking lieutenant.

Tyler knew Thomas personally from several tours of duty. Judging by his slightly greying temples, he had only aged a decade at most.

"He must still have a functional cryopod. But I can't imagine how his mental state is if he is waking and sleeping often," Tyler said.

"He is undamaged," Shale said, terminating the hologram.

Tyler stood quietly for a moment, thinking. Everything was starting to make sense. The Tekian patrols were intent on his capture and not on his death. It would take two officers of the UEA to bring the ship fully online. Whatever was wearing Croyan's skin apparently knew enough to keep Tyler alive if it had any hope of leaving Acrea. The thought left an ashen taste in his mouth.

Given the twisted anger the evil that wore Croyan's skin had displayed, followed by the all-out assault on Moonlit Waters, Tyler had doubts. Perhaps the plan was not that simple. Maybe it was never about leaving at all. The main guns that the *Spero* possessed would make quick work of the planet. All life would end in a firestorm. Was Armageddon more Shade's style?

Tyler felt the warmth of the crystal that Celest had given him pulse in his pocket. Pelagos needed power, and he needed a communications terminal. Shade must not have known about Thomas, or Tyler imagined Shade would have found a way into orbit long ago with intentions of forcing his way onto the ship. Tyler needed to work quickly. Shade would return to Moonlit Waters, and Tyler wanted an appropriate welcoming party hovering over the castle. His ship. The *Centaur*. Two officers were needed to bring the *Spero* back online, but only his authorization was needed to free the *Centaur* from its slumber.

"What are you hiding from?" Crylona asked, her voice barely above a whisper.

Tyler jumped slightly, forgetting for a moment where he was.

"I don't know how much of the past the people of Pelagos know, but we fled our home planet of Earth to escape an alien invasion. We didn't have the means to defend our world, so we ran," he said.

Crylona stared at the deck.

"Everyone on this planet is a descendant of human beings from Earth. I haven't quite sorted out how the balans or Sogra came to be yet or most of the other amazing races that I have witnessed, but everything is pointing at a disaster during landing," Tyler said.

"Technically, Commander, none of us should be here," Shale said.

Crylona looked up with her eyes narrowed.

"Yes, Shale. This is not Yar887. While I am interested in how we ended up here, that is for another time. Crylona and I were just about to rest for a while," Tyler said.

Shale chimed in compliance and came to attention.

"I will await your instructions."

Tyler motioned for Crylona to lead the way back to the bridge. He heard Shale follow a short distance behind them and glanced as they entered the cabin. The drone had turned and taken up a defensive stance in front of the doorway. His chest swelled with pride. He was proud to serve the UEA and only hoped that there would be a UEA to go back to someday.

They had a few hours of restless sleep under Shale's watchful eye. Something about wearing the mask kept Tyler from falling fully asleep. Every time he would start to drift into a deep sleep, he felt like something wriggled in his throat. The sensation was uncomfortable. When he could no longer stand trying to sleep, he gathered up his belongings and nodded as Crylona did the same.

They cycled through the air lock one by one, with Shale going first, Tyler second, and Crylona third. Polaris provided the same shimmering bubble as before, with Starmist doing the same for Crylona. It would take pressure far beyond the deepest Acrean ocean to damage Shale.

The shelf where the derelict UEA vessel rested upon overlooked a trench that disappeared into the darkness.

"The Barrens," Crylona said.

The Barrens proved to be an accurate description of the wide scar that ran the length of the ocean floor. The water was motionless and was missing even the most basic small plant and animal life. The result was a seemingly endless stretch of clear water and barren ocean floor as far as the eye could see. Tyler felt noticeably more hungry than he had since submerging.

Crylona led the way as before, with Tyler in the middle and Shale bringing up the rear. Tyler marveled at the cleverly engineered thrusters placed all down the drone's back, legs, and feet. The thrusters appeared to be nothing more than glowing slits that released thin blue jets of propulsion. Shale was easily keeping up as Starmist increased speed and darted deeper into the Barrens.

They encountered the first sentry after a time, and it was Tyler who noticed it before the others. He had caught the flicker of movement out of the corner of his eye, but it had faded as quickly as it came. When the movement occurred again, Tyler confirmed the glittering of scales even at a great distance.

"Warning, multiple life-forms detected," Shale said. Shale's voice thumped against the dome around Tyler's head like a sea creature's sonar.

Tyler squinted, and his ocular implant flipped the spectrum into infrared. Instead of the one creature he had expected, a half-dozen shapes burned brightly in the distance. "I see them," he said.

"They are Riders," Crylona said, her voice sounding far away. "We must hurry before they summon their Herald."

The crystal clear waters around them began to streak and churn as they accelerated. Tyler looked at the yawning trench below. It was a perfect hiding place for an ambush. Somehow, the Riders kept pace with them and stayed just close enough to confirm that they were indeed following. He glanced at their pursuers again, and there were twelve shapes this time.

"How far until we are across?" Tyler asked.

"We have just begun the crossing. I doubt we will make it without confrontation," Crylona said.

They continued surging ahead for several hours but failed to put any real distance between the Riders and themselves. Tyler couldn't help but notice that their numbers continued to grow until he could no longer distinguish individual shapes anymore. They simply looked like a horizon of heat that was getting larger.

"Crylona, this second outpost you mentioned. Does it have any defenses?" Tyler asked.

"I don't know. It is just like all the rest. None of them speak anymore like the ones in Pelagos," she said.

Tyler tore his gaze from the gathering swarm of heat and urged Polaris faster. They had better hope the next outpost had stronger walls or a functional shield array. He could sense that Polaris was tired from the exertion of keeping the pressure from killing Tyler and acting as propulsion. The balanite would be of little use in a fight beyond what it was providing now.

"Just get us there, and soon," Tyler said with more calm than he felt.

Several more hours passed before the derelict frigate came into view. Half of the ship was hanging precariously over the trench. The only thing that had stopped it from going completely over was a jagged fragment of the ocean floor that had smashed the engines and wedged them under the rock. What was left of the ship was the triangular hull and one of the wings. It had seen better days.

Crylona, in a rush, set them stumbling across the ocean floor under the ships wing to the air lock. Tyler glanced from the way they had come and could clearly make out a large group of scaled creatures charging toward them. Crylona cycled the air lock manually and urged them all inside. It was a tight fit, and it took the chamber what felt like an excessive amount of time to empty. They stumbled weakly into the dimly lit interior of the frigate, drained of strength from the breakneck journey across the Barrens.

"Shale, go to the engineering bay and give me a diagnostic. I want to see what, if anything, still works on this bird," Tyler said.

"Aye sir," Shale said and disappeared towards the aft of the ship.

Tyler surveyed the long central corridor and noticed a similar state of disrepair to the interceptor. There was rust, decay, and rot everywhere. He motioned for Crylona to follow him before he realized that she had probably been on this ship more times than she could count. She didn't argue and fell into step behind him.

The double door to the bridge was open, which was not a good sign. Tyler stepped through the hatch and noticed familiar bedding in the corner of the bridge. The consoles were dark, and many had melted after centuries of exposure to salt. An unexpected glimmer caught his attention, and he moved to where the pilot would have once sat. The chair and frame had long ago rotted away and in doing so, had covered one of the bridge system consoles.

He wiped away the grime once again, glad he couldn't smell anything, and was pleasantly surprised when a ship's diagnostic flickered to life on the still functional pad.

A surprise bang broke his concentration, followed by a series of louder impacts on the hull.

The Riders had come.

"Commander?" Shale's voice crackled to life in his ear.

"Report," Tyler said.

"The reactor is online, and life support is still functional. The shield array is not responding, and neither are the point defense cannons. No engines," Shale said.

Tyler sighed. He didn't even know why he had gotten his hopes up, given the conditions of the exterior of the ship. The banging outside continued, followed by a blast that shook the deck. Something larger had joined the fray.

"I sense a Herald," Crylona said softly.

Tyler unfastened his pack and dropped it to the deck with a thud. He rummaged for a moment until he found the two items he sought. Warsteel whispered against his back as he flung the cloak over one shoulder, followed by the buzz of the heavy repeater as he thumbed the weapon to life.

"We need to control as much of what is about to happen as we can," Tyler said.

Crylona was wide-eyed and nodded.

"I am going to go jam the air lock and open the outer door. The ship is going to flood slowly, and with life support still online, we are going to keep the water out as long as possible," he said. "The only way to even the playing field is to keep them coming from one direction."

"I understand," Crylona said. Starmist rippled around her middle, looking ready.

Tyler nodded and moved to jury-rig the air lock controls. It took him longer than he would have liked to manually manipulate the outer door controls. When the warning klaxon finally sounded, he was worried. Based on the banging on the hull, there could be a breach forming where they couldn't control the flood of water. He stepped back and slammed the manual release button for the inner door.

The life support field flickered as the outer door cracked open and water rushed in to fill the air lock. The field crackled and bowed inward before pushing back against the torrent. Dark shapes floated just beyond the outer door, and a single hunched form slipped between the doors and emerged into the flooded air lock. A Rider passed through the field and blinked in confusion either from the sudden atmosphere or because of Tyler's heavy repeater blasting shrieking bolts of sonic energy into its scale covered torso. The Rider rocked backward and tumbled into the open ocean with a smoldering hole in its middle.

Three more Riders with dark green scale covered bodies pressed through the opening, and Tyler squeezed the trigger of his heavy repeater. A volley of shrieking sonic energy leaped through the Riders like sound waves passing through smoke.

"Commander, I have downloaded repair schematics for this ship. What are your orders?" Shale asked, her voice crackling to life in his ear.

"Weapons," he said, blasting another Rider with a face similar to that of a fish.

"Aye, sir," Shale said.

Tyler felt Polaris just within reach, gathering strength.

Rest, my friend, Tyler thought.

His heavy repeater continued to cough compressed bolts of sonic energy, cutting Riders down as quickly as they came. When the charging creatures paused, and the watery curtain lay still, Tyler stood on his toes to get a better look at what was beyond the breach. He had a strange thought when a bone spear as long as a man, slid through the life support barrier and impaled him against the rusted corridor behind.

I always thought I would die on my feet, not on my toes.

17 – SHOW ME

"Again!" Samson said. "This time with more intensity."

Lanadari sat cross-legged on the sweet-smelling purple grass in the great gardens of Castle Forgotten. VAST streamed from her skin like ice melting to vapor in the Acrean sun. She held only a fraction of the VAST Samson knew she could command, but brute force was not the purpose of today's lesson. This particular training session was about control.

Samson glanced at the Deru, standing a short distance away. It watched them with its intense blue orbs of cold flame. How was he supposed to train something he couldn't speak with? Could its race even hear the sweet song of the VAST? These were some of the many questions he had tried in vain to get answers to.

He held his own silver blanket of VAST against his skin like warm shifting grains of sand. They had been sitting like this for hours, and he sweated freely. Lanadari barely looked winded. He had already surpassed his previous record by a full hour and was beginning to feel the strain.

Who, after all, was training whom?

His command of the VAST had grown aggressively over the last few weeks, and he wondered just how much further he could go with Lanadari as his student.

The training at the Temple of Spero had been suspended following the attack by Shade, and no new acolytes had been admitted since. He wasn't even sure that what he was showing Lanadari would have been sanctioned by the elders. Most of what Samson knew had been self-taught anyways or had been passed down from one village shaman to the next.

Samson felt his breath catch in his throat, and he fought the urge to cough. He had to maintain his concentration. He was, after all, now a teacher. It wouldn't do if he couldn't outlast his student.

"I am tired," Lanadari said. She let the VAST stream away softly and opened her eyes.

Samson exhaled sharply, not even realizing he had been holding his breath. The VAST crackled with energy against his skin and faded slowly into the air around him in a shimmering nimbus. He stood up, which was starting to take far longer with every year that passed.

"Very well, let us rest," Samson said, hoping he had kept the weariness from his voice.

Lanadari stretched and yawned and then leaned back to lay against the slight grassy hill, staring up at the sky. The Deru lumbered over and mimicked her posture exactly, shaking the ground as it fell unceremoniously onto its back. Twigs and leaves shot out in all directions and dissolved into dust as quickly as they had appeared.

"I like it here," Lanadari said. Her eyes were closed, and the warm Acrean sunlight caused her runes to glitter brightly.

"As do I, young one. While I do long for the fresh mountain air of Tonu, I can think of few places better than this," Samson said.

"What is Tonu like?" Lanadari asked.

Samson felt a pang of homesickness and loss as he thought of his village. An image of Bresh, stoic with arms crossed, came to his mind. He hadn't thought of his brother in the chaos of the last few weeks. But now, an innocent question from a young woman had put tears in his eyes.

"Ah… well…" Samson stammered. "It is a small village cradled in the southern mountains. A few days from Arabellum."

Samson noticed Lanadari wince when he mentioned Arabellum. She had been Lady Dark at the time, Shade's huntress.

"The air is crisp and clean with many rivers and fragrant grasses, much like what you are lying on. The people are simple and hardworking." Samson said.

"I think I would like that too," Lanadari said with a sigh.

The Deru rustled in agreement.

"Someday, I will take you there," Samson said. He stretched until his old bones creaked and settled down next to Lanadari to stare at the grey-green sky.

A gentle breeze stirred the garden, and complex smells from hundreds of different plants wafted through the air. Samson closed his eyes for a moment and listened to the wind. The sound that he kept hearing was the rhythmic movement of the leaves, branches, and vines of the Deru. There was a faint pattern to the sound.

"Samson?" Lanadari asked.

He jumped in surprise at her voice. "Yes, child?"

"I would like to go for a walk outside the city. There is a place I need to see," she said.

Samson had a hunch at the place she had in mind. The coast of Arral was dotted with hundreds of fishing villages. When he had touched Lanadari outside Kent's Gate and been flooded with memory, one painful reoccurring vision had pushed through all the rest. The destruction of her village by the Tekians.

He stared at the sky and considered his options. He knew it would help with her healing, and the road might present more dynamic training than the Moonlit Waters gardens or sparring arena.

"What about you, Deru? Does a walk sound like something you would also enjoy?" Samson asked.

The Deru lay silent on its back, staring at the sky as if it hadn't heard or didn't understand the question.

"He is content here in the garden," Lanadari said as she pushed herself to her feet.

Samson felt color rise to his cheeks. "How do you know this is a fact, child, when he does not speak?"

Lanadari shrugged and spread her hands in a helpless gesture.

They left the Deru lying in the sunshine and exited the garden. Samson grabbed his walking stick that was leaning just inside the archway that led to a maze of corridors that housed hundreds of workers, visitors, and lesser nobility of the castle.

He guided Lanadari down the most direct route out of the castle and onto a series of rope bridges that connected with the great central staircase in front of the council chamber. They stopped only briefly for Samson to catch his breath and to buy a quick meal and a skin of water that they could enjoy on the road.

When Moonlit Waters faded into the distance behind them, Lanadari finally spoke again.

"You know where we are going, don't you?"

Samson nodded. "I suspected you would want to see it."

Lanadari sighed and stared at the ground. "I don't know why I need to go, but I need the closure that will come with standing amongst the ruins."

"Perhaps a new village has grown in place of the old?" Samson offered hopefully.

Lanadari remained silent.

They walked for a time on the well-maintained highway that stretched along the coast to the south. They reached a stone signpost after a few hours of walking and turned down a faint path that led towards the sound of the ocean. The village they expected to find was not far.

The village was little more than overgrown ruins. A few stone foundations were all that was left of the homes that once stood, and most of them had been scorched by fire. A few of the stones bore signs of heavy weapons fire, most likely from one of the Tekian flying machines. The place radiated cold and loss.

In the center of the village was a large chunk of shattered crystal. Many fragments dotted the ground around the aqua-colored pyramid-shaped crystal. It looked to have taken a single hit from something heavy at its base, radiating cracks and breaking across its surface.

Lanadari approached the ruined crystal pillar and touched it with a delicate hand. A faint light stirred in the depths of the crystal.

"No one can undo the damage that was done here," Lanadari whispered. "But I can make it safe again for those who come next."

She placed both of her hands on the crystal pillar and closed her eyes. The faint light that had stirred within flared brightly and began to pulse like a heartbeat. The stray fragments of crystal that littered the ground glowed with the same aqua-colored light. Several of the fragments leaped from their resting place and clanked back into place from where they had fallen as if pulled by a magnet.

Lanadari's light violet-colored hair danced free of its cord and flowed around her face like she was underwater. More crystal fragments drifted up from the ground and spun around the pillar until they found the matching opening. When the final fragment clicked into place, and the crystal pillar was once again whole, she removed her hands and stepped back.

The spiderweb cracks on the crystal's surface fused and released small rivers of steam into the air. The crystal pillar throbbed audibly, and Samson felt the chill in the air vanish. Lanadari knelt before the crystal pillar and bowed her head. She remained perfectly still as the crystal pulsed a final time and then took on a steady inner light like a crackling torchstone.

"I want to be alone for a while, Samson. Please," Lanadari said.

"Take all the time you need. I will be close by," Samson said.

He hobbled a short distance away, leaning on his staff more than he had in a long time. It was surprising how much the walk from Moonlit Waters had taken out of him. The last few weeks were certainly hard on his body, and he hadn't healed properly. The care he had received in the city was the best available, but there was only so much that could be done for a Balan of his years.

He found a small boulder sticking out of the ground that was within sight of the village and sat down heavily. His bones hurt. He often thought of the amazing things that could be done with the VAST and wished for the thousandth time that healing was within his powers.

A cool breeze from the sea filled his nostrils with the sweet smell of the ocean and chased away some of the aches in his bones. He could hear sea birds calling and waves crashing against cliffs. The sky was clear, and the Acrean sun had many hours left in the heavens.

Samson stretched and sighed, wondering how the rest of his companions were doing. Had Tyler made it to the Deep with the mysterious Crylona? A smile found its way to his lips when he thought of Razmal shouting at Ralon, who usually wore a roguish grin. He missed the adventure but wondered just how his body would have allowed him to go with either party had Celest demanded it.

Instead, here he was, sitting on a rock in the Acrean sunshine. He was doing something important, whether it looked like it or not. Lanadari's mental health was the key to her continued training. She had volatile emotions, and any kind of closure she would find in her ruined village was worth the effort.

Or lack of effort on his part, he thought, sitting comfortably on a rock.

He looked towards the village again and shaded his eyes with one of his hands. He could make out very little from where he sat, but he hoped to see Lanadari heading his way any minute. The more he stared, the quieter the village seemed. Nothing moved.

Samson leaned against his walking staff and rested his cheek against his hand. His eyes felt heavy sitting in the warmth of the day. What would closing his eyes for a few moments hurt?

"Samson," a soft voice said, snapping him awake. He blinked in confusion, and his eyes met the square, swirling silver irises of Lanadari's. "You fell asleep."

Night had fallen, and Yalonia hung large and rust-colored in the sky. Samson winced as he tried to stand up. Sitting on a rock for such a long period of time made his bones hurt, not to mention that both of his feet were asleep.

"I am embarrassed, lady," he said, leaning heavily on his staff to stand.

Lanadari looked him up and down and frowned. "I have been so preoccupied that I didn't realize how injured you are."

Samson waved her off with his free hand, not daring to take his other hand off his staff, else he land facedown on the grass. "Old bones is all."

"May I?" Lanadari asked, taking a step forward. Her eyes were kind and sparkled with an inner light.

Samson nodded and tried to keep the suspicion he felt from reflecting on his face.

Lanadari placed a cool hand on his head and another on his chest and closed her eyes. The runes on her skin shimmered and took on a reddish hue.

"Oh, Samson," she whispered. "What have they done to you?"

He raised an eyebrow. Sure, he had been through his fair share of battles over the last few weeks, but the healers had done what they could.

"I would say they did their best with what they had," he said.

Lanadari opened her eyes to meet his. "I can do better."

A feeling of cold spread from her hands and rapidly propagated across his skin. He gasped and struggled to draw breath as the cold turned to numbness and sank deeply into his muscles and through to his bones. His blood felt like shards of ice had entered his veins. His eyes widened as the runes on Lanadari's skin increased in radiance.

A ring of energy flashed around her feet and shot upwards in a pillar of blue fire. The fire pulsed and flowed upward, burning a perfect ring into the ground. The numbing feeling in his bones rapidly faded and was replaced with an agonizing blast of heat. He opened his mouth to scream, but the only thing that came out was billowing steam.

"This is pain leaving the body," Lanadari said, her voice deep and sounding like several voices speaking at once.

Samson was fairly certain she was killing him.

When he felt like he could take no more, the burning was replaced by an amazing feeling of euphoria. He had never felt more alive. Every muscle in his body flexed as if made new. The bones that had minutes ago caused him constant pain felt remade. The blue pillar of flames around him swirled silently and pulled into his body like breath filling his lungs.

"Samson?" Lanadari whispered softly. "How do you feel?"

He opened his eyes, not realizing he had squeezed them shut at some point during his ordeal.

"Alive," he replied and then burst into joyous laughter. He flung his staff aside, which had splintered and broken down the middle, and wrapped Lanadari in a bear hug. He heard her giggle softly, and then the breath whooshed from her as he picked her up and twirled her around. When they were both good and dizzy, he set her down and smiled.

Samson noticed that the runes that normally glittered on her exposed skin were greatly diminished. They were still there but looked more like light-colored tattoos instead of embedded crystal fragments. Her skin was paler than usual, and her eyes looked sunken.

"Lady, are you well?" Samson asked, reaching out to steady Lanadari as she swooned.

"Just tired. Can you help me back to the village? I wish to bask in the light of the healed crystal," she said.

Samson winced in habit, thinking about how he would manage to hobble and help her walk. He nodded and scooped her up in his arms. She felt like she weighed next to nothing with his renewed vigor. Balan, after all, prided themselves on physical strength. He had, however, become frail with the time spent with the VAST.

He carried Lanadari back to the village, inhaling the cool ocean breeze in great breaths as he walked. It took them a short time to reach the crystal, and he carefully set Lanadari against its smooth exterior. She nodded in thanks and placed both hands on the glowing surface. The runes on her arms flickered, and she sighed.

She sat touching the crystal for half of Yalonia's climb through the evening sky. Samson studied the darkness above, all the while appreciating the billions of twinkling stars in the heavens.

"I am ready to go home," Lanadari said, startling Samson from his stargazing.

She stood, leaning on the crystal with one arm, and reached for Samson to take her other. When the two of them touched, a great sound of thunder shook the ground. An overwhelming presence invaded the area, compressing the soil, crumbling ruined buildings, and flattening the grass. Samson knew the presence immediately.

Celest.

"Lady," Samson said, dropping to one knee.

18 – BONES

Roarc opened his eyes, feeling as if he had just closed them moments before. Zuh'Erg was across from him, resting on his haunches and staring down at the city. The sounds of Mazoris snoring broke the silence that otherwise permeated the rocky shelf where they rested. The same perpetual light from the glittering stars above confused any sense of time having passed.

I was beginning to wonder when you would awaken, Zuh'Erg said in his mind.

Roarc pushed himself up against the wall to stand. It took him a few moments to massage the pins and needles of sleep out of his legs and back. A few stretches later, he felt more or less well-rested. He wondered what the wolf had in store for them today.

The city is deceptively far away. It will take us hours to reach the cavern floor and still more to the gates, Zuh'Erg projected. The wolf was still crouched, staring at the city.

Roarc stepped forward to stand beside Zuh'Erg and followed his lupine stare with his own. The dark tower seized his gaze, and he felt an unseen force pull his eyes to look at the flickering blue ball of flame suspended above it. The flame whispered long-dead words. Words that Roarc could feel in his body but that his mind could not comprehend.

"We need to go. Now," Roarc said. The voice coming from his lips sounded like someone else. Someone desperate.

They woke Mazoris and were met with a great deal of hissing and spitting of Sogra curses and were headed down the winding stone steps within the hour. Oppressive silence hung in the air, and no one dared to break its heavy enchantment. There was something ancient and enormously powerful emanating from the city, and a general sense of dread at breaking the silence kept them moving one quiet step after another.

The temperature since entering the tunnels from the surface had been constant. Roarc noticed with each step from the platform down to Starlit Waters that the temperature was dropping. It wasn't long before they could all see their breath steaming and swirling. Mazoris looked increasingly miserable as the temperature plummeted. His blood was cold enough and didn't need help from the elements.

When they reached the floor of the cavern, the size and scale of Starlit Waters pressed in on them. Even from a distance, Roarc could gauge that the place was massive. As promised, it took them the better part of a day, which they estimated by how often Mazoris had to stop and chant warmth back into his body with various beads and fetishes that wafted into smoke once consumed.

The gates of Starlit Waters were a sight that left Roarc breathless. As a half-giant, almost everything he encountered was too small. Even the half-giant villages in Teka were minimal, with just large enough tents and barely adequate bones for construction. What stood before him was a gatehouse so large that he felt like a Balan must have felt when standing before the mighty gates of Arabellum.

Starlit Waters had been built for giants.

Initially, the gate of the barbican from such height and distance had looked closed. Up close, the twisted black metal gate was slightly open, which meant Roarc and his companions could stand shoulder to shoulder with room to spare on either side. The massive curtain wall that stretched endlessly in either direction appeared to be crafted of a single piece of grey stone.

They crossed into the gloom under the barbican, and Roarc considered bringing out his torchstone. The vastness of the fortification would have easily swallowed his light. The portcullis came into view, backlit by the perpetual starlit sky. The dark gate of ornate metal was raised to half position, which left plenty of room for Roarc to walk fully upright.

They emerged into the outer city that was protected by the curtain wall they had just passed through. The inner curtain wall and lower bailey of the tower were far off in the distance.

The silence of the city was deafening.

The air was perfectly still and frigid. Roarc glanced at Mazoris, who had a thin sheet of frost adorning his scales. He had never witnessed a cold Sogra before. The sight was pathetic. Should an invading army want to conquer the whole of Teka, they needed only to bring cold and let it wipe out the entirety of the lizard population.

As pathetic as Mazoris was, Roarc knew if they didn't somehow warm him soon, they would be a band of two warriors instead of three.

"We need to get you warm," Roarc said, looking down the broad boulevard that led to neat rows of solid buildings. Each building was topped with stained glass and had multiple stained glass windows. The glass twinkled a variety of colors in the light from the starlit sky.

Mazoris hissed weakly and expended another of his beads in a flash of light and smoke. The ice that clung to his scales steamed and fell away. By the looks of his beaded necklace, he was running low on the fetishes that were keeping him alive.

Zuh'Erg broke into a loping run towards the building with a simple mental projection of, *Scouting,* that echoed in Roarc's mind. Mazoris picked up his pace with a look of fear in his eyes. Roarc knew how to recognize that look better than most. He was generally the compelling event leading up to the fear others felt.

"Keep going. We aren't far now," Roarc said. He hoped his words were encouraging. He wasn't overly fond of Mazoris, but the thought of being alone with Zuh'Erg made him intent on the Sogra's survival.

By the time they reached the outer spiral of the buildings, Roarc was half carrying Mazoris. Zuh'Erg stood in a tall and wide doorway that looked identical to all the others. They hustled through the doorway, and the sound of a heavy stone door booming closed echoed through an empty vestibule.

The inside of the building was dimly lit by an unseen light source. White marble floors with rough gray stone walls formed a large central chamber. Several corridors led off into unknown areas. Roarc caught sight of a jagged crystal hearth that looked intact.

He crossed into the chamber, leaving Mazoris hunched against the wall. Zuh'Erg disappeared down one of the corridors, leaving Roarc to study the crystal hearth. The face of the finely crafted hearth was covered in fine gold flakes with a single rune carved in the giant language.

"*Impels,*" Roarc grumbled aloud, tracing the rune with his finger.

The crystals within the hearth roared to life and blessed warmth expanded outward. He heard scurrying, and then felt the impact of a frigid, scaled body that bounced against his own. Mazoris grabbed at the hearth and spread his arms and legs wide to drink in the warmth. The Sogra sighed with pleasure and sank to his knees. His spear clattered from his limp fingers to the marble floor and his heavy pack quickly followed.

Roarc allowed himself a moment to bask in the warmth and soothe his stiff muscles. He sensed Zuh'Erg before he saw the Erew. It was unnerving how he could materialize out of thin air next to someone. His hood shadowed his face and his wise yellow eyes missed nothing.

"What can we do for him? It's not like we can take the hearth with us," Roarc said.

Sogra can endure a great deal when they are warm. Like any lizard, he needs to soak as much of it in as he is able. He needs a short time here and will be able to resist the cold for the rest of the journey to the tower, Zuh'Erg said in his mind.

Roarc felt anxious at the mention of the tower. He needed to get there, and the delay made his palms sweat.

"I should just go ahead. You two can catch up," Roarc said. He felt hopeful that Zuh'Erg would agree.

The wolf crossed his arms and remained unmoving.

I need YOU to open something for ME, do not forget that, Zuh'Erg projected. The volume in Roarc's mind made him flinch.

He felt the half-giant berserker rage build in his chest for a moment before a quick look at Zuh'Erg's particularly long and sharp-looking claws calmed him. He refused to think about what he wanted to do to the Erew, knowing that the wolf was always in his head. He forced a smile, turned, and walked into the vestibule.

Roarc stared at the door for a long while. He wanted to be defiant and throw open the heavy stone and charge into the street. Instead, he stood perfectly still and breathed. He needed a clear head for what was to come. There was obviously something of value that Zuh'Erg wanted and he needed to keep his wits about him to figure out how he could use it to his advantage.

The tower called to him again. The sensation made his bones feel wrong in his body. His mouth was suddenly rife with saliva and tasted metallic. A sheen of sweat covered his bare forearms, and he could feel his breastplate stick to his back. The compulsion was getting worse and every moment he resisted was physically painful.

He turned back and found Zuh'Erg in the doorway, his head cocked as if listening.

We need to get you to the tower, he projected.

Roarc had a vicious comeback on the tip of his tongue but held it. The look in Zuh'Erg's eyes was not unkind. It was almost as if the wolf felt sorry for him.

"What do you know?" Roarc asked.

The wolf remained silent.

Roarc sighed and shook his head. Would Zuh'Erg save him from certain death just to deliver him to a similar fate? Maybe. But he doubted it. There was something about the way that Zuh'Erg looked at him. Like he had hope.

Mazoris had begun to stir and had even ventured away from the hearth a short distance. He was looking over at them, his predatory eyes watching the scene unfold. Leave it to a Sogra to find potential carrion. Roarc didn't intend to become a meal today.

"A tasssk," Mazoris said.

He returned to the hearth, pulled his heavy pack over, and knelt down. His tail swished back and forth as he rummaged through the pack. When he found the items he was looking for, he hissed and clicked in victory.

Roarc, against the compulsion of the tower, walked over to see what Mazoris was doing. In the Sogra's clawed hand was a small seashell bowl. He was crushing various herbs into the bowl and pouring acrid-smelling liquid from a small clay flask with a stiff-looking stopper into the bowl as well. The smell was horrendous.

Roarc turned away and retched, trying to hold down the meager contents of his stomach. He covered his face with his hands and blinked his watering eyes. What could possibly make such a foul smell? He hoped that the Sogra wasn't going to eat it.

Mazoris set the bowl on the floor and let the now smoking and bubbling liquid waft vapors over him. He dipped one of his talons into the bowl, and when it emerged, the end was covered in something thick and dark green. He began to trace crude runes on his chest scales and spent the next several minutes dipping his talon back in the bowl and then covering more of the scales on his body. After a short time, Mazoris was covered head to toe in rancid-smelling runes.

"Protections," he hissed.

"I can imagine. Nothing will want to come within twenty feet of us," Roarc said, choking and striding quickly to the vestibule away from the horrible fumes.

"Protections from the cold," Mazoris said. He gathered up the materials he had pulled from the bag and placed them back where they had come from.

Zuh'Erg stood looming in the doorway and pulled his cloak tighter around his head. It looked like the smell was bothering even the stoic Erew when he threw the stone door open and slipped silently onto the street.

Roarc adjusted his wall shield and maul and followed Zuh'Erg into the cold. He heard Mazoris follow them out, the faint clicking of his talons on the cobblestones telling the quickness of his strides. At least the Sogra had recovered quickly and had thought of a way, albeit a stinky way, to keep himself warm.

No matter what happened next, Roarc would not be stopped from entering the tower.

They passed identical-looking buildings with the same stained glass windows, large stone doors, and domed glass roofs. If there had been any twists or turns beyond the spiral that led ever inwards, Roarc would have been hopelessly lost. Their Erew companion was a constant shadow in the distance that vanished for several steps and then appeared at a different location after several more.

When they reached the inner bailey and found the gates thrown open, Roarc was relieved. The tunnel through the inner gatehouse was much shorter than the reinforced gatehouse of the outer bailey. The shadows felt the same, and he resisted producing his torchstone. Sometimes, what lurked in the dark was better left undiscovered.

The tower loomed large when they emerged from the tunnel. Roarc stared up, no longer able to see the blue flame that had called his name and set his bones on fire. He knew it was still there and it was all he could do not to break into a run to reach the shadowy archway that led inside.

There didn't appear to be a door, only a large archway of polished black-pearl colored stone. They approached the opening and Zuh'Erg stopped as if struck by an unseen force. Roarc turned and noticed that Mazoris had stiffened and appeared to be frozen. Whatever was affecting his companions didn't seem to affect him.

He grinned as he passed Zuh'Erg, and felt the yellow lupine eyes on him. When he stood in the shadow of the tower's doorway, a sparkling field of energy sprang to life. The thin field of blue energy swam with floating rune in the giant language that twinkled to life for an instant and then faded, only to reappear again. Roarc knew in his core that if he touched the field, it would kill all three of them violently.

Roarc looked around the archway for a way to bring down the field. He searched for a long while and felt a similar sensation to the one he had felt the last time he had spent hours searching for a way to open the first door leading to the underground city. He took a step back and drew his heavy maul with practiced ease. Perhaps the energy would behave similarly to solid stone.

He swung his maul lightly, and it bounced off the wall with crackling blue sparks. It felt like the field had bowed inward. He glanced back at the waiting yellow eyes of Zuh'Erg. He could read nothing from their frozen depths.

Roarc squared his shoulders and brought his maul backward and then slammed it forwards with all of his considerable strength. The maul crashed into the rune field with a tremendous boom. Blue fire raced along the head of the maul, and runes appeared and then shattered as a shock wave traveled across the surface of the barrier. A great groan sounded like the twisting of metal.

He looked on in horror as the head of his maul flexed and began to melt like wax of a burning candle. The runes crackled along the barrier and surged inward as if attacking the foreign metal. A high-pitched humming noise split the air, and Roarc lost his grip on his violently shaking weapon. The explosion shouldn't have been a surprise, but when his maul erupted into a ball of fire and threw him backward, the sense of loss was overwhelming.

Roarc landed painfully and smelled his crisped flesh strongly. He closed his eyes and sucked in a hot breath, fairly certain he had just been killed. It took him a few moments to realize that he was, in fact, still living. He struggled to his feet and glared at the archway.

The runic field and his maul were gone.

Zuh'Erg and Mazoris stumbled forward as if their steps had never been interrupted.

What happened? Zuh'Erg projected.

"I opened the door," Roarc said. He kicked a chunk of still glowing metal that hissed when it touched his boot.

So it seems, Zuh'Erg projected as he moved smoothly into the shadow of the tower.

"Broke your hammer?" Mazoris asked. He sounded almost apologetic—if a Sogra was even capable of that.

"Yeah," Roarc said quietly.

"Find a new one," Mazoris said, slinking off to follow Zuh'Erg into the tower.

"Yeah," Roarc said absently and followed them into the darkness.

They found themselves in a perfectly round chamber. Roarc had expected to see a stairway of some kind, but instead, the tower rocketed upwards as far as his eye could see. At the end of his gaze burned the blue flame.

It took his eyes a few moments to adjust before the first skeleton came into view. Huge yellowed giant bones stood perfectly preserved in the center of the chamber. In fact, three complete skeletons were facing each other, their clothing long since rotted away. One held an enormous silver hammer poised over its head as if it were about to strike down on an anvil. The second skeleton held a pair of tongs designed to grasp hot metal. The third skeleton was kneeling and held a large scabbard as if it was presenting it to someone.

The scabbard caught Roarc's attention and held it fast. The black leather with red stitching was whispering something he knew he should understand but was just out of his reach. The scabbard had intricate silver runes running along its center that oozed power.

What was this place?

His gaze drifted to the center of the tower and fell upon a sword made of pitch-black metal, suspended in midair by four thick chains of dark iron. Roarc felt himself compelled to take the blade that seemed to drink in the light from all around. It was then that he knew the sword by name.

Moira.

19 – WEIGHTLESS

"What do you mean the commlink went down?" Thomas asked, pacing the deck like he was going to wear a hole in it.

"The alignment module has not been used in several hundred years. All of the recent use has overloaded the mechanism that allows us to properly orient the array for communication," Morgan said.

"So it's broken?" Thomas asked, obviously knowing the answer.

"It requires maintenance," Morgan corrected.

"What if Commander Tor is trying to contact us this very instant? Are we going to give the savior of this entire doomed expedition a busy signal?" Thomas said. He was shouting again.

"It will keep ringing," Morgan said, matching him with his ancient earth phone metaphor.

"Then open a path for me to fix the alignment module on the comms array," Thomas said.

Morgan's avatar flickered for a moment. Every time he did that, Thomas knew he wasn't going to like the answer.

"That particular system is on the underbelly of the *Spero*," Morgan said.

Thomas placed his face in both of his palms. The underbelly of the ship had been damaged irreparably during the failed landing attempt of one of the colony modules. The resulting explosion that had broken up the module had rendered most of the decks on the underside of the ship exposed to space.

"So you are telling me I am going *outside*," Thomas said through his fingers.

"Unless, of course, you can find yourself another drone to play with?" Morgan said.

Was that sarcasm?

Thomas dropped his hands and stared at the AI. Morgan stared back at him impassively.

"I am going. Right now," Thomas said. He spun away from the middle of his quarters and grabbed his uniform jacket off the bed. He had taken to wearing his uniform again after Commander Tor had been found alive.

"You should eat something. My scans indicate it has been some time since you nourished your body," Morgan said as the doors to Thomas's quarters opened.

"I am sure I can grab something on the way," Thomas said with an absent wave of his hand. No way was he going to eat. Not before strapping into a space suit and heading into the scariest environment he could think of. His stomach lurched at the thought.

Thomas hadn't done particularly well in any of the space simulations. In fact, he had barely gotten through boot camp. He had done even worse in officer school. He had been thankful when he had earned his commission, but he always felt like he had simply passed by default versus earning his stripes.

Space was terrifying. A small crack in your helmet? Dead. A torn suit? Slowly dead. Explosive decompression? Quickly dead. How about a blast of radiation? Grow a third eye, and then? Dead.

Regardless of how he felt, everyone still sleeping aboard the *Spero* and all of the people below were counting on his next move. None of them even knew any of it was happening, but the choices he and Commander Tor made in the coming days would make all the difference. The continuation of the human race was at stake.

Thomas jogged through the corridors of the ship, not really seeing anything. He was preoccupied and running on what he often called autopilot. When he stepped into one of the central lifts and the doors closed, he allowed himself a moment to steady his breathing. The people mover chimed, requesting a destination, and he took another deep breath.

"Habitation B," he said quietly.

The people mover made an error sound and refused to move.

"Get me as close to what is left of Habitation B as possible," he said.

The people mover chimed in compliance and lurched with what felt like a diagonal direction. The hum of the lift always helped to calm him. Today, it didn't have the desired effect.

When the people mover stopped and the doors slid open, he expected to see flickering lights and damage. Instead, the corridor beyond was pleasant, well lit, and clean. Apparently, Morgan had restored life support to this area of the ship.

Thomas stepped out of the lift and started walking the only direction the corridor led. When he came to a section of the corridor that split left, right, or continued straight, he stopped.

It wouldn't have made sense for Thomas to lug a heavy space suit around the ship, so he looked for the lighted directional indicator on the ceiling to guide him. The indicator glowed green and pointed to the left. It felt like hours of walking before he finally stopped at an nondescript doorway that was missing markings of any kind. He stood in front of the door and spread his arms in annoyance.

"Morgan?" Thomas said, sighing.

The door slid open soundlessly and the opening revealed a storage closet. The closet was small and held a single space suit, tool kit, and helmet.

"Strange place to keep a suit," he said, pulling the heavy kit out of the closet and onto the deck.

UEA space suits came in one size and had a variety of self-fit options. It took Thomas a great deal longer to don the suit by himself. It normally took three people to get someone suited up properly. By the time Thomas stood up with the suit on his body he was sweating freely. The gloves of the space suit were magnetically bound tightly to his forearms until he needed to swing them over his clammy hands.

The storage closet door snapped shut and he bent down, awkwardly, to pick up his helmet and repair kit. He looked up at the ceiling and the green arrow showed him his heading. Hopefully it wasn't far. Thomas swallowed hard and walked heavily down the corridor.

By the time he reached the maintenance shaft that would admit his bulk he felt like he had run a marathon wearing a jogging suit stuffed with weights. His legs shook and he sweated freely. This wasn't going to work. If only he could have some artificial intelligence turn off the gravity like the old sci-fi books that he had read in the ship's database.

Optional physics and all.

Thomas pulled open the manual release on the maintenance hatch and prepared to prime the handle to open it. Something tickled his senses. He paused, donned his helmet, and lowered his gloves onto his hands. The space suit clicked and sealed tightly. He heard a slight hiss of air and his view screen that was built into the helmet displayed his vital signs and oxygen levels. His heartbeat and blood pressure were off the charts according to the readings.

He pulled the primer with his gloved hand three times and pushed the release lever. The hatch slammed open and the vacuum of space on the other side sucked him down the maintenance tube like a murderous slip and slide. He clawed at the tunnel with his blunted too-large hands as it whizzed by but to no avail.

Thomas wasn't at all surprised when the maintenance tube disappeared and was replaced by a sparking and madly spinning debris field. Oddly, it was the debris that saved his life for the moment. When he slammed into a particularly large piece of what had probably been a water reclamation unit and felt a rib crack, he knew that his momentum had stopped enough to keep him from entering a decaying orbit that would have plunged him into the planet's gravity well.

"Morgan," Thomas gasped. He could taste blood in his mouth.

No reply.

Thomas clung to the debris like a life raft and looked around. He was technically still aboard the *Spero* from what he saw. The problem was, it was just barely. He was dangling from a breach that had gashed a gigantic canyon-sized tear in the ship's hull. Bits and pieces of debris continued to rain down from the wound, entering the atmosphere below like shooting stars.

He activated his nav system with his helmet's intuitive eye controls and navigated a series of menus until he found the map he was looking for. A wireframe of what the underside of the ship was supposed to look like appeared and settled over what he was actually seeing. Augmented reality had its uses.

A red blinking dot appeared far off on the other side of the ship. His destination was on the wrong side, or rather, *he* was on the wrong side of where he was supposed to be. Thomas swiped his eyes through a series of menus to run oxygen scenarios. He would barely make the repairs with enough oxygen to reach an accessible hatch on the other side. That was, if nothing went wrong.

Thomas stared at the chunk of slag that had broken his fall and realized something had already gone wrong and he hadn't even really started yet. The good news was that the magnetic system in his gloves and boots had engaged and had kept him from floating off the debris when he became weightless. At least gravity wasn't an issue anymore.

He turned his body enough to see the connecting braces that led to a piece of the torn gash in the ship's hull. He needed to pull himself along the braces until he could attach his boots to the hull and walk, somewhat eerily, upside down with the planet filling his view below. He fought back panic, reached up, and began pulling himself along the braces.

When his oxygen level blinked eighty percent he flipped himself from the brace and attached solidly to the hull. He was standing upright staring at Acrea. It really was beautiful. But he had more important things to do right now than to appreciate the scenery on his spacewalk.

"Morgan?" Thomas asked, swiping his eyes through the limited band range of his suit's communication system.

No response.

He walked across the underside of the hull and skirted the canyon-sized chasm that had spilled the innards of the ship to the planet below.

When his oxygen level blinked fifty percent, he found himself standing before the massive planetary communications array of the *Spero*. It was a wonder that something as large as what he was looking at had a fine motor system for critical orbital adjustments. The schematics were easy enough to find in his suit's database and he quickly brought himself up to speed on how to access the maintenance panels to service what appeared to be a pretty simple tooth-and-groove system.

His hypothesis was that one of the gears had worn out with the passing of nearly one thousand years. He located the first of a series of panels and began to disassemble the system. He was sweating in his suit by the time all of the panels were removed and tethered to a static line that kept them from floating off into space. The primary gear in the system was indeed worn down, but not to the point where it should have been causing a complete failure.

Thomas pulled a tool out of his maintenance bag and began servicing the gear and the rest of the connected systems. When his oxygen level flashed twenty-five percent, he was fairly certain he had found and fixed the problem. A fragment of metal had broken off from one of the grooves and had wedged its way into one of the secondary gears. Removing the fragment proved to be an enormous challenge in the weightlessness of space.

It took Thomas until his oxygen sensor blinked ten percent to remove the fragment, test the array, and replace the panels. Everything was in working order.

"Morgan?" Thomas said.

"Well done, Lieutenant. Please expedite your return to the *Spero*. I am reading critical oxygen levels from your suit," Morgan said over his suit speaker.

"You don't have to tell me twice," Thomas said absently.

"Why would I say anything twice? Perhaps your suit communications device is damaged. Shall I repeat?" Morgan said.

Thomas sighed. "Never mind."

The schematic for the ship's external maintenance access points leaped on his view screen. There were several close by and he chose the one that looked the closest. He stowed his tools and attached his tool kit to his waist strap to keep it from floating and getting snagged on anything. He walked as quickly as he was able with magnetic boots that clung just long enough to be unnatural. It was hard not to look at the red blinking oxygen warning in the lower right-hand corner of his heads-up display.

Acrea spun serenely as he bounced across the ship's hull. He longed to set foot on the surface and breathe in air that had not been recycled by machines. He wanted to hear the sound of the ocean instead of artificial systems making his water and providing his light. He felt like he was getting closer to escaping the ship that had become his prison.

When the maintenance hatch came into view Thomas breathed a sigh of relief. He approached the hatch and reached his gloved hand into the recess that held the manual release. He grasped the handle and pulled.

Nothing happened.

He repeated the same process and pulled the handle. The hatch didn't respond. He wished he could hear the noise, if any, that it was making. It would be easy to diagnose the error if he could hear what sound it was making. He tried to feel a vibration through his thick gloved hand without success.

"Morgan, I can't get the door open," Thomas said. He was forcing down panic.

"The sensor grid for the lower decks is offline," Morgan said. His synthetic voice sounded matter of fact. Like he was saying, *you already know what I am telling you.*

A critical red oxygen-depletion message filled his heads-up display, stealing his vision of what was in front of him. He had a few minutes at best before he asphyxiated. He dismissed the alarm with a flick of his eyes and looked for another access point. When the closest one appeared on the map, he felt a crushing wave of defeat.

He would never make it in time.

"Morgan, I need options," Thomas said. He wasn't even trying to keep the panic out of his voice.

"I am assessing the situation. Please stand by," Morgan said.

Thomas gritted his teeth. He wasn't going to stand by when he had minutes of breath remaining. He stared at the map again thinking through the panic. A radical idea began to form and he broke into the fastest run he could manage with his magnetic boots trapping one boot at a time and releasing too slow.

He tried hard to breathe only when he had to, but the exertion from running had him trying to gulp in more precious air than he had. It started to happen slowly. Each rattling intake of air was less satisfying than the last. Noxious gas alarms began to blare in his helmet. His own breath was killing him.

When he reached the fastest velocity he was able to he disabled his magnetic boots and rocketed forward. He sailed weightless over the hull, his momentum carrying him like an arrow across the curved surface. He was gasping now, and each intake of poison brought him closer to blackness. His vision was starting to blur and he swore he was looking down a long tunnel just to see what was right in front of him.

He crashed into the deck and deployed both the magnets in his boots and hands to halt his motion. It took the magnets several bounces before they fully engaged. Had he not stopped when he did, his momentum would have carried him into space and then the gravity of Acrea would have embraced him and torn him from the sky. Maybe he should let the planet have him.

Thomas shook his head against the thought and held his poisoned breath until his lungs screamed. He disengaged his glove magnets and put his boots back to "stride" mode with a flick of his eyes. The map swung back into view as he staggered forward. He was within a hundred yards of an access point. The distance seemed impossible.

He blasted out the breath he had been holding and gasped in what was left in his suit. It wasn't oxygen. His body revolted against the poison he drew in and his chest felt like someone had stabbed him. The pangs of agony intensified with each step and by the time he had the hatch in view he knew that he wasn't going to make it.

It was a strange feeling being so close to surviving a moment and knowing that your body had nothing left to give. He staggered and collapsed against the hatch. The agony in his chest had been replaced with a warmth he had never felt before. The feeling spread across his body and he felt an involuntary smile reach his lips.

He felt an overwhelming sense of tiredness wash over him. Maybe it wouldn't be so bad to take a quick nap. Perhaps when he woke up his oxygen situation would have resolved itself? Who was he to resist such a profound feeling of peace? He yawned, yawned again, and then yawned a final time before passing into darkness.

20 – DEAR LADY DARK

Celest enveloped what was left of Lanadari's village like a crushing wave of force. Samson couldn't move under the tremendous weight of her presence. Lanadari still had her hand on the crystal pillar, but he could tell that she was powerless to move as well.

"Ah, here you are," the voice of Celest boomed like thunder. "You left the Deru in the garden by itself."

"Yes Lady, we invited it to follow but it seemed content where it was," Samson said through clenched teeth.

"You are to train. The three of you must train without distraction," Celest said.

The voice was painful.

"Yes, my lady," Samson gasped.

"Return to the city," Celest said, her presence fading like a thunderclap.

Lanadari leaned heavily on the crystal pillar, sweating and shaking. Her cheeks looked sunken and dark circles ringed the underside of her eyes. Her light lavender-colored hair stuck to her damp neck and her breath came in ragged gasps.

Samson felt a pang of pity well up in his chest.

"We can rest awhile and start our way back when you are ready," he said.

"I am fine," she said, her voice barely above a whisper.

Samson bowed and nodded, expecting her to sit down any moment. When Lanadari moved her hand with a wave and the night was chased away by a flash of light, Samson staggered in surprise.

They were standing in the fragrant garden of Castle Forgotten as if they had never left. The Deru was still lounging where they had left it, both arms behind its head, one leg kicking to an unheard rhythm.

"H… how?" Samson stammered.

Lanadari shrugged and walked out of the garden heading for the inner courtyard. "I am going to bed," she called over her shoulder.

Samson stood with his mouth open and a finger in the air with an unasked question on his lips. The Deru craned its neck of tightly woven vines as if to ask where she was going.

"I don't quite understand the day I have had, Deru. But nonetheless, a day I will not forget for some time to be sure," Samson said.

He sat down heavily on the ground across from the Deru and pulled his legs up to his chest. He couldn't have dreamed of sitting like this a day ago, let alone ten years ago. The healing Lanadari had worked on him was miraculous. He knew he should be tired or at least affected profoundly from teleporting. Not to mention an ancient crushing down on him with an enormous presence. To be honest, it was all starting to feel like all in a day's work to him.

The Deru sat up and stared into him with its flickering blue orbs of dancing fire.

"We are to train," Samson said, moving his hands in the motion of two finger creatures doing work.

The Deru tilted its head, looking curious.

"You know, train? I will show you the wonders of the VAST," Samson said, moving his hands to try and show the Deru what he meant. Apparently the sweeping gesture of what he imagined the VAST to look like surprised the Deru and it leaned back as if trying to get away from a cloud of insects.

Samson rubbed his chin and thought back to his first lessons as a boy when the elder of his village had begun his own training. He could still see the wizened Balan bent over a walking stick of yellowed bone, just as twisted as his old body had been. He could still smell the leather of the elder's robes and the minty scent of the herbs he once used for the pain in his bones. It seemed that all Balan at a certain age had the bone pain.

"Observe," Samson said, holding out his hand and focusing on the middle of his creased palm.

A small bright light winked into existence.

The Deru leaned forward as if to see better. Samson fed a small amount of VAST into the flickering light until it tripled in size. The silver radiance danced and surged, demanding to be grown. He resisted the urgings and instead turned his gaze upon the Deru.

"Can you sense it, Deru?"

The Deru held up its own hand made of vines and roots and turned its flickering eyes to its palm. The silver light that floated above Samson's palm pulled slowly towards the Deru as if it had been caught in a slow-moving current. When the light reached the Deru, it expanded outward into a perfect sphere and turned a brilliant shade of green. Samson knew his mouth was hanging open but he didn't care to close it.

The predictable song of the VAST, the one he had immersed himself in for most of his life, had changed. The notes were the same but the whispers had stopped and were replaced by a rhythmic sound like waves gently lapping against a distant shoreline. He could smell the VAST and the scent was loamy and ancient.

The green orb of shimmering VAST appeared to catch the current again but this time it flowed back to Samson. He caught and held the orb with his own will and stared into its crystalline depths. His light was still inside. The Deru had not replaced it but had instead layered it with something profound.

Samson looked up and met the Deru's intense flickering blue stare.

"I understand," Samson said, barely above a whisper.

He called to the new song, the one that had revealed itself as readily as a new voice joining a choir. The soil around him surged and the Deru took a step back. Samson continued to focus, knowing he was close to an understanding. Hundreds of vines burst from the ground and wrapped him in a delicate embrace. He was not afraid and let the vines wrap him from head to toe as the new song of the VAST enveloped his mind.

"Good," said a voice that sounded like shifting Acrean soil. Samson knew at once that it was the Deru speaking.

"This is amazing," Samson said, feeling an energy pulsing through the vines encircling his body.

"Glad," came the same gravely voice.

Samson drank in the warmth from the vines and closed his eyes, feeling his way along a network very different from the one he had known before. He opened his eyes and felt a truth had revealed itself through contact with the primal forces of Acrea.

"You aren't here to be trained, are you?" Samson asked.

The Deru made a sound like bones rubbing together. "Shepard."

Shepard.

The image of the Deru standing on the docks, the crook they all carried strangely absent. A surge of emotion coursed through the vines around Samson's torso. He gasped and winced as the vines squeezed the breath from his lungs.

"I understand," Samson said through clenched teeth. The Deru was here to earn his crook. "Please, show me more."

The vines encircling his head squeezed like a mother's embrace.

"Prepare," the Deru said.

Images hammered into Samson like physical blows. He felt them, smelled them, and witnessed them at an alarming pace. It was impossible to process the flood of information and the longer it went on the more helpless he felt. He knew that he should be trying harder to comprehend but the embrace from the vines was so relaxing that he simply *allowed* the deluge of information.

When the images suddenly stopped it felt like plunging into an ice-cold river after working all day in the hot Acrean sun. He gulped for air and shook violently, his skin covered in sweat. The vines eased their grip on his head and began to recede en masse. He dropped to his hands and knees, staring at the disturbed soil beneath him.

He pushed himself to a crouch and stood up on unsteady legs. The Deru stood, its flickering blue eyes holding a newfound understanding. Samson knew they had exchanged a profound moment of information exchange.

The last of the vines had retreated early when a whisper of VAST came at his call. He took a step back, his robes blowing in an unseen wind, and slashed the air with one of his hands. A section of the retreating vines oozed dark sap as a lash of shimmering air cut through them cleanly. With his other hand Samson turned his wrist like he was turning a door handle and spun the vines with silver energy that poured from his fingertips.

The vines spun as if of their own accord, tightening and hardening as they layered one after another. Samson sensed the new song the Deru had taught him just within reach and opened himself to it. Green energy pooled and rippled under his feet and curled its way up his legs and torso and came to rest as a swirling ball of radiant energy that bobbed in front of his chest.

The twisted vines, fully formed into a long crook, rotated in midair. Samson braced himself and widened his stance, keeping the green energy between himself and the crook. He cupped his hands around the energy and whispered a silent prayer that he wasn't about to destroy the crook and in turn the Deru who stood intently studying the scene.

Samson called to the VAST and gritted his teeth against the avalanche that answered his summons. A great shell of silver energy poured over the floating green orb. With each passing moment he felt his control slipping. But he knew he didn't need long. When he could resist the pull no more, Samson thrust his palms outward and sent the crackling ball of silver and green careening into the crook.

A blast of force threw Samson sprawling to the ground. Plants and flowers erupted upwards into the air and distant wind chimes went berserk. A boom so loud that Samson feared he would no longer be able to hear came a moment after. Dust and debris showered him like gentle rain.

It took a few moments for the cloud of dust to clear and when it did Samson struggled to his feet. He blinked his eyes and beheld an awe-inspiring sight. The Deru stood tall, with its new crook in hand. Samson felt a sense of pride when he laid eyes on the crook that he had helped create. He knew the knowledge the Deru had imparted had allowed for its creation.

"I was wondering what all that noise was about," came a soft voice from the archway beyond the garden. "I could feel the immense power even as I slept."

Lanadari stepped from the cover of the arch, looking somewhat recovered. How long had Samson been outside with the Deru?

"Ah, well, I don't know about *immense*," Samson said. He felt the heat in his face and hoped he wasn't bright red.

"You underestimate your abilities," she said, stepping past him to stand before the Deru. She reached out and touched the newly formed crook with her slender hands. The runes that lined her flesh glowed a faint green hue and she nodded.

"Celest spoke to me of the Deru's prowess in battle. Care to test your martial skill against mine?" Lanadari asked.

Samson choked on his own breath and was about to object when Lanadari produced two angry-looking batons from under her voluminous sleeves. Celest's words rooted him in place. She needed to work through her demons. But what if she injured the Deru? Samson blinked and shook his head after staring at the towering Deru. More like Lanadari would be the one injured.

The Deru rustled and leaped backwards, landing in a deep lunge with its newly formed crook extended outwards towards Lanadari. Samson couldn't believe how fast the Deru moved.

Lanadari unclasped her robes and shrugged them off. She wore her plain tan jerkin and her skin glittered in the Acrean sunlight. Her long violet-colored hair was bound by a single strip of cloth and hung down the center of her back.

She approached the Deru slowly, spinning her batons with practiced ease. She closed the gap quickly and the Deru waited. When the crook and two batons met in rapid succession, Samson blinked repeatedly in order to keep pace with the eye-watering sparring match. The movement of weapons was nearly a blur as each combatant tested the defenses of the other.

The Deru was clearly the stronger and more agile of the two, but Lanadari had a deviousness to her fighting style that had Samson raising an eyebrow. She twisted and kicked out, solidly connecting with the Deru's oaken hide. The blow had the opposite effect and she staggered back when the Deru shrugged off the impact like a bird landing on a branch.

Lanadari was breathing hard and the look on her face was one of sheer joy. This was the happiest that Samson had seen her and he smiled in spite of the violence. She leaped forward again and weaved around the Deru's crook, delivering several rapid jabs to its thick, armored torso. The Deru bent at an impossible angle and nearly folded itself in half as it leaned back and struck out with the vine-covered trunk of one of its legs.

Lanadari crossed her batons at the last moment in an attempt to absorb most of the impact. She would have had similar success blocking an avalanche. Her batons went flying and she crumpled backwards in a heap. When she landed heavily and pinwheeled awkwardly across the grass, Samson thought she had been knocked unconscious. When Lanadari lifted her head and glared at the Deru, her once light-silver irises had turned black.

"There you are," a voice like oily smoke said from all around them. "Lady Dark, where *have* you been hiding."

The intricate runes around Lanadari's throat darkened and became consuming darkness. A purple stain crept down to the nape of her neck where it met silver runes that flared and fought the spreading taint.

"You cannot be here," she said through clenched teeth.

How could they all have been so foolish? Of course Shade and his influence couldn't be stopped by the mere destruction of a dark crystal choker. How could Celest have been so naive? Samson called to the VAST and they answered in a wave of crushing energy, eager to burn away the darkness. He paused, thinking back to something the ancient had said. Lanadari would need to face the darkness or it would consume her.

Instead of hammering Lanadari with VAST, hoping to expel the growing taint, Samson rushed in front of the Deru and thrust out his hand, palm out. A shimmering silver veil snapped into existence shielding both Balan and Deru.

The Deru put a colossal hand gently on his shoulder and looked down at him with haunted and smoldering eyes. It shook its head no, and then stepped through the veil of VAST. Two long strides brought the Deru to Lanadari's side where it knelt and hammered both of its trunk-like legs into the dirt. Tender vines erupted from the ground and encircled her ankles. Green pulses of light poured into her skin and the runes drank it in hungrily.

Samson watched as the light in the garden changed and the shadow Lanadari cast twisted and crawled to the other side of her body like a scuttling insect. The shadow frayed and purple mist swirled around the edges as it swelled to twice its original size.

"Strange, I cannot tell where you are child. Tell me, how is this possible? I haven't been able to sense you and now its like you are standing before me shrouded in mist," the shadow whispered.

Lanadari stood trembling. The fear in her dark eyes was painful for Samson to look at.

"You cannot hurt me anymore," she whispered, balling both of her hands into fists and glaring down into the shadow.

The shadow took a step, flipped upward, and settled on barely formed boots. The ethereal apparition of Shade, Master of Midnite hovered before her.

"I don't like what you have done with your hair," Shade said through a mocking purse of his ghostly lips.

Lanadari let loose a feral scream and swung her batons savagely at his smoky form. Her weapons passed harmlessly through the apparition.

"Now now, calm yourself. I have so many questions. Why haven't you come home?" Shade asked.

Lanadari stood panting, her hair hanging raggedly in her face. "I am home."

Shade made a clicking sound with his tongue that Samson found incredibly annoying.

"Regardless, I will not squander this opportunity. Tell me, did my gift of smoldering hero go over as good as I had hoped it would?" Shade asked.

He didn't know. Samson tried hard not to think, just in case Shade could read his thoughts. How could he not know that Tyler still lived?

Lanadari stood silent.

"You WILL tell me what I want to know," Shade hissed.

The black runes around Lanadari's neck appeared to turn red around their edges and she screamed. The vines around her ankles convulsed and the grass blackened in a wide ring around her and died. She gritted her teeth and clanged her batons together. Blue lightning snarled along their lengths and they hummed in anticipation.

Shade raised a ghostly eyebrow. "Good luck with that. Please wake me when you are finished fanning me with your helplessness."

Lanadari stared back at him with hate in her eyes. "Oh, these aren't for you,' she said softly.

She slammed both batons against her throat and raging lightning crashed into her. The apparition of Shade looked surprised as it tore into fragments and drifted away with the wind. The black runes encircling Lanadari's throat smoked and faded to match the color of her pale skin. Her black irises turned green and then back to silver just before they rolled back in her head and she crashed into the arms of the Deru, smoke rising from her still form.

21 – PELAGOS

Tyler grabbed the haft of the spear that had pinned him just under his arm with one hand and used his other arm to snap the quivering bone with a well-aimed strike. The spear cracked near the tip that had buried itself several inches into the decayed steel of the frigate wall behind him. His Warsteel cloak had detected the projectile before he could have hoped to react and tugged him just high enough for the spear to pass harmlessly into the crease between his arm and chest.

"Cutting it a little close," Tyler said, pushing himself off the wall and back onto his feet. The gash in his Warsteel shimmered for a moment and became whole again. He checked the charge on his heavy repeater and made a mental note. Half a charge left.

A vibration so intense that he nearly lost his footing hammered the ship's hull. The only way he could describe the noise was like that of an enraged whale. The Gale was close and clearly upset about its Riders corpses chumming the waters outside the air lock.

A large dark shape loomed outside the partially open external doors. A clawed hand appeared and gripped the door, crushing the decaying metal like baked mud.

Another hand appeared, followed by the glaring visage of the Herald. It didn't look particularly happy.

Lightning roared from the Herald's outstretched palm and struck Tyler squarely in the chest. The energy crackled against his armor and the blast sent him scraping against the corridor wall. The Warsteel cloak he wore drank in the excess energy and he didn't feel that much worse for wear. Until the second, third, and fourth blast followed in rapid succession.

His powered armor, overwhelmed by the repeated volleys, seized up with a belch of failing seals and the normally fluid Warsteel cloak became heavy and still. Tyler dropped to the deck, a prisoner in his own defenses. His thoughts went immediately to Polaris. He knew the balanite would answer his call. He reached out with his will but became distracted by a blur of movement. The Herald's head snapped back from a savage blow of flowing silver.

Crylona stood looking small between Tyler and the Herald. Starmist coiled around both of her wrists like an angry serpent. The Herald croaked and struck out with its meaty clawed hand. Crylona swayed and grasped the much larger creature by the wrist and twisted. She struck with the index and pointer fingers of her other hand in rapid succession against the Herald's thick, scaled hide. She released the creature's wrist and in one fluid motion spun and kicked the arm she had just held, connecting with the elbow.

An audible *crack* filled the ship and the Herald screeched in pain.

Lightning leaped from its open maw and hammered the deck where Crylona should have been standing. She had moved with such ease to avoid the blast, as if she knew it was coming. She sprawled into a roll and then sprang forward with her elbow leading, slamming into the Herald's middle. Green blood splattered the walls and deck of the ship as bones crunched and a ragged exhale splashed precious fluid.

Crylona swayed back to avoid a clumsy swipe from the enraged beast and then snapped off a rapid series of punches. Starmist flowed over her fists and empowered her strikes. Hide, scales, and bone crumbled like dried seaweed. The Herald stumbled and leaned forward, grasping at its chest. Crylona seized its lurching form by the back of the head and cried out with raw emotion. She slammed her knee with tremendous force into the Herald's face.

The sound of breath leaking from a mortal wound whistled agonizingly through the nearly silent ship's corridor.

"Commander, we have weapons," Shale's voice crackled in Tyler's ear.

"Light them up," he said, hardly able to form the words from the crushing weight of his unpowered armor.

"Aye sir."

The Herald slid unmoving to the deck, its head bent backwards at an unnatural angle. As the creature fell, the ship lurched as its long-silent point defense cannons thrummed. The hull reverberated back each shot from the cannons, and muted explosions shook the long-dormant craft violently.

Tyler felt himself starting to black out from the crushing pressure of his armor. He had never thought about how much of a curse technology could be. He would give anything just to be able to move his arm and shift his weight to draw breath. When tiny pinpoints of light began to swim across his vision he knew that he was in trouble. Blackness threatened to take him and he gasped loudly.

Crylona, appearing to have heard his distress, knelt beside him. Starmist slithered from her outstretched palm and Tyler felt tingling around his middle. He was raised up like a mother lovingly embracing her child and then leaned in a sitting position against a crumbling wall panel. A moment passed and Tyler drew his first agonizing full breath in what seemed like hours.

"Nearly suffocated by my own armor. What a story that would have been," Tyler said.

Crylona blinked at him from behind her mask. He thought he noticed humor in the way her eyes narrowed.

"A song to be sung for all to hear," she said.

The ship rocked again as an enraged blast of sonar, presumably from the Gale, tore into the hull. Water was beginning to leak in from cracked seals all along the walls and ceiling.

"This was a good outpost," Crylona said. Her voice sounded sad. "It has served its purpose."

Tyler tried to nod but his Warsteel had his neck kinked.

Enough of this, he thought.

Polaris hummed into existence across his lap where his fingertips were just able to touch the quicksilver Warquarter. He felt strength surge through his fingers, crawl up his arms, and sink deeply into his bones. His Warsteel twitched and became weightless and his powered armor hissed as its seals tightened and allowed him to move again. He scrambled on all fours to retrieve and holster his heavy repeater and then unclasped the Warsteel cloak, stowing it in his pack. He wasn't about to risk in the open ocean the same helplessness he had just experienced.

"It's time to get out of here," Tyler said, struggling to his feet. He leaned on Polaris, thankful for its strength. He felt fond emotions emanate from the Warquarter. They really had come a long way from the cavern where they had first met and where Tyler's mind had been broken. He hoped over time he would heal completely. There was still so much he had forgotten.

"Shale, let's go," he said, touching his ear for private communication. "Can you set the defenses to auto?"

Shale was quiet for a moment. "Negative, Commander. Suggested action is for you to withdraw while I provide covering fire."

Tyler knew the protocol. A drone would sacrifice itself to ensure the survival of its crew. Under normal circumstances and perhaps before his time on Acrea, he would have left the drone to complete its programming. Something told him he was going to need Shale in the future.

"Shale, I am ordering you to abandon ship and follow us out. We won't make it without you," Tyler said. "Polaris is running on fumes."

The Warquarter crackled slightly under his grip in protest but settled down almost immediately. They both knew that Polaris would be hard pressed to keep the ocean from crushing Tyler, let alone pull him along at the speed they would require to escape an angry Gale.

"Acknowledged, Commander. Stand by," Shale said.

The ship lurched violently again, this time from a sustained outward barrage from the cannons that sent cracks along the entire hull. Water sprayed inward and was quickly flooding the ship, soon reaching Tyler's waist. Polaris flowed like a melted candle up his arm and formed the protective layer across his body and bubble around his head. It was about to get cold again.

A final barrage from the point defense cannons was all the ancient ship needed to finally let go and succumb to the crushing weight of the ocean. A groan followed by the rush of water signified the death of the unnamed UEA frigate. Tyler and Crylona shot out into the open ocean amid a torrent of bubbles and debris. Crylona grabbed Tyler's hand and he felt them surge through the chaotic and churning wreck.

A blast of biological sonar hammered Tyler like a hammer on an anvil. His teeth rattled in his skull and Polaris strained against the barrage.

"I think we pissed it off," Tyler said, craning his neck to search the darkness.

"I don't know what that means, but it sounds about right," Crylona said. She tightened her grip on his hand and slipped her fingers between his own.

He felt his heart skip a beat. He hadn't held another woman's hand other than his wife's in years. Roughly nine hundred years if one was going to get technical. She squeezed his hand as if to tell him it was alright.

"We will be across the Barrens soon and should see the first sentry post. The Gale will not follow," she said.

Flashes from the darkness caught Tyler's attention and he squinted to try and get a better look. The flash repeated and looked like it was getting closer. It took only a few moments for Shale to appear, slicing through the water like she was native to it.

"Haste, Commander. We must make haste," she said, grabbing his other hand.

A jolt and a maddening stream of bubbles was the only indication he had that they were moving at a tremendous rate of speed. He looked back one last time to see if he could get a look at the broken wreck of the ship. He squinted as a small dot of light flashed for a moment and then expanded like a supernova. The Gale, a good distance away, framed the picture perfectly.

The sphere expanded aggressively outward and the shadowy figure of the Gale looked to get caught in the shock wave. The solid figure stood out starkly against the white-hot energy for a moment before tearing at the edges and flinging apart.

"Faster," Tyler gasped, kicking his feet like it would make a difference.

"I failed to mention that I rigged the reactor core housing to open as I left. It does not mix well with water," Shale said.

"That was an important oversight," Tyler said.

"Sorry, Commander," Shale said. Her tone didn't sound very sorry.

When the shock wave did wash over them it was like a gentle changing of currents that didn't do any real damage. Tyler breathed a sigh of relief. He and his companions had emerged from another brush with death relatively unscathed. It was like someone was watching out for them.

The crystal in his pocket pulsed and warmed for a moment. He closed his eyes and shook his head in wonder. Celest was with them, guiding them. She had a stake in the journey just as much as the rest of them. Would they have survived without her intervention? Maybe he didn't actually want to know the answer to that question.

****

The sentry post came into view after what felt like an endless journey through the darkness. Nothing else challenged them and the monotonous momentum through the water was mind numbing. Tyler noticed the light before the others. Crylona obviously knew where she was taking them, but she seemed surprised when Tyler pointed it out. They passed by the lights but were too far away to see what they were. He did feel eyes upon them and shook off the sudden feeling that he had just had countless weapons pointed at him, ready to fire.

They moved quickly through a shallow canyon that twisted and turned through terrain that held a complex maze of coral. Tyler had visited the coral reef off the coast of Australia back on Earth when he was a cadet and the experience had never left him. The comparison to what he passed through now was like calling the Great Barrier Reef bland in color and shape. In fact, he felt nearly overwhelmed with the sheer amount of different colors, shapes, creatures, and flora.

In short, it was utterly beautiful.

"The Garden," Crylona said, her voice barely above a whisper. "We are very close now."

The scenery moved slower now as Shale pulled back on the full burn of her thrusters. It was strange how Tyler was beginning to think of a drone as having a gender. Shale was in fact molded in the shape of a woman and had a gentle feminine-sounding voice with what someone from Earth would call an "English" accent.

Tyler drank in the color around him like a sun-stroked man lost in the desert. There didn't appear to be anything remotely predatory about the plants and fish that crowded the canyon on all sides. In fact, there was a harmony to the place that he had never before encountered. Great shelves of coral grew as far as the eye could see in as many shapes and colors as one could imagine.

The plants that swayed in the ocean current resembled kelp that Tyler had seen on Earth, but they varied in size, shape, and again—color. Many fish and fishlike creatures darted along the plants, not hunting as one might expect. Instead, they appeared to be playing games and enjoying a beautiful day lit by an unknown light. In fact, the light was coming from everywhere.

Everything in the canyon was emitting a soft glow that joined together to form a radiance that reminded Tyler of moonlight from a full moon. He certainly was feeling nostalgic moving through the Garden and only had things he had seen on Earth to compare it to. He was struggling to really compare it to anything he had seen before the deeper they went.

After a time, a much brighter light set the horizon ablaze, and Tyler had to squint as they approached it.

"The gates of Pelagos," Crylona said as they became enveloped in the light.

Tyler would have had his mouth hanging open if it wasn't already forced open by the shell creature keeping him alive. Before him, two pristine-looking UEA fighters hovered before a cavern wall with a gigantic maw that led into darkness. Twin spotlights from each craft were the source of the blinding radiance that had led them to the gates.

"Halt and prepare for scanning," came a firm but not unfriendly voice. The voice had been broadcast and then picked up by Tyler's ear implant. Apparently, they were still using UEA channels for communication. He paused for a moment to consider if Crylona also had a communication implant.

"Oh calm yourself Benjamin, you of all people know what I went to the surface for. As you can see, I was successful," Crylona said, her voice crackling slightly in Tyler's ear.

So she did have a comm device.

"I am not as concerned with the Sleeper. What has our scanners going crazy is that metallic thing you have with you," said the same voice, Benjamin, by Crylona's designation. "It is heavily armed."

Shale released Tyler's hand and then held up both of her synthetic arms. "My arms are not so heavy, and I only brought two."

The commlink stayed quiet for a moment and then open laughter split the silence.

"I don't know where you found it, but I will trust that its intentions are good with a sense of humor like that," Benjamin said.

Shale turned to Tyler and dropped her arms down. "What have I said that is funny?"

"Never mind," Tyler said, followed by a mock sigh. He really was starting to enjoy the company of the drone.

The two fighters moved off slightly in a spray of bubbles and allowed them through to the cavern beyond. Polaris seemed rested enough to propel Tyler under his own power the rest of the way and he followed Crylona into the darkness. Shale brought up the rear, silent and observing.

It was totally unexpected when they broke through the surface of the water into open air. Tyler blinked as the bubble that had protected him from the pressure and cold faded away and he gazed at a distant lighted city.

"Pelagos," Tyler said loudly, beating Crylona to the words he was certain were on her lips.

The city was comprised in bulk by the UEA colonization module. Habitation domes, farming domes, and grow lights. There were a good many lights coming from what looked to be homes carved right into the cavern walls that held the colony module like a lover's embrace. Point defense weapons lined a long beach that held a great many people that looked like they were streaming out of the colony module to greet them.

Several more fighters were moored on either side of the large bay and in the center, floated a sight that Tyler never thought he would see again in his lifetime came into view.

The UEA *Akasuke.*

22 – CRUEL WORLD

Razmal and Ralon were dumped unceremoniously into a large chamber moments after finishing the climb that had left their muscles screaming in agony. Razmal was still having trouble feeling his fingers and it wasn't just from the cold. Gripping the ladder for what could have only been a couple of hours had sapped his strength completely.

"Welcome, most esteemed guests," came a voice, shrill and squawking. It came from back the way they had been dragged from.

Razmal forced himself into a sitting position and found himself on display for hundreds of Avians that ringed the chamber. A raised platform complete with a large throne made of bone took up most of the far side of the chamber. On the throne sat the fattest and most hideous-looking Avian Razmal had ever laid eyes on.

The Avian on the throne had feathers every shade of the rainbow. It wore a thin crown on its head made of an exotic metal and rested its taloned hands on either side of the throne. It wore long white robes made of fine cloth with green glittering runes adorning the robe's edges. Dark black eyes regarded him with curiosity and a downturned curved yellow beak shined in the light from torchstones that flickered all along the chamber.

"I am Skylord," the fat Avian croaked. He waved his arm and his brilliant plumage danced in a kaleidoscope of color. "One is welcome here. The other, is slave."

Razmal raised an eyebrow. The Skylord didn't speak the Acrean dialect very well for being nobility.

"Slave?" Razmal asked, not yet daring to rise with so many hostile glares coming from the assembled Avian ranks.

"What gift?" the Skylord asked, disregarding Razmal like he hadn't even spoken.

Ralon had also struggled to a sitting position and studied his surroundings looking bored.

"We brought you a most precious offering from the kingdom of Moonlit Waters. However, I am afraid that because of our rough treatment it may have been broken," Ralon said. He was being very formal and Razmal stared at him in wonder. It took him a moment to realize the Acrean was using big words that the Skylord probably didn't understand.

Razmal could have sworn that Ralon caught him staring and winked at him.

"You see, the item that was entrusted to us to present to you is none other than an egg from the Moonlit Cliffs, laid by one of our Avian noble families."

The chamber buzzed with chirps, hoots, and squawks as those that spoke the trade language translated for the rest. Northern Avian nobility had an infamous reputation for inbreeding, which was producing less viable offspring and more muted-colored plumage which automatically relegated them to a life as a commoner. Only through breeding widely would a royal line continue its purity.

The Moonlit Cliffs had broken off from Avian society long ago and now had a completely different and desirable genealogy. The gift that Ralon was teasing the Skylord with was truly priceless.

"Bring!" the Skylord shouted, almost rising from his throne. Razmal was very certain due to his bulk that he was flightless and also unable to walk on his own.

Two Avian brutes hopped into the chamber and dumped Ralon and Razmal's packs unceremoniously to the rough stone floor.

"With care!" came a chorus of shrill voices from various parts of the chamber.

Both of the brutish Avians hunched their shoulders like they had been struck. The old Avian that had used what Razmal only could assume was the VAST limped over to the packs and turned them over with his walking staff. A small bundle, wrapped in purple velvet, tumbled out of Ralon's pack and came to rest on the floor. A hush settled over the crowd and the fat Skylord craned his thick neck to see.

The old Avian bent low to retrieve the wrapped bundle and let his walking staff tumble forgotten to the floor with a clatter. He tenderly unwrapped the velvet cloth and cooed with tenderness when the egg was finally revealed. The egg was large and white with a slight rainbow hue that changed color when the old Avian appraised it.

"An amazing gift," the old Avian said, turning and inclining his vulture-like head and neck in what could only have been an attempt at a bow.

The Skylord made a satisfied sound in his throat and settled back in his throne, fixing Ralon with a beady stare. "The price?"

Ralon spread his arms wide and bowed, his long hair brushing the floor.

"A true gift, mighty Skylord. We wish only to speak of a profitable alliance between our two kingdoms and to warn you of an impending invasion," Ralon said, standing from his deep bow, tall and straight.

"We know of the shadowed one," the old Avian said, still cradling the egg. "Our kingdom has reach even as far as the shrouded island."

"Then you know of his failed invasion of our lands?" Ralon asked.

The Skylord laughed loudly in his meaty throat and shook his head. "Invasion. Funny."

Ralon tilted his head and looked puzzled.

The old Avian walked over to a group of attendants and handed the egg to a very wide female Avian with white feathers that looked as if she had never flown a day in her life. When the egg was safely delivered and the attendants shuffled out of the chamber, the old Avian walked back to retrieve his walking staff and leaned against it.

"That was only a skirmish, Acrean," he said.

Ralon took a moment, looking like he was considering the words carefully before responding. "Then join with us against the coming attacks that are sure to follow."

It was the old Avian's turn to consider, and he rested both hands on his walking staff.

"It is customary to present the Skylord with a gift before making such a request," the old Avian said.

Razmal felt angry and he knew his face had flushed bright red. What did they think the egg they had just presented was for?

"Not just any gift. If you are asking the northern kingdom for help against an enemy, only a weapon will do," the old Avian said thankfully before Razmal did something he would regret. He was still processing the fact that he may have been called a slave. It didn't sit well with him.

"What did you have in mind?" Ralon asked.

The old Avian cocked his head to one side and bobbed his shoulders up and down. Razmal had once been told this was the equivalent action to that of a smile for an Avian.

"The gift of the egg has granted you and your sla… er… attendant safe passage through the city. We will show you to your accommodations as I am sure it has been a long day. I will send for you and we will talk more of the gift the Skylord requires," the old Avian said. He waved his hand and wing dismissively and the two burly Avians that had upended their packs seized Ralon and Razmal by the shoulders and hustled them aggressively out of the chamber.

Razmal fumed as the Avian guards led them from the audience chamber and across a rope bridge. He kept his eyes forward and refused to look at the dizzying drop below. Ralon was a few steps ahead, uncharacteristically silent.

Razmal couldn't shake the disrespect and scorn they had both been shown thus far. The Moonlit Waters Avians were a wise and gentle people. The contrast to the dirty and mocking Avians of the northern kingdom brought his blood to a boil.

His thoughts moved quickly to Gryphem. What had happened to the young Avian noble? The thought sent a pang of panic shooting through Razmal's chest.

"Stay calm and we will get through this alive," Ralon said over his shoulder. He had spoken in the Balan dialect with perfect inflections. "My bet is they don't speak Balan."

One of the Avian guards slammed a polished club made of bone into Ralon's rib cage regardless of understanding the words he had spoken. Breath blasted out of him in a long, misty grunt of pain.

"You will regret that," he gasped, drawing another savage blow to the ribs by the Avian guard.

Ralon leaned heavily against the rough spun rope handrail of the bridge. He spit blood over the side, turned, and smiled bloody teeth at Razmal. He winked and turned away, feigning great injury. Was he drawing the Avians ire on purpose?

Of course he was.

Razmal felt a club prod him in the back from the second Avian guard. He refused to give the guard any indication that he had begun moving again because of the not so gentle impact that sent a wave of agony up and down his spine. He stumbled between the uneven bones that made up the floor of the bridge but managed to keep his feet with the help of the rope handrail.

A cold wind started to blow as they crossed the wide chasm that was exposed to open air. Tall peaks climbed into a low ceiling of clouds. The wind turned bitter and small flakes of snow tumbled down in chaotic sheets. Visibility declined and in moments the bridge and far peak disappeared into the falling snow.

Razmal shivered. Not just from the biting wind, but from the anger that glowed in his middle. They needed a plan and they needed it soon. Ralon always seemed to be one step ahead of everyone else. Why was he going along with the abusive treatment? The image of the gates of Arabellum would forever be etched into Razmal's mind. It seemed that if Ralon wanted to, he could bring down the entire Avian city single-handedly.

Instead, Ralon trudged ahead of him in the now ankle-deep snow, hunched and holding his robes around him against the biting wind.

When they reached the end of the bridge and the Avian guards prodded them into a tunnel that looked to be naturally occurring, Razmal sighed in thanks. The wind was no longer able to claw at him and suck every remaining shred of warmth from his body. He cupped his hands in front of his mouth and blew on them to try and get feeling back in his fingers. He looked around as they moved deeper into the mountain, memorizing their route. If there was one thing Razmal was exceptionally skilled at, it was his sense of direction.

They walked for a time before stopping before a doorway that looked like several others they had passed along the way. The lead Avian guard pointed into the doorway with his cudgel and squawked rudely. Ralon ducked his way inside and Razmal followed. He looked over his shoulder and noticed the guards turn and stand sentry on either side of the door.

The room they walked into was a large chamber that sloped downward and was packed with huddled bodies. Razmal squinted as the only light in the room came from above where the cave opened to the cloudy sky. Snow drifted down from the ceiling in small eddies. It took his eyes a few moments to adjust and he sucked in a breath of surprise. The huddled masses before him were Balan.

The anger he felt before was replaced by something even more powerful. Rage. The condition of the Balan in the chamber was nothing short of barbaric. The smell of unwashed bodies and waste permeated the cavern. Groans and coughing sounded like a twisted symphony and somewhere towards the back a child was weeping. At least, it sounded like a child weeping.

"What in the name of Spero is going on," Razmal hissed through his barred teeth.

"Slavery from the looks of it," Ralon said. His voice sounded strained as if he was in physical discomfort.

"Could they be from the lost caravans?" Razmal wondered aloud.

An emaciated Balan a short distance away from where they had come in scurried over to them, having overheard their conversation.

"Many of us, at least the ones of us that are left, are from Itinif," he said, his breath reeking of rot.

Itinif was a Balan city that served as a gateway between the northern kingdom and the hill country of Arral. It was a trading settlement with minimal defenses, counting on the mercantile skill of its inhabitants over military might. Razmal knew of it only by reputation, having never traveled that far north beyond Moonlit Waters.

Razmal recoiled slightly and brought his hand to his face to cover his nose and mouth. "How long have you been here?" he asked.

The emaciated Balan chuckled and shook his head. "Time doesn't mean anything here."

"What is your name?" Ralon asked.

The emaciated Balan paused as if trying to remember. What could be done to a person where they forget their own name?

"Most just call me Mos."

Razmal stuck out the hand that wasn't covering his nose and mouth. "Well met."

Mos stared at his outstretched arm like it had the head of a viper and backed away a step.

"Apologies," Razmal said. He felt foolish.

Mos glanced up at him with fearful eyes. His irises were the color of pearls, giving him the appearance of someone blind.

"Is this everyone?" Ralon asked, sweeping the chamber with his gaze.

Mos looked around and visibly relaxed. "Oh no, this is one of countless places just like it."

Razmal closed his eyes. Countless places just like it? How many of his people were enslaved in the northern kingdom?

Mos cocked his head suddenly as if listening for something. He hissed and cursed and scurried away. Razmal reached out a hand as if he could stop him to speak more when a noise from behind got his attention. He turned and noticed the old Avian with the staff standing in the doorway.

"No, no, no. These are not accommodations fit for our guests!" he shrieked, bashing both guards just out of sight with his walking staff. "Come guests, come. I will take you the rest of the way myself."

Razmal didn't move. He was fighting hard to control his breathing and had balled his fists at his side. He felt a light touch on his back and jerked his head to look up at Ralon.

"We will be able to help them, but only if we learn more about what we are dealing with here. It is hard, but we must play along," Ralon said softly.

The old Avian made a sound like a strangled chicken in his throat like he was trying to politely tell them he wasn't going to wait. Razmal scrubbed his face with his hands and took a deep breath.

"Thank you, kind host," he forced himself to call cheerfully as he picked his way back up to the doorway. Ralon was only a few steps behind him.

The old Avian made a sweeping gesture as if to present the way and they fell into step behind him, the two Avian guards taking up the rear.

"Are you not afraid they will run away?" Razmal asked, referring to the slaves in the chamber.

The old Avian chuckled like he was gargling stones. "Where would they go?"

The two Avian guards from behind made similar chuckling sounds.

They walked for a very long time, following a twisting tunnel that led them deeper into the mountain. When the tunnel became dark and the torchstones lining the wall became few, the old Avian whispered something to his staff and the stone at its head flared to life, casting warm light in a sphere around them.

When Razmal felt like he could walk no more, they came to an ancient-looking stone door that closed off the tunnel. The old Avian turned and shooed the two brutish guards away with his arm and wing. They dropped the equipment packs they had been carrying and hooted at each other as they hopped back the way they had come, disappearing from sight.

Ralon looked around and shrugged his shoulders. "Some accommodations. You really shouldn't have."

The old Avian blinked rapidly and bobbed his head in an expression that Razmal could only assume was mocking.

"Listen well. You do not have time for rest. You are lucky that the Skylord allowed you to walk from his presence alive," he said.

Razmal should have known.

"Beyond this door is a place we do not speak of. It is an ancient place, guarded by angry spirits. Inside is an artifact that is your only hope of leaving Alya Cheyl alive. There will be no alliance. The only bargain that will be struck is your continued life and leaving our city in one piece," the old Avian said.

"What of our Avian companion?" Ralon asked, looking at the ancient door with a bored expression.

The old Avian shrugged as only an Avian could. "Good breeding stock. He will be well cared for."

"What is the artifact?" Razmal asked. His mind was whirling. Celest had bade them to the northern kingdom to secure an alliance. Now they were being used as pawns for an artifact that the fat Skylord would accept as payment only for their lives. What had the ancient guardian missed?

The old Avian placed a hand reverently on the stone door and closed his beady eyes. "I only know it from old stories. It is a spear that shines brighter than our most polished crystal and can pierce any armor."

Razmal quirked an eyebrow. It sounded similar to the weapon Tyler carried. But what would it be doing buried beneath a mountain? He didn't believe in ancient spirits either. After all he and his companions had been through in the past couple of weeks, he had a hunch it was more of what Tyler called "technology." Perhaps there was something beyond the ancient door that was the real reason Celest had sent them.

"Open it," Razmal said.

23 – MOIRA

Do not approach the sword, Zuh'Erg cautioned in Roarc's mind.

Roarc wanted not only to approach the sword, but he also wanted to free it from its bondage and claim it as his own. He could almost taste the power that was throbbing from the blade. It called to his most primal nature.

Zuh'Erg padded swiftly around the perimeter of the circular chamber to the far wall where he stopped and examined something. Roarc tore his gaze from Moira and narrowed his eyes to see what the Erew was doing. It was then that he noticed several archways at even intervals carved into the stone.

There were four archways, counting the one they had used to enter the tower. Each had an intricate set of runes carved in the frame of the archway. At the top of each archway was a square piece of stone with a thick glowing rune that stood out from the rest. The one that Zuh'Erg inspected looked like two circles, one dark and one light, that were about to touch and become one.

Roarc looked at each archway in turn, his curiosity momentarily keeping him from the insistent calling of Moira. The archway to Zuh'Erg's left had a rune that looked like a pool with a radiant circle of pearl. The archway to Zuh'Erg's right looked to have been gouged by the claws of an angry beast. Someone, or something, had done their best to scratch out the central rune that looked like a large rust-colored circle.

This is your ticket home, Zuh'Erg projected, touching the rune that was two circles becoming one.

The tower rumbled and shook like something had come alive. The burning blue flame above dimmed considerably and three crackling beams of energy leaped from its center and crashed into the stones of the tower. White light spiraled down the walls and sank into the rune-covered archways. The solid stone centers inside the archway cracked like broken clay and bright light leaked into the chamber.

The smell of ozone permeated the tower and the cracks in the archways became fissures that steamed and groaned. As one, the stones blew apart and sucked inwards, revealing rotating multicolored mist where solid walls had once stood. A complex menagerie of sounds spilled from each misty passage.

Home, Zuh'Erg projected, motioning for Roarc and Mazoris to join him.

Mazoris rushed across the short distance and clattered to a halt, stopping short of plunging into the mist.

"Sssafe?" the Sogra asked.

Zuh'Erg nodded from under his hood.

Mazoris backed up a few steps and then charged forward into the misty gateway, vanishing with the whisper of someone passing through a thin curtain.

Zuh'Erg turned to Roarc expectantly.

Roarc, however, only had eyes for Moira. The blade sang to him and begged for release from its prison.

Snap out of it, we don't have time for this, Zuh'Erg projected. The words were forceful and Roarc had to shake his head to resist the sudden compulsion to obey.

"Get out of my head!" Roarc shouted, taking a heavy step towards the giant skeletal smiths. He knew he was going to have to knock the chains off with something heavier than what he had. His eyes settled on the large metal hammer and he committed himself to the act with a forward rush.

The blur of movement wasn't nearly as much of a surprise as Roarc was sure Zuh'Erg had hoped. One moment, the Erew was standing before the swirling archway and the next he was charging through the air at Roarc, claws flashing.

Roarc had anticipated the move and knew his wall shield, while still strapped to his back, was still a potent weapon. He dropped into a lunge and bent at the waist and flexed his powerful leg muscles. When he sprang forward, the resulting momentum hammered Zuh'Erg in the chest with the edge of the wall shield.

Any other enemy would have gone down hard, but not Zuh'Erg. The Erew took the impact as if it was expected and slid down the wall shield like a sled. His momentum continued and he slid along the cobbled floor, his claws digging lines into the stone as he went.

Roarc didn't stop to see what was happening behind him and instead charged at the femur of the giant smith holding the hammer. Inches before he connected with the yellowed bone the entire leg moved. Unable to reverse his momentum, Roarc barreled into the side of the massive forge and banged his chin hard on its surface. He turned just in time to see a skeletal face peer down at him, twin coals of red burning in long-dormant eye sockets.

The giant skeleton shuffled backward and swung the glimmering hammer in a two-handed chop towards Roarc. The half-giant scrambled out of the way and would have surely been crushed had it not been for a sudden blur of movement and flashing claws that tore chunks of bone from the giant's forearm. The skeleton roared silently and shook the hooded and cloaked form from its arm.

Zuh'Erg tumbled through the air but before he hit the ground, vanished in a burst of wind that stirred long-settled dust like a whirling dervish.

Roarc struggled to his feet and shrugged his wall shield off his back. He felt naked without his maul but was determined to do whatever was necessary to free the dark blade from its prison.

Maybe it is restrained for a reason, half-giant! The words in his mind were sharp. Zuh'Erg was not happy.

You are right. I am not happy. The blade was not supposed to be here. The guardian wanted only for me to return the two of you to Teka.

Roarc rolled out of the way as a skeletal foot kicked at his face. "Can we talk about this later? I am a bit busy," he said. He strapped his wall shield over his forearm and jogged around the forge to try and put some distance between himself and the hammer-wielding giant. As he reached the other side, the head of the skeleton with the tongs turned and then looked down at him.

Roarc muttered a curse and raised his shield just as a yellowed bone arm wielding the tongs whistled towards him. The long metal implements shrieked across his wall shield, showering him in sparks. The impact numbed his arm and staggered him to one knee.

This isn't going very well, he thought.

The tower shook violently and he looked up into the burning blue ball of fire. It continued to feed raging torrents of energy into stone walls at an alarming pace. Stone was beginning to turn molten and smoke billowed skyward in ragged sheets.

The archways were not meant to be opened for such a long time. Please, Roarc. Flee from this place and live! The mental barrage from Zuh'Erg was pleading and genuine.

Roarc looked up at Moira again and felt the pull of the blade urging him on. He charged forward with a bellow and evaded another swing of the tongs that crashed into the side of the forge with a *clang.* One of the chains that bound the sword in midair came into view as he skipped away from another savage blow.

The chain looked to be spiked to the wall by a stout peg and the links were suspended twice as tall as Roarc. He could hear the two giant skeletal figures shuffling towards him and he made his decision. Without his hammer, the only option left to him was his wall shield. He hefted his shield, turned it horizontal, and flung it with all his might towards the chain.

The wall shield zipped through the air and wobbled slightly before it struck the chain, snapping the ancient links with ease. His shield bounced off the wall and skipped a short distance away. Roarc turned towards Moira again and was satisfied to see the blade had sagged slightly lower. He was also alarmed at how close the giant skeletons had gotten, their red eyes smoldering.

He ran to scoop up his wall shield and just before his fingers found the metal surface, a cloaked and hooded figure appeared and kicked the shield away with a furry and clawed paw. Roarc growled in anger and chased after the shield while avoiding the skeletal giants that were bent on crushing him. Did the Erew want him dead?

Of course I do not want you dead, but I do need you to LEAVE, Zuh'Erg said gruffly in his mind.

"Not going to happen," Roarc said just as he snatched his wall shield from the ground and turned to find the next chain that needed breaking.

As luck would have it, the hammer-wielding skeleton ended up doing part of the job for him. In its haste, the giant had gotten itself tangled in one of the dark chains and was trying desperately to extract its thin neck and forearm. When the hammer managed to strike at its captor, the chain shattered into a rain of broken links.

Moira dropped another couple of feet but still remained out of Roarc's eager grasp.

The tower bucked and quaked as more energy poured down from the flame above. Roarc nearly lost his footing and fell, but instead slid a short distance, barely keeping himself from tumbling into the archway with the scratched rune and mangled frame. A convenient booted foot had halted his momentum.

Roarc looked at the boot for a moment and then followed it up with his eyes to a rough leather legging, up to a thick hide belt, and finally to a crooked mouth grin complete with horrific teeth. A single eye stared back at him. A Yalon had come through the gate.

"Zuh'Erg!" Roarc bellowed in panic just before slamming his wall shield into the creature's mouth of crooked, blunt teeth.

The Yalon roared in pain and swatted Roarc away with a club made of gristly bone. The club connected soundly against his breastplate, but it blasted the breath from his lungs regardless. The Yalon clutched its bent jaw with one hand and turned towards Roarc with murder in its eye.

Zuh'Erg materialized in a flurry of claws and teeth on the Yalon's back, raking and biting the creature. The Yalon clutched suddenly at its torn throat and pitched forward, thrashing. Zuh'Erg rolled away and sprang back to his feet, whirling around as if he was looking for more prey.

The archway with the badly damaged rune flared and the swirling mist inside reversed direction for a moment as three Yalon spilled out, blinking in confusion. They all wore the same leather and hide garb as the first, but each held a different weapon. In all, Roarc had eyes only for the Yalon that clutched a heavy-looking stone hammer in its two massive hands. He ignored the one with the stone two-handed sword and disregarded the other that wielded two jagged hand axes.

He was going to get the hammer.

The skeletal giants chose the exact moment of the new Yalon's arrival to rejoin the fight. The skeleton wielding the tongs struck the Yalon with the hand axes hard, pinning the creature against the wall next to the archway. Sensing the danger, the Yalon with the two-handed sword bellowed and charged forward, cutting the blacksmith's-hammer-wielding skeleton deeply in the femur. The skeleton roared in silent agony and knocked the Yalon off its feet with a sweeping, backhanded slap of its bony hand.

Roarc used the chaos around him as an opportunity to charge the Yalon with the hammer who was staring up in shocked awe at the angry giants. His wall shield, tilted slightly inward, cracked painfully against the Yalon's shins. The Yalon grunted in surprise and then collapsed in a spray of gore as Roarc reversed his shield's momentum and drove the edge up under the beast's chin. The stone hammer dropped from the creature's limp grip and into Roarc's waiting embrace like it belonged there.

The skeletal giants engaged the Yalon's fully. Where their eye sockets had merely smoldered moments before, now they roared brightly like an inferno.

Roarc used the opportunity and broke into a sprint, headed towards the second-to-last chain holding Moira, suspended out of reach. A well-aimed throw of his acquired war hammer cratered the far wall just under the spike securing the chain. The stone groaned and thin spiderweb cracks spread quickly across the surface. The spiked chain lost its hold and fell away, swinging wildly. He turned just in time to watch Moira drop and accelerate towards the opposite curve of the tower wall.

The battle to his left looked to be nearly over as the last of the Yalon invaders fell bloody and unmoving before the blacksmith's hammer of the skeletal giant. It looked like neither giant had taken any critical damage beyond a few missing ribs and hacked femurs. The kneeling giant with the scabbard still had not moved and remained frozen in time.

Roarc crossed the tower floor and had Moira in his sights. The blow that lifted him off his feet and sent him reeling was a surprise. He crumpled painfully to the dusty tower floor and rolled like a runaway barrel. He came to a jarring halt when he slid into the wall and felt blood leaking from his nose and tasted it in his mouth.

"Not now," he groaned, sensing the bloodlust roaring through his veins.

He turned to see what had felled him and his eyes settled on the blacksmith's hammer laying crimson-stained, just within a few paces. The giant skeleton, now hammerless, moved quickly to retrieve its weapon and presumably to finish off one very angry half-giant.

Roarc didn't feel particularly like being finished off.

The bloodlust surged through his muscles, and he sprang forward, snatched the hammer in a roll, and ended in a crouch. The blacksmith's hammer felt incredibly long and heavy in his hands, but he hefted it defiantly regardless.

The tong-wielding giant circled around the far side of the forge and the hammerless giant thundered directly towards him around the other side. Roarc struggled with each passing moment to remember what he was supposed to be doing. In his bones he wanted only to kill, maim, and destroy.

Stay with me, Roarc, a familiar voice said in his mind.

Roarc barred his bloody teeth and surged forward from his crouch into a leap that carried him straight into the weaponless and reaching skeletal giant. He let loose a feral cry of rage and swung the blacksmith's hammer with both hands gripping its length in an overhanded chop. The giant crossed its arms in front of its face to ward off the blow. It might as well have had a shield made of smoke.

The hammer pulverized bone from hands, to wrists, to skull, and down through an ancient spine. The skeleton collapsed backward in a heap and Roarc's momentum carried him through his swing. The blacksmith's hammer connected with the tower floor, vibrated painfully, and broke apart in his hands. He raised his palms in amazement and watched the metal dust slip through his fingers and fade away.

He turned just in time to catch a heavy foot of bone to his chestplate. He felt the armor cave in and crush against his sternum and he struggled to breathe. He dropped to one knee and wheezed. The tong-wielding skeleton had joined the fray and Roarc worried this fight would be his last. The bloodlust had all but left him.

Roarc, not yet defeated, reached out with both hands and grabbed the giant's ankle. He pulled hard and twisted his body, attempting to topple his foe. His reward came in the form of a large metal tong across the back. His breath blasted from his lungs and lights danced before his eyes. He coughed and resigned himself to the next strike that he knew was coming and would be the last.

A blur of silver fur and a firm shoulder shoved Roarc out of the way just as stone fragments erupted from where he had knelt moments before.

Run! Through the portal, now! Zuh'Erg roared in his mind.

Roarc felt compelled to obey and staggered to his feet. He looked across the room and found the archway with the rune of two circles becoming one. It was then that he noticed the portal in the middle of the archway flickering weakly. He looked up at the blue flame above and cursed as it began to gutter and die. He sucked in a breath at the pain all over his body and limped across the seemingly impossible expanse. He knew his time was short.

When the black metal chain swung and bumped his shoulder he swatted at it, annoyed. He gasped and turned in time to see the marvel that was Moira, spinning in a wreckage of chain back towards him. Roarc raised his hand like a patient pupil in a lecture hall and closed his fingers around the bloodred leather-wrapped hilt.

Roarc, no!

The words echoed endlessly in his mind as the ageless darkness of Moira consumed him.

24 – UNREST

Shade emerged from the endlessly lapping waves like a shipwrecked sailor washing ashore on a deserted island. Thankfully, the island before him was *his* island, Teka. He fell to his hands and knees and touched his head to the gritty sand of the southern shore. This part of the island was the only part that ever received direct Acrean sunlight since the mists began farther to the north. The day was warm and pleasant and smelled like rain.

Shade hated it.

Allen crashed through the waves, his taught leathery hide steaming as water trickled and dripped to the sand below. He still wore an oversized pack that contained the precious communication equipment from the transport. He coughed and retched like a drowning animal and collapsed after only a few steps up the beach. He looked like a morbidly shaped turtle.

Three Immortal Guard emerged a moment later, followed by the new guard. The new recruits looked ragged and confused at how they had survived the ship hitting the ocean and breaking into more pieces than Allen could ever hope to put back together. The three Immortal Guard didn't appear to be bothered in the least, their faces hidden behind visored helms.

"Well then, a bit of a walk to stretch the legs," Shade said, starting up the beach towards the thick jungle in the distance. He didn't look to see who would follow. None of them had a choice after all. They *had* to follow.

Shade moved with purpose now that he was home. There would be much work to do in the coming days. He would need to get a full inventory of the remaining jump craft, airships, soldiers, and slaves from his considerable forces. What had happened on the shores of Arral would not happen again. He would throw every last resource he possessed this time.

The experience of being repelled by the Acrean defenses left him with anger in his belly, but it also taught him a valuable lesson about the current lay of the land. His invasion by air or by sea was doomed to fail, regardless of how many were under his command. No, next time, the invasion would come by land. The temple defenses would be useless if the plan that Shade had been hatching for the last several days bore fruit.

Shade led his new guard, Allen, and the three remaining Immortal Guard into the swamp as the Acrean sun hit the midway point in the sky. To call what they were walking into a true swamp was a misconception. There were no trees in an Acrean swamp, regardless of the continent. Shade couldn't recall the exact reason why the seedlings they brought from Earth never took root, but they had made do without trees regardless. The swamp they walked into now was made up of tall thick grass, noxious vines, stagnant rivers, and oppressive mist.

Home.

They walked for a time and the mist embraced them like an angry lover, oppressive and heavy. Shade could hear the others crashing behind him, especially Allen who cursed and slashed at thick undergrowth with his razor-sharp claws. He nearly leaped out of his skin when he felt a cool hand on his arm and he turned to a certain red-haired woman with freckles.

"I never did get a chance to thank you properly for freeing us, Master," Kushora said.

Shade raised an eyebrow.

The look she was giving him was like the one a cat gave a mouse before it pounced.

"I was foolish and confused. I am thankful for your lesson," she said.

Shade found himself speechless and more than a little suspicious. He would, however, play along.

"Oh yes my dear, I am glad you are coming around. There is so much to do and so little time," he said.

Kushora traced a delicate finger up his arm and tickled at his neck. Shade tried hard to force down the laughter in his chest. What did she think she would accomplish with this little game?

"What are you playing at, kitten?" Shade said.

"Oh, I am just admiring my handsome master and letting him know that I am sorry," Kushora said.

Shade grabbed her delicate wrist and resisted the strong urge to break it. He instead patted her hand with his other hand and smiled at her as sweetly as he could manage. Facial expressions were difficult. Especially the ones that didn't involve rage.

"Apology accepted. Just a misunderstanding, yes?" Shade asked.

"Yes," Kushora said coyly, tilting her head down and then looking back up with her big red-tainted eyes.

"Perhaps we should—" Shade started to say when a presence he thought dead thundered into existence in his mind. He felt himself push Kushora away roughly and then he stood perfectly still, reaching out with the darkness within.

"There you are," Shade said. "Lady Dark, where *have* you been hiding."

The jungle dissolved around him and he felt his presence transport an incredible distance to an unfamiliar place. He couldn't see the background of where he stood and it took his eyes a few moments to focus upon a figure he had studied since she was a girl.

Lady Dark.

At least, she looked like his dark lady. Her hair was different and much lighter colored and she had glittering runes covering every inch of her exposed skin. He noticed that the intricate runes around her throat had darkened, the same color of all-consuming darkness. A purple stain crept down to the nape of her neck where it met silver runes that flared and fought the spreading taint.

"You cannot be here," she said through clenched teeth.

Shade focused on Lady Dark and smiled as the light in the place changed and the shadow she cast twisted and crawled to the other side of her body like a scuttling insect. The shadow frayed and purple mist swirled around the edges as it swelled to twice its original size.

"Strange I cannot tell where you are, child. Tell me, how is this possible? I haven't been able to sense you and now its like you are standing before me shrouded in mist," Shade said in a whisper.

Lady Dark stood trembling. The fear in her dark eyes was delicious.

"You cannot hurt me anymore," she whispered, balling both of her hands into fists and glaring down into the shadow.

Shade took a step, joined with the shadow, flipped upward, and settled on barely formed boots.

"I don't like what you have done with your hair," he said through a mocking purse of his ghostly lips.

Lady Dark let loose a feral scream and swung her batons savagely at his smoky form. Her weapons passed harmlessly through his apparition.

"Now, now, calm yourself. I have so many questions. Why haven't you come home?" Shade asked.

Lady Dark was panting and her hair hung raggedly in her face. "I *am* home."

Shade made a clicking sound with his tongue. What had they done to his lady to make her so incredibly annoying?

"Regardless, I will not squander this opportunity. Tell me, did my gift of smoldering hero go over as good as I had hoped it would?" Shade asked.

Lady Dark stood silent, and Shade could tell she was struggling with something. What was it she was holding back?

"You WILL tell me what I want to know," Shade hissed, turning his dark will fully upon her.

The black runes around her neck appeared to turn red along their edges and she screamed. She gritted her teeth and clanged her batons together. Blue lightning snarled along their lengths and they hummed with anticipation.

Shade raised a ghostly eyebrow. "Good luck with that. Please wake me when you are finished fanning me with your helplessness."

Lady Dark stared back at him with hate in her eyes. "Oh, these aren't for you,' she said softly, slamming the batons against her throat.

Shade roared in agony as his link with Lady Dark collapsed under rivers of crackling fire. He wasn't sure when he had fallen to his knees or when his clothing and hair had started burning. The normally quick-to-react darkness within him seemed almost afraid for a moment before healing shadows wrapped him like a fire blanket. He felt disoriented and dizzy and there was an absence in his mind where something should have been.

Shade couldn't feel his Immortal Guard. Any of them. He could normally feel their cold presence and even the presence of his new guard, but right now there was only emptiness. It took him a few steadying breaths before he felt well enough to rise and when he did, only four people were standing with him. Allen and the three surviving Immortal Guard stood confused, but still loyal. The new guard were gone.

"Where…" Shade croaked and fought back a fit of coughing.

"They left. Something happened when you cried out and they all went berserk," Allen said.

Shade could tell a fight when he saw one. A few scuffs and dents on armor that hadn't been there before, fresh blood on Allen's claws and maw, and bloodstains all over the swamp.

"This looks hours old," Shade said, touching a slightly sticky drop of blood on the purple grass.

"You have been screaming in agony for hours," Allen said. "Kushora led them against you and we held them off. Given the look of her, they will be back."

Shade stood for a time, drinking in the healing shadows as well as considering his options. The new guard were instrumental in his plan to take the mainland. He could do it without them for now. They wouldn't last long in the wilderness without the cryogenics that would keep their hot blood from consuming them fully.

"We move. With haste!" Shade snapped, feeling recovered enough to set a determined pace through the swamps of southern Teka.

Shade remained silent as they trudged through the treacherous landscape, letting his body move mechanically while his mind wandered. Betrayal was becoming a somewhat daily occurrence and it was really beginning to cramp his style. How had Lady Dark turned on him in such a short period of time? He had imbued her choker when she was young to constantly ensure her obedience. He had always assumed that obedience would become habit. She was, after all, spoiled beyond her station.

They walked on through the night and into the following day without rest. At least without the new guard to pine over, they could make better time. The denizens of the swamp appeared to know what was good for them and they received no challenges from the hostile creatures that lurked. On several occasions, Shade felt eyes upon him.

Human eyes. He was fairly certain it was not any of the new guard, and that meant it had to be Marsh People. They, however, knew better than to challenge him. Even with an army.

On the fourth day of uneventful travel since arriving on the beach, the fortress of Midnite Waters came into view. Even from a great distance, the giant pit behind the city could be seen from where his precious transport had been buried, recently unearthed for the first time in nearly a thousand years. That same transport now littered the bottom of the Acrean Ocean in thousands of pieces.

It looked like much of the walls and towers of the fortress had been repaired and there was still an army of Sogra, half-giants, and Avians working to restore the dark stone monolith. It even looked like they had enlisted one of the monstrous winged abominations from the Pens to move heavy things.

"Home, Master," Allen said, his hellish voice thick with what Shade imagined was emotion. It actually just sounded like Allen was stepping on a cat.

The only thing Shade could think about was a hot shower, warm meal, and sitting in his favorite chair. He nodded absently and they walked toward the hardened and heavily defended main gate of the city.

***

Shade sat on his throne, freshly bathed and wearing new dark-colored robes. While he didn't physically need to eat, for some reason he had sat down on returning from the swamp and eaten enough to feed several people. The meal had been extravagant and primarily composed of juicy meat. He took sincere pleasure eating meat since he knew that Croyan despised it. How could anyone live on vegetables alone?

He craned his neck to see what Allen was doing for what felt like the hundredth time. The engineer was still working on integrating the communication equipment with the fortress defense grid. Shade wanted to have a chat with the annoying ship AI of the *Spero*. He had been unable to try his weapons control override for quite some time. Statistics were against him, but time was still on his side.

"We are just about ready, Master," Allen said from under a hidden panel that sat on the bottom of the wall where it met the floor behind the throne.

"Good," Shade said, thrumming his fingers on the arm of his throne.

A gong sounded in the distance, announcing someone seeking audience. Shade sighed and rolled his eyes. Did no one understand he was busy?

"Come!" Shade shouted, hoping the annoyance in his voice would deter any future interruptions.

An Immortal Guard strode confidently into the room. Shade looked at him and clucked his tongue. What a shame that there were so few left. He had lost so many on the Moonlit Waters beach. It bothered him that he wasn't actually sure how many Immortal Guard still remained in addition to the three that had survived. Dozens? A hundred?

"Yes?" Shade asked, steepling his fingers and resting his chin.

The Immortal Guard dropped to one knee and a rasping voice emerged from his full-visored helm. "Lord, I bring news from our Avian scouts in the swamps."

Shade leaned forward. He had sent scouts into the swamps to locate the new guard. Even though they would eventually come to him, he didn't want them ravenous and bloodthirsty when they did. He was, after all, trying to run a prosperous kingdom.

"And?" Shade demanded.

"The one with the red hair leads them. There are still as many as you said and none have gone out on their own," the Immortal Guard said.

Shade smiled thinly. At least Kushora was fulfilling her leadership role that he had instilled in her upon being converted. She might hate him and want to rip him to pieces, but she had to obey the basic primal commands imparted to her.

"How far away?" Shade asked, absently tapping his index finger on his knuckles.

"They have been heading steadily towards Marsh People territory," the Immortal Guard said. He looked like he was flinching behind his helmet, ready for Shade's famous temper.

"Ah," Shade said, standing quickly from his throne. He walked down a few steps and patted the Immortal Guard on the shoulder. "Well done, please keep me posted on their movements."

Shade could sense the surprise and the relaxing of tense muscles through the Immortal Guard's armor. The man stood, quickly backing his way out of the throne room. He paused, bowed a few times, and fled the throne room before his good luck ran out.

Allen chose the moment strategically, Shade was certain, to emerge from his tinkering and stand to watch the Immortal Guard leave.

"What's his problem?" Allen asked, rubbing his oil-smudged talons with a dirty rag.

Shade waved his hand dismissively and walked in his customary philosopher's pose around the room. Why were the new guard walking directly into hostile territory? Was it because they could sense Shade and were heading in the opposite direction? The pull to be at his side would increase as the days passed, but Shade found himself concerned. While the Marsh People were merely an annoyance to him, what damage would they inflict on newly made Immortal Guard?

The Marsh People were a collection fragmented tribes divided into numerous clans. Shade had never cared to learn much about them beyond their inability to be subjugated. They had been human once, and still looked it. However, something had changed them enough to be useless for most of his ambitions. They wore primitive armor and fought with primitive weapons but if you got enough of them together perhaps they could do lasting harm to his new guard.

"I am going to have to go after the fools," Shade said, stopping and shaking his head in disgust.

The gong sounded again in the distance.

"Grand Central Station, baggage department," Shade said in a growl. "Come!"

He hurried up the steps and sat once again on his throne, trying to look threatening. A dirty and muddy-colored Avian hopped into the chamber looking like it had been through hell and back.

"Mighty Midnite Lord," the Avian squawked and attempted an awkward-looking bow.

Why was everyone always bowing anyways? Who started that?

"Go on," Shade said, trying hard to hold his temper.

The Avian looked up at him and blinked its beady black eyes rapidly.

"It… uh… you see… I… uh," the Avian stammered.

"Out with it!" Shade roared.

"The Tyrant lives," the Avian hooted loudly.

Shade cocked his head, not certain he had heard the dirty bird correctly. Who was *The Tyrant*?

"Am I supposed to be shocked or care who you are talking about?" Shade asked.

The Avian looked genuinely confused.

"I fought in the Battle of Moonlit for you, Lord. I watched you destroy the tower where The Tyrant rebuked you, and I watched him fall."

Shade was suddenly very interested.

"Go on," Shade said, his voice low and venomous.

"I roosted in the Moonlit Cliffs until my wounds had healed enough, hidden and out of sight. It was when I was leaving that I heard that The Tyrant had survived and seeks an alliance with the norther kingdom."

Shade leaned forward and glared down at the Avian.

"Did you see him?"

"Yes Lord, a tall man in strange armor holding a shining staff," the Avian said.

"Lives of a cat," Shade sighed, feeling strangely elated.

25 – COLLATERAL DAMAGE

The ancient door swung silently inward and the air behind them rushed past like the corridor beyond had drawn breath. The old Avian limped back up the way they had come making gestures as if to ward off evil spirits.

"Return with what has been asked or don't return at all," he called over his winged shoulder.

Razmal shook his head in disgust and Ralon mimed what the Avian had said with his lips but made the sound of an unintelligent goat.

Razmal couldn't help himself and covered his mouth to stifle the smile and deep laugh. It felt good to laugh. No sooner had the sound escaped his lips than he felt tremendously guilty. He couldn't get the enslaved Balan out of his head. His people were suffering and here he was laughing.

He scrubbed his face with his hands and motioned towards their equipment. It took them awhile to sort through the gear since it had all been mixed together. After a time, they shouldered their proper belongings and Razmal hefted his familiar hammer and shield. The whispering of the VAST wasn't nearly as bad underground.

Ralon had yet to draw his sword and instead conjured up a series of floating and sparkling wisps that illuminated the tunnel. The small globes of light whirled around their heads, dropped down to their feet, and shot just far enough ahead where they could see.

The tunnel looked to have been cut with rough hand tools and was missing the polish from the tunnels up above. There were no torchstones or even a place to rest a stone. As they walked, the tunnel became gradually shorter and thinner, and they had to walk single file with Ralon hunched over so as to not bang his head on the thin braces. By the look of the architecture, it had been dug by Balan.

They wandered for a time, steadily moving deeper into the mountain. A light up ahead that didn't belong to Ralon gave them pause and they crept carefully forward. Ralon extinguished his lights and they let their eyes adjust to the gloom before walking to where the tunnel joined a large open chamber that shot upward as far as the eye could see. In fact, given the distance, the eye wouldn't be able to see how far up it went.

At the bottom of the cavern lay a shining object that looked like a smaller version of the Temple of Spero. How could there be another temple this far underground?

"It's a ship," Ralon said, studying the gloomy cavern.

Tyler had told Razmal of the ships from his home planet and the ones he had encountered on Acrea. They had also suffered the onslaught from the ship Shade had laid siege to Moonlit Waters with. The way he understood them was that they were all dangerous. But how had one gotten here?

Ralon stared up into the gloom, licked his index finger, and raised it above his head.

"I bet that goes all the way up to the surface," he said, motioning up.

"So it fell in?" Razmal asked.

Ralon shrugged.

Razmal looked down at the ship with suspicion. He hoped it was friendly to Balan like the Temple of Spero.

They picked their way down a broken and flaking slope. It appeared that few had traveled any further than the tunnel mouth, at least, nothing that didn't have wings. The way was treacherous and by the time they reached the cavern floor they were sweating and dirty. Razmal had scraped his palms and knuckles on the sharp rocks after nearly falling down a steep slope.

The cavern floor was relatively smooth in comparison and the walking was a great deal easier. Razmal kept looking from left to right, expecting an evil spirit he didn't believe in to jump out at any moment. They continued walking without issue right up to the nose of the ship. It appeared to be undamaged like it had been set down were it lay versus crashing.

Ralon motioned he would walk on one side of the ship and he motioned for Razmal to take the other side. They split up and Razmal swung his hammer in a small circle to work out the kink that had been building up in his shoulder and moved his shield higher up his forearm. He was still expecting trouble.

When Razmal found a familiar opening, he was cautious. He had watched the Temple of Spero vaporize unbelievers before and wondered if this temple would find him undeserving. He stood before the opening, staring at the recessed hatch. This was a ship, he reminded himself. Not the temple.

Ralon walked up to him as if he was out for a leisurely stroll and turned to the opening with his hands in his hip pockets.

"I've seen bigger," he said dryly.

"Have some respect," Razmal said, raising up on his toes to peer through the squat window in the center of the hatch. The glass had begun to cloud with age, but he could see what the Avians were after. Sitting in one of two chairs was an armored figure. It leaned heavily to one side and was supported by a long spear with a wide blade and wicked-looking point. The hand that held the spear looked like brittle bone as did one of the legs that was exposed when the armored boot that had held it decayed to dust.

The armor looked similar to what Tyler wore, but it was much bulkier looking. The person wearing the armor was long dead and ancient but seeing them sitting and leaning on the weapon instilled an image of timeless strength. How many Avians had tested themselves against the ship in hopes of retrieving the weapon and armor? Countless slaves was a more likely scenario. Razmal looked around and winced at a thick layer of ash on the ground in front of the hatch.

He took a deep breath, attempted to clear his mind, and stepped forward into the opening. He spread his arms and waited for the light of judgment that he expected would come. A low hum filled the air and a firm male-sounding voice in the holy language demanded his obedience. He dropped to one knee and threw down his weapons.

The voice repeated and Razmal felt the probing light again, this time accompanied by a blast of heat.

"I am worthy," Razmal said, gritting his teeth as the heat intensified. He felt movement beside him and a clang of something metal against metal. The intense heat and light vanished and the alien voice said something sounding far more kind.

Ralon stood with his hand against a glowing plate next to the hatch. The light caught his hand and wrist just right and Razmal noticed the skeletal metal glove he wore. He had noticed it on Ralon on several occasions but never knew what it was for. Apparently, it opened doors.

The hatch slid open noiselessly and the ship yawned as if taking a breath for the first time in centuries. As the air hit the seated figure, the frail bones holding up the armor disintegrated and the armor, along with the spear, clattered to the deck.

Ralon and Razmal carefully entered the ship, looking around for any potential danger. The entirety of the ship was a single room with only the two chairs, a row of blinking consoles, and a wall that had a picture that moved and appeared to mimic the shape of the ship with multiple red and yellow lights blinking.

"This was surprisingly easy," Razmal said, looking down at the pile of crumbling armor. None of it would do them any good given its condition.

"Lets just get what we came for and go," Ralon said, his voice having an edge to it. He looked uncomfortable, almost like they were robbing a crypt.

Razmal nodded and slung his shield over his shoulder and looped his hammer through a cord on his pack. He bent down and reverently lifted the spear that reflected the light from the ship that came from everywhere and nowhere at the same time. He flinched as a precaution, expecting the alien weapon to shock him or turn him to ash as Tekian weapons were rumored to do.

The metal of the spear felt cool in his hands.

Razmal whispered a prayer of thanks and turned to Ralon who had stepped back outside the ship. He was looking around the cavern and had a hand on his sword.

"Let's move. There are eyes on us and I would rather not be caught out in the open," Ralon said.

Razmal gave the interior of the ship a final longing stare and then strode out to catch up with Ralon who had already started back the way they had come.

They picked their way back up the slope and Razmal found walking much easier by holding the spear like a long walking staff. The weapon was well balanced and durable. Regardless of how many times he scraped it on the ground or banged it against a rock, the surface of the spear remained smooth.

"What do you suppose the ancients called a weapon like this?" Razmal asked, breaking the silence as the tunnel back to the surface came into view at last.

Ralon didn't slow and didn't even look at him. He was distracted and the look on his face told of some inner conflict.

"It's a Warspear," he said.

Razmal exhaled with a raise of his eyebrow. Was everything about war when it came to Tyler's race?

"How do you know so much about all of… this?" Razmal asked, sweeping the spear in an arc indicating the metal hand Ralon wore and the silent ship below.

They reached the tunnel and Ralon visibly relaxed and turned to Razmal with a sly look on his face. "Noble born, remember? I am supposed to know everything."

They stood in uncomfortable silence for a few moments and Ralon leaned against the tunnel wall casually and asked, "So now what?"

Razmal looked at him with what he was sure was a look of confusion to mask his insides.

"What do you mean? We go and give the Skylord the Warspear and try one more time to broker an alliance. I am sure with the gift in hand he will come around," Razmal said, not quite believing the words as they came out of his mouth.

Ralon remained leaning and stared at him with his quicksilver gaze that shifted and flowed in an ever-moving square around his irises. Razmal found it unnerving, like the Acrean was looking into his soul. But what would he be looking for? Their course of action was clear. They needed the Avians for the coming campaign.

"Let's go," Razmal said, unable to take the piercing gaze any longer.

Ralon grunted, summoned his floating like before, and started up the tunnel.

The two companions moved at a steady pace back up the tunnel. When they passed the ancient door and torchstones appeared at regular intervals, Ralon let his small spheres of light fade back into the ether. The tunnel was eerily silent and the longer they walked the more

Razmal felt that an Avian would come into view. The slave quarters came and went but this time, instead of huddled masses, the chambers were empty.

Where had everyone gone?

They reached the rope bridge and weak Acrean sunlight filtered in through gently falling snow. The wind moaned through the peaks and the air was crisp and smelled of heavy moisture. A commotion from up ahead could be heard when the wind calmed enough to allow the sound to carry. It sounded like a large number of Avians cut with the sound of someone or something screaming in agony.

Razmal and Ralon hurried across the bridge and into the tunnel beyond. They followed the roar of a large crowd and had to stop short of the massive throne room as the tunnel was jammed full of slaves and dark-feathered Avians standing shoulder to shoulder. The crowd in the tunnel was looking at something going on in the central chamber. Razmal stood up on his toes and craned his neck around the press of bodies to get a look. His eyes settled on that of the Balan he had spoken with in the slave quarters being thrown from the raised throne.

Razmal pushed his way through the crowd, using the Warspear as sufficient encouragement for any that would not move. He charged through the last of the unwashed masses, encircling the Skylord and his attendants.

He stopped short and stared down at the torn and bloody body of Mos. His wounds looked to have been inflicted by beak and talon. Razmal knew the Balan was dead, but he couldn't tear his gaze away from his fogged-over eyes, locked in an endless stare.

"Slave! You bring gift, yes?" said the voice of the Skylord. He sounded very far away.

Razmal felt empty inside, like he had failed Mos and the rest of the Balan slaves of Alya Cheyl. The feeling crept from his gut into his chest, and his shoulders slumped. He turned and approached the throne, cradling the Warspear. The old Avian appeared from the crowd and flapped his ancient wings to land just to the Skylord's left-hand side. He banged his polished bone staff on the floor and called for silence.

The crowd noise became a dull roar as Razmal knelt before the Skylord.

"Mighty Skylord, please accept this gift in the spirit of peace from the kingdom of Moonlit Waters. We ask for your participation in an alliance against the Tekian threat and help in defending against their next attack," Razmal said.

The Skylord chuckled and Razmal stood from his kneeling position. He caught the look that he and the old Avian exchanged.

"No. But gift, still mine," the Skylord said, leaning forward.

It was at that moment that Razmal noticed the blood on the Skylord's beak. Rage boiled over within Razmal's chest, and he bared his teeth. He glanced over at Ralon, who stood tall, and their eyes met. An expression was shared that defied logic. Ralon nodded at him as if knowing and agreeing with what was in his heart. He crossed his arms and his quicksilver eyes settled on the Skylord expectantly.

"Give him the spear, slave!" the old Avian snapped.

Razmal exhaled and a wave of calm washed over him.

"Gladly," he said.

He moved with practiced grace, extending the Warspear fully and gashing open the old Avian's throat. In the same motion he spun the spear in a shallow arc and caught the Skylord in his bulbous chest with the wicked spears tip. He stepped into his swing and drove the Warspear deeper into the Skylord, twisted, and kicked upward on the haft. The spear sang and blood misted the air as the glittering blade exited the Skylord. He rotated the blade again and separated the old Avian's head from his torso. Two Avian bodies hit the floor as one, and the audience chamber erupted into chaos.

Hooting and screeching Avian guards pressed in from all sides in a flurry of crude weapons, clacking beaks, and reaching talons. Ralon drew his slender blade and slashed open an Avian guard that came too close. With his other hand he summoned a chaotic ball of compressed air and shot it into the crowd. Feathers, debris, and screams of pain filled the air.

"Fight them! Free yourselves!" Razmal shouted in the Balan language. He struggled to free his dented shield from his pack with his one free hand and kept several Avians at bay with the Warspear.

A satisfying battle cry repeated from hundreds of his people as they lashed out at any Avian that had not taken flight. Razmal dodged a spear that had been thrown from somewhere up above. A great many Avian had taken to the air and were raining down arrows and spears into the crowd below. He nodded in satisfaction as a spear hurtled upward from a squat Balan and knocked an Avian from the chaotic air.

"This can't be what Celest wanted from us!" Razmal said, grunting as he pierced another Avian with the Warspear.

"Perhaps the Warspear was the goal all along. Either way, we must leave this place and soon. The riot will spread and Alya Cheyl will burn," Ralon said.

Razmal shook his head no. They couldn't just leave.

"What of the egg? What of Gryphem? We can't just leave!" Razmal said.

A blinding pillar of white light erupted from the throne and an angry female voice answered any additional questions he might have had. "You have done quite enough Razmal of Tonu! You will return home. Now."

Celest.

"So, maybe not the spear then?" Ralon shouted over clashing weapons, the boom of the white light vanishing.

Ralon slid across the floor, wet with Avian blood, and grabbed Razmal by the shoulder.

"Time to go," he said.

Ralon dropped to one knee and drove the point of his sword against the stone floor. He whispered and the buzzing of VAST filled the space around them. A thin shield of wind rotated in the area around them, deflecting spears and arrows away from the duo.

"You are going to need to help me with this," Ralon said, his voice strained.

Razmal could see the fuzzy outline of a portal forming but it looked like Ralon was struggling.

"I can't," Razmal said softly.

Ralon closed his eyes and then reached out his hand. "Take my hand," he said.

Razmal looked at his companion's hand like he held a serpent and recoiled.

"Take it!" Ralon demanded.

Razmal growled and switched the Warspear to a cradle under his shield arm and took Ralon's hand in his own.

The VAST sounded loudly in his ears and he felt power roar through him like an inferno. Ralon's eyes grew large in surprise and the portal snapped into existence fully formed. They rushed through the opening and left the beginning of the end of Alya Cheyl far behind.

26 – MOOD

A contingent of armed soldiers met them as they emerged from the frigid waters of the ocean. The soldiers were dressed in familiar-looking UEA battle armor, but the underclothing was colorful instead of the usual camouflage fatigues. Each of the soldiers held gauss rifles and had a sonic pistol holstered on their hip. The sight nearly brought a tear to Tyler's eye.

"Attention," called one of the soldiers wearing chest armor that bore a sergeant's insignia.

The line of soldiers, roughly thirty in all, came to attention. A young-looking lieutenant, judging by the insignia on her chestplate, saluted and then stepped forward.

"Welcome to Pelagos, Commander Tor, sir," she said in a rush.

"At ease, Lieutenant…?" Tyler said, letting a question hang in the air.

The curly blond-haired lieutenant blushed. "Lieutenant Parker, sir."

"Well Lieutenant Parker, thank you for the honor guard. All of you, at ease," Tyler said.

The soldiers approached one by one to shake his hand. The custom appeared to have changed over time and instead of grasping hands, the soldiers of Pelagos embraced forearms. It reminded Tyler of the ancient Roman greeting from the historical records on Earth.

Tyler noticed that Crylona was hanging back from the greeting and Shale was standing beside her, quietly scanning her immediate surroundings with a soft blue light that others wouldn't be able to see.

"Can I take this thing off now?" Tyler asked, scratching around the edges of his seashell mask.

Crylona walked over and nodded, grasping his mask on either side. She brought her masked face close to his and hummed quietly.

"This will be uncomfortable," she said.

"Oh I am sure it can't be any worse than the——" Tyler started to say and then gagged and coughed as the mask released its hug on his face and something wriggled up his throat and out of his mouth. He doubled over and retched repeatedly. Stars danced before his eyes and his ears rang. When he felt he had nothing left in his stomach he braced his hands on his thighs and pushed himself upright.

Wide-eyed stares met his own and he waved them off like nothing had happened. Crylona stashed the mask in her satchel and looked beyond the crowd of soldiers. A brightly colored procession moved slowly from the city down to the beach. Tyler took a deep steadying breath and walked up to meet them.

The procession stopped and a man with salt and pepper-colored hair walked the rest of the way to meet Tyler. He wore a brightly colored orange robe of cloth that had gold accents around the neck and sleeves. His eyes were a dark brown and his smile was warm. He extended his hand and the two embraced forearms.

"Commander Tor, I presume," the man said. "I am Tadashi Akane, welcome to Pelagos."

Tyler's eyes went wide. "Akane?" he said.

Tadashi smiled warmly. "If the stories are true, you knew one of my distant ancestors."

"Knowing your ancestor, only some of what you heard is true," Tyler said with a wink.

Tadashi laughed and embraced Tyler like a long-lost brother.

"Come, we have prepared a meal and some tea." Tadashi said, motioning up the beach towards the weakly twinkling city. "Well done, Crylona. Thank you for your dedication. Please, join us.

Crylona shrugged and stared down at the sand, appearing uncomfortable. She nodded and moved to stand next to Tyler.

"You never struck me as the shy type," Tyler said, leaning towards her and speaking quietly from the side of his mouth.

"I don't like crowds and I especially don't like the attention," she whispered back.

"Come," Tadashi said, motioning with both hands and turning to walk up the beach. His attendants, four in all, wore flowing lavender-colored robes and turned as one to follow him. Tyler turned and thanked the soldiers again before joining Tadashi.

The path they walked was well traveled and made of dull-colored cobblestone. Prefabricated, grey, UEA, single-story buildings lined the path on either side. Curtains covered a single window on the front side of each of the buildings. Most were dark.

The path widened into a roadway that led steadily towards a large central dome structure. There were several domes from what Tyler could see and the brightest light came from the ones on the outer edges of the city. Grow lamps, from the look of how the light leaked out from the multifaceted domes.

When they arrived in front of the central dome that climbed high into the cavern, Tadashi turned around and motioned for his guests to enter what Tyler knew was one of four intake areas that served as air locks and scrubbing chambers. He would be amazed if everything was still in working order. He hadn't been bombarded by greasy solar atoms in ages.

The thick air lock door was open and the inner door was closed. The chamber inside was white and spotless. Seven people crowded into the room and Tyler noticed that Shale remained outside.

"Are you coming in?" Tyler called over the heads of the others in the chamber.

"Negative, Commander. I will remain outside. I am not permitted to enter," Shale said.

Tadashi spread his hands helplessly. "It is by no rule of ours. She? Is it a she? No? It, is welcome."

Shale remained in place, her blue orb glowing softly.

Tyler shrugged and signaled he was ready. The outer door of the chamber boomed as it closed and a bright light filled the room. He squinted against the bombardment of energy and knew when the light faded he would be cleaner than he had been since his cryopod opened so many weeks ago.

The bright light switched off and was replaced by a softer radiance that appeared from the window of the door that led inside the dome. Tyler looked down at his armor as it steamed and nodded in satisfaction. The inner door swung open and Tadashi led the way inside.

They transitioned from the scrubbing chamber into the dome and the air became humid and fragrant. The landscape inside was that of a grassy meadow one would find on Earth. The first green grass Tyler had laid eyes on since arriving on Acrea grew under massive lights designed to mimic the yellow sun of Earth. There were crops growing in neat rows as far as the eye could see. A single tall tent made of orange fabric was placed a short distance from where they stood.

Tadashi led them into the welcome cover of the tent. Tyler shook his head in amusement. He had been near freezing for several days and now a few moments under an artificial sun and he was scampering for shade.

The tent contained a single long table with twelve chairs. The setup looked like a standard UEA prefabricated conference table with a finely made table runner of blue silk. Tyler had spent countless hours sitting and planning at conference tables just like it. The nostalgia he felt for something as simple as a meeting table was surprising.

"Come, sit," Tadashi said, moving to take his place at the head of the table.

Tyler took the chair to Tadashi's left and Crylona took the one to the right. The four attendants that had accompanied Tadashi disappeared back out into the bright grow lights.

"They will be back with refreshments," Tadashi said, apparently having noticed Tyler gazing after them.

"To be honest, Tadashi, this is all a bit surreal for me," Tyler said.

Tadashi smiled and nodded. "I can only imagine things from your point of view. I am honestly fascinated by how you arrived on the surface in the first place."

Tyler shrugged. He wasn't even certain how any of it had come to pass. "I wish I knew. One moment I was aboard the *Spero*, preparing for cold sleep, and the next moment I woke up crash-landed on the surface."

Tadashi was staring at him with rapt attention. "Fascinating. I am sure you have an amazing tale. I only wish we weren't in such a dire situation and could take time for you to tell it properly."

Tyler quirked his lip. Right to business.

"Go on," Tyler said.

The attendants reappeared, one carrying a heavy grey pitcher that dripped with condensation. Two others held clear glasses and plates. The fourth carried a tray heaped with what looked like rice cakes, meat, and vegetables. When the smell of the tray reached Tyler's nostrils he inhaled deeply and his stomach growled audibly. Tadashi grinned and motioned for the attendants to set down the bounty and to serve them.

When the meal was served and the cool tea poured into glasses, Tadashi took a savoring sip while Tyler hungrily devoured a plate of food, using the rice cakes to pick up the savory meat and veggies.

"As I am sure you know, our power situation has become critical," Tadashi said, taking another sip of tea.

Tyler nodded between bites and paused for a moment when he noticed that Crylona still wore her seashell mask and sat in front of an empty plate and empty cup.

"The Deep is a dangerous and unpredictable environment and the only thing that has kept us alive and thriving is the colony reactor," Tadashi said.

Tyler's gaze lingered on Crylona a moment longer before he looked back at Tadashi, who was staring at him intently.

"I have what you are looking for," Tyler said, producing the glowing shard that had been entrusted to him by Celest. "This will extend the life of the reactor."

A look of relief washed over Tadashi and he sat back in his seat and sighed.

"I had anticipated a search for a viable power source taking time," Tadashi said, absently stroking the hem of his robe. "The fact that you are here with a solution so readily is amazing. We were all worried about having to scavenge parts from the Vault."

"The Vault?" Tyler asked, his food forgotten.

Crylona shifted uncomfortably in her seat. "Lord Akane, perhaps a story for another time," she said.

Tyler shot her a questioning glance and turned back to Tadashi.

"I will hear it now," Tyler said firmly.

Tadashi looked at Crylona nervously and then back to Tyler. "Perhaps *vault* is the wrong term. It is a supply freighter that would have been scuttled to build the starport. That is, if things had gone to plan."

Tadashi paused and took a drink of tea. "But the danger involved with reaching the vault ship has kept us from any salvage operations."

"Do you know what condition the ship is in?" Tyler asked. Every ship he had come upon thus far had been damaged, derelict, and decaying. He remembered that each colony pod came equipped with a variety of maintenance vessels designed to perform initial colony tasks and then would be scrapped to build upon the colony infrastructure.

"It is in perfect condition," Crylona whispered.

"How?" Tyler asked, his heart beating fast. "You have seen this with your own eyes?"

She nodded and stared down at her plate.

"The freighter possesses heavy shielding, and they are still functional," Tadashi said. "The UEA built the starport freighters to last."

It was Tyler's turn to lean back in his chair and sigh. He looked across the table at Crylona who was still acting strangely.

"What do you know, Crylona?" Tyler asked.

Tadashi cleared his throat softly. "We lost her brother some years ago attempting to access the Vault. Its energy signature has been a beacon for the darkest creatures that haunt the Deep."

"I am sorry," Tyler said, feeling bad for pressing the issue.

"It's fine," Crylona whispered.

"We nearly lost you as well, young one," Tadashi said with tenderness in his voice.

Crylona stood suddenly, tears in her eyes, and hurried from the tent. Tyler looked helplessly at Tadashi and the man smiled. He reached across the table to squeeze Tyler's armored shoulder. "She just needs some time."

"I have rested enough, and I thank you for your kindness" Tyler said. "Can you please show me to the reactor?"

"With pleasure," Tadashi said as he stood.

Tadashi led Tyler back into the bright artificial sunlight and across the wide green meadow. The only thing missing was a blue sky, light breeze, tall trees, and the sound of birds. It would have been perfect with just a few small additions. But no, this was not Earth. He still had a mission to complete.

"Tadashi, may I ask you. Is the *Akasuke* still operational?" Tyler asked.

Tadashi walked a few steps ahead of him with his hands clasped behind his back. "Very much so. It is our primary defense when one of the bigger creatures gets the bright idea of encroaching on our territory."

"Is it still space worthy?" Tyler asked.

Tadashi nearly stumbled and it took him a moment before he answered. "Not likely. We have had to make significant modifications over the years to keep the ship running. Antigravity harnesses are usually the first things to go. None of our ships have a functional harness anymore."

Tyler grunted in acknowledgment and walked in silence for a time. He was willing to bet the freighter had a stockpile of harnesses and a variety of other useful items he was going to need.

"Have you had any word from Lieutenant Caledon?" Tyler asked. He needed to make sure the second officer he would need to fully activate the *Spero's* systems was well.

"Who? Oh yes, Thomas. Apologies. We stopped calling him by his military rank a long time ago. He was well the last time we checked in with Morgan," Tadashi said.

The name of the *Spero's* AI brought a pang of excitement to Tyler's chest. He was finally starting to get somewhere.

"We usually only have enough power to check in with the *Spero* every few weeks. I hope that what you have brought remedies the issue for us," Tadashi said.

"You apparently have never met Celest," Tyler said dryly. "This will remedy your power needs and more."

They were nearing the perimeter just before the interior of the dome wall when Tyler spotted what looked to be a bunker entrance. Two soldiers stood on either side of a recessed hatch that looked heavy and weathered with age. The soldiers stood a little taller when they recognized who approached.

"Lord," the first solider said with a bow.

"Commander Tor," the second soldier said with a salute.

Tyler returned the salute and Tadashi bowed. Tradition and protocol were alive and well after a thousand years. Both soldiers turned to the hatch and grabbed metal wheels that had been hidden by the way they were standing. Both spun the wheels at a rapid pace and the thick metal hatch split down the middle and banged open. Dim light flickered from the beginnings of a tunnel that sloped down.

"If you will follow me, please," Tadashi said, ducking into the slightly cramped tunnel.

Tyler had to nearly double over and duckwalk as the tunnel was far too small for him.

"Built for utility and not comfort as you can see," Tadashi called from over his shoulder.

The tunnel walls, floor, and ceiling were made of rough metal grates. Small lights that flickered slightly were spaced at even intervals along a central conduit that ran down either side of the tunnel. They walked for several minutes before the tunnel gave way to a tall and spacious room with a variety of consoles displaying habitation information. The center of the room looked identical to that of a starship engine room, complete with a reactor core and housing.

"Welcome to the heart of Pelagos," Tadashi said, followed by his usual pearly-white smile. "I hope you know what to do next as I have no idea what you are going to do with that crystal."

Tyler pulled the crystal out again and approached the reactor core. This was the part that Celest had been a little vague on details about. Was he supposed to open the reactor core and flood the entire dome with radiation? That seemed doubtful.

As he got closer to the reactor core, the crystal warmed in his hand and began to hum. He came within a few feet of the core and the crystal vibrated violently and cracked. Wisps of white light began to leak from the crystal and pour into the reactor housing like bees violently defending a hive. Alarms blared from several consoles and Tyler had a moment of doubt.

The crystal darkened in his palm and most of it turned to dust. A small sliver, pulsing with energy, was all that remained. Apparently Celest had given him a little extra for a rainy day. He pocketed the sliver and turned back to a beaming Tadashi.

"We are at full power for the first time in five hundred years, Commander!"

Tyler grinned back at him and his eyes settled on the console he had been waiting to see. The central computer hub of Pelagos waited.

"May I?" Tyler asked, approaching the console.

"By all means, please. You have open access as long as you need," Tadashi said, hurrying to a wall panel that looked to display defensive statistics of the Pelagos perimeter.

Tyler placed his palm on the console scanner and felt the link establish between the central computer and his implant.

The central computer greeted him and began to transfer information at a rapid pace. A great deal had happened in a thousand years. He used what the computer gave him to fill in the gaps from his own download that he had done what seemed like years ago when he had awoken in his cryopod.

"Computer, open a channel to the *Spero*," Tyler said, removing his hand from the scanner.

"Commlink established," a female voice replied.

The largest of the wall screens flickered for a moment and displayed the seal of the UEA for a moment before a smiling face appeared.

"Hello Commander Tor," Morgan said. "Would you like me to release weapons control?"

Tyler tilted his head slightly in wonder. Had he just heard hope in the AI's voice?

"No, that won't be necessary. This world has seen enough hardship. The last thing it needs is a barren surface or a quake that swallows half a continent. We will leave the cannons of the *Spero* to their rest," Tyler said.

The AI almost looked disappointed.

"How is Lieutenant Caledon? Oh, I mean, Thomas?" Tyler asked. "The two of us have a great deal to discuss."

Morgan stared back at him with a blank expression.

27 - THE GAMES WE PLAY

"How can he be alive?" Shade whispered, leaning back numbly in his throne. "I watched him burn. I watched him fall."

"He is stronger than you think," said a familiar voice.

Shade groaned. Not again.

Croyan stood directly in front of him, his green eyes bright and clear.

"You aren't going to push me away so easily this time," Croyan said, crossing his arms over his chest.

"Fine, fine. I don't actually have anything else to do today," Shade said with a sigh.

The Avian standing at the bottom of the throne glanced nervously from side to side. "Are you speaking to me, Lord?"

Shade ignored the dirty bird and instead focused on Croyan. He hadn't had the man appear to him this focused for nearly eight hundred years. Perhaps a lengthy conversation would glean a secret he had yet to pillage. Especially given that Tyler was alive. Again.

"So tell me then, what would you have us do?" Shade asked plainly.

"We have to complete the mission!" Croyan shouted, taking a step up the dais to shake his fist at Shade.

"Come now, it has been so long, you really think it would even make a difference now if we did? Time defeated all things." Shade said.

Croyan paused and his mouth worked soundlessly as he struggled with the uncomfortable truth.

"Now, if you are done grandstanding I have some scheming to do." Shade said, waving his hand dismissively.

The Avian scout, still standing petrified, took the sudden pause and wave as permission to leave. It scrambled across the smooth floor, leaving a trail of molted feathers in its wake. Avians were so sensitive. Shade often wondered how they had any feathers left at all with how many they lost.

"You don't have to kill him," Croyan said, his voice pleading. "There is no need to kill anyone else. We can still atone for what we have done."

Shade clucked his tongue in annoyance. "Now where is the fun in that?"

Croyan growled and charged up the remaining steps and vanished as his hands closed around their shared throat.

"This is still *my* body," Shade said, locking Croyan back behind a roiling wall of darkness.

Lady Dark had certainly done a number on the fragile balance he had kept with his volatile inner prisoner. The appearance of Tyler had been the opening volley in a desperate inner struggle and Lady Dark severing herself from his influence had only exacerbated a delicate situation. It would take time, but he would once again gain mastery of Croyan.

Shade sat thinking quietly for a time. The sound of rebuilding could be heard outside. It was symbolic for the inner walls that he needed to construct in the coming months. Croyan had been right about one thing. Shade had been hasty in trying to kill Tyler. The rage had overcome his better judgement.

There was a far better way to get what he wanted and perhaps a lengthy military campaign wasn't what was needed. What if he forced the fight to be brought to his own doorstep? The swamp would do most of the job for him, regardless of the forces the Acreans somehow managed to ferry across the sea.

"You know, Croyan, you did bring up a good point. Perhaps it is time to put the final piece into play," Shade said, his voice cold and dripping with sarcasm.

"Leave her out of this!" Croyan sobbed, his voice sounding like it was coming from the bottom of a deep well.

"Make me," Shade said, leaping from the raised platform of his throne and landing lightly on the polished floor with a savage grin.

He strode from his throne room, the plan solidifying in his mind as he walked out into the central square of Midnite Waters. There was a bustle of activity repairing the damage his long-buried transport had caused after its resurrection. Once they were finished repairing the fortress, he would redirect them to hardening the city's perimeter defenses and call in the sky ships that patrolled the northern and western borders of Teka.

The key to long-term survival on the island was keeping the Marsh People from coming together. He had spent the better part of five hundred years keeping them fragmented and tribal. It took a great many troops and resources just to keep his kingdom from being overrun. Had he pulled back all of his forces for the battle of Moonlit Waters, he was certain he would have been victorious. But he wouldn't have had a home to come back to.

Marsh people stink was notoriously difficult to get out of the draperies.

Shade crossed the large central square, dodging workers when he was able and knocking others clear off their feet when there was no where else to go. He was, after all, the supreme leader here. He had a reputation to uphold. It wouldn't do for anyone to see him kindly giving way for someone to pass.

He walked unhurried to the Tekian portion of the city. He passed every size, shape, and color of human imaginable. If there was one thing that Shade could say about his reign, it was that he took care of his people. Every one of them was descended from a large contingent of colonists that had mutinied with him oh so long ago. There had been enough to keep the gene pool diverse, but still, something had happened where they were no longer fit to become Immortal Guard.

A dirty boy in ragged clothing ran in the street before him and when the boy caught a glance of who was coming, he ran screaming into a well-kept house made from salvaged ship materials. Was that any way to greet his lord and master? He gave these people everything.

Most of the buildings in the Tekian quarter of Midnite Waters were makeshift shelters scavenged from hundreds of years of collected debris. The sky still rained at regular intervals burning and smoking wreckage from the *Spero* and one of the failed habitation modules. They had found useful material over the years on Teka, but its planetary position caused most of the rain of debris to hit the mainland instead.

Shade grinned as he passed more homes made of scavenged hull plating and partially burned, prefabricated habitation huts. Most of the material had been stolen from the Acrean people in coastal village raids. He may not have been able to safely steal the riches of Moonlit Waters, but the vast coast of Arral held untold spoils.

The homes gradually gave way to the warehouse district where a wide variety of goods were stored. Two Immortal Guard stood at the only entry and exit point which was a surprisingly intact metal gate that still opened and closed. He approached the checkpoint and the two guards saluted him as one. Shade nodded and they opened the gate.

A pang of regret sat heavily in his belly as he passed through the checkpoint. The Immortal Guard were now a fragment of their former glory. He thought again of the new guard running bloodthirsty and unchecked in the Tekian wilderness. There was very little that could actually kill them, but the possibility did exist. Shade could not let that happen.

But first things first.

Shade walked past several rows of neatly kept warehouse modules. The warehouse kit had come over on the transport with Shade and his rebellion over nine hundred years ago. Most everything that the UEA manufactured was built to last. The warehouses were a testament to human engineering. The fatal flaw of humanity, however, was that of life.

The thought rattled around in his head and caused his darkness within to roil and seethe. Humanity didn't live long enough to enjoy its labors. Shade had identified the problem long ago and set about to come up with a solution. Borrowed cryogenic technology coupled with his gift would grant any pure-blooded human eternal life.

At the low *low* cost of absolute loyalty to him.

Shade smiled at the thought.

Yes, he wanted weapons control of the *Spero* above. But what he really wanted was to convert the hundreds of thousands that he was certain still slept aboard. The Acreans would stand in his way and they needed to be eliminated. He was sure that everything necessary for a journey to the ship above was kept in the impenetrable rock below Castle Forgotten.

Who forgets where they put a castle, really? Shade mused, shaking his head.

Tyler was still the most direct way to accomplish his goals. Thousands of years might pass before he guessed the override codes to reduce the Acreans to dust. He certainly had that amount of time, but there was an itch within him that demanded immediate action. The darkness wanted out.

Shade reached the end of the row of warehouses and came to the perimeter wall that stretched around the entire city. The wall had also been a gift from the original colonists and had been intended to protect the main settlement on Arral. None of the *Spero* bridge crew could have known the surprising turn that landing would bring them.

He looked around, making sure no one was within sight, and searched the wall for the hidden mechanism he'd had installed. Along one of the wall seams was a small gap that would fit a hand. On the back side of the opening was a hidden button. Shade felt around, found the button, and pushed it down.

The wall swung silently inward, becoming a door with well-kept hinges. Shade didn't come this way often, but when he did, maintenance was always performed. He stepped inside and swung the door closed behind him with a gentle backwards kick. The door closed with a solid *boom*. He didn't need light to see by as he knew the way by heart and took the steps that he knew were there two at a time.

When he reached the bottom of the stairwell, automatic lights kicked on and a corridor made of a salvaged ship's innards led a short way to a single heavy hatch with a wheel-locking mechanism. The hatch had belonged to a frigate engineering bay that had met an unfortunate end at the hands of Acrean gravity and a crushing impact that rendered the vessel inoperable.

Shade grasped the wheel and spun it easily, hearing the satisfying *clunk* as the lock opened and the hatch swung inward. He stepped into a sizable room littered with storage containers, racks of weapons, and the crown jewel of his treasure, a single cryotube. He closed the door behind him and wheeled the lock once again closed.

Finally, alone.

Shade busied himself with cleaning the stray containers and half-finished projects he had been working on that lay strewn across several long metal tables. He wasn't exactly sure why he was going to all the trouble to make the area neat and tidy, but something tugged at him on a basic level he didn't exactly understand. Croyan was huddled in the back of his consciousness, incredibly displeased with what was about to happen.

"Oh, it won't be THAT bad," Shade said, putting a modified gauss rifle on a waiting wall mount.

He looked around and nodded at the neat space. He smoothed his robes and rapidly combed his dark hair with his fingers. A particularly glossy tabletop served as a makeshift mirror and he smiled to examine his teeth. Everything was in order.

Shade crossed the room to the cryotube and stood before it for a long while. The view port was frosted over as they often were when not exposed to natural sunlight. He could picture the woman, lying perfectly still and achingly beautiful. Her brown eyes would be closed and he assumed she still kept her blonde hair chin-length and layered. He took a deep breath and reached over to prime the release mechanism with three quick pulls of the red handle.

The cryotube hatch groaned in protest and swung open, releasing a large cloud of cryogenic gas. A woman lay perfectly still dressed in a formfitting cryogenic suit. Tubes full of shimmering blue liquid sprouted from various places along her body. The tubes drained quickly of the blue fluid and then filled with the milky-white reanimation liquid.

Shade waited patiently, refusing to rip her from the cryotube like he had the woman with the red hair and freckles. No, this woman deserved his very best. He stood like a long shadow, waiting for the liquid to do its job. His heart skipped a beat when her chest expanded with her first shuddering breath and she opened her eyes.

"Pistos? Where… Where are we?" she asked, blinking and looking as if she was trying to focus.

The woman squinted as if seeing him for the first time, and a grin made her brown eyes dance. The relief on her face drained away and was replaced with a frown when Shade did not return her smile. She raised her arms weakly and looked like she was trying to cover herself from his piercing gaze.

"Where is Tyler?" she asked, struggling to sit up but obviously still weak from being juiced in a cryopod for nearly a thousand years.

It was then that Shade smiled and took a step to bring him close. He reached up and traced a long boney finger along her delicate jaw, brushing aside a lock of blonde hair.

"Hello, Amanda."

EPILOGUE

The probe watched as another world burned. It had witnessed countless mass extinction events as bleeding planets leaked life, giving air and water into the depths of space like a sliced throat spurting blood. When the planet gasped its last breath and became cold and barren, the probe prepared all it had recorded and transmitted the data into the galactic expanse.

The Reish Ayen fleet that had gutted the celestial body under the probe's watchful eye turned and roared silently away. The probe logged the fate of the world to its data bank and scrolled through an endless list of hunting grounds, looking for the next solar system.

A strange thing happened. The list, once thought to be without end, blinked and would scroll no further.

The probe had never encountered such a profound moment. What was its purpose to be when the list ran out of names? It sat in front of the barren world and rechecked the list. The same outcome repeated after years of scrolling. It had been to every planet and solar system in its data bank. The probe, unable to accept a life without purpose, did something unprecedented.

It broke the law.

In the deepest recesses of the probe's memory was a forbidden data file that contained ancient star charts deemed too dangerous to explore. The charts contained known star systems of the ancients. While the Reish Ayen hadn't encountered their mortal enemy in several thousand years, they still marked any suspected bastion, no matter how abandoned, as off limits.

The probe broke through the relatively easy encryption that wrapped the data file and loaded the forbidden star chart data into its navigational array. Thousands of new solar systems and planets flowed into the probe's list.

It had purpose again.

The probe retracted its detection equipment and became long, sleek, and nearly invisible to prying eyes. With one final look at the dead world, the probe used its decaying gravity well as a much needed boost and slid silently into the deep of space.

The passage of time meant very little to the probe. Hundreds or even thousands of years could have passed before it finally reached the first solar system on the new list. As protocol dictated, the probe started passive scanning with the intent to find celestial bodies. Four rocky and two gas giants returned telltale signatures that life was not present. The probe logged the data and sped off to its next destination.

Several solar systems over countless years returned similar data. Rocky planets, no signs of life. Gas giants, no signs of life. Asteroid belts, no signs of life. The probe logged the data each time and continued down the new list.

The probe, after a particularly lengthy travel time, entered a solar system just like any other. The probe started its passive scan and found two rocky planets locked in a symbiotic dance, an asteroid belt, and three gas giants on the outer edge of the solar system. Both of the rocky planets returned the telltale signatures of life.

The probe logged the data and unfurled its detection array to begin looking deeper at the planets.

The first planet was rust-colored and did not appear to possess any surface water. The signatures of life were thick in its atmosphere. The detection array would take time to bring the surface into clarity. The danger with looking closely at any world was that the probe's energy signature increased astronomically.

Anyone looking would know that it was there.

The second planet was azure blue in color, mountainous, and covered in liquid water. The atmosphere was veritably glowing with signatures of life. It would take time to scan both planets and the probe was linear in the way it did discovery, so it turned its full attention onto the rust-colored planet.

The probe opened fully and deployed its full arsenal of detection tools. An image of a mayfly, part of the Ephemeroptera family, flickered in the probe's memory. The data had been taken from a slave world known as Terra, and was an accurate picture of what the probe looked like. It was that very world that had triggered the massive hunt for the species that had escaped the fate of the Reish Ayen occupation.

The probe was purpose-built to find humanity and to bring down the full wrath of the fleet upon wherever they were found hiding.

The rust-colored planet, while teeming with alien life, appeared far too primitive to bother with occupation or enslavement. The probe logged the data and put the planet in the "extermination" folder in its data bank. It was time to move on to the second world.

One of the sensitive pieces of equipment on the probe's array tingled and the probe paused. Had it just detected a power signature? The array tilted towards where the signature appeared to have come from and focused in. After an intensive scan, it found nothing. Perhaps it should get closer?

Protocol dictated that the probe stay well outside a solar system while it was doing initial reconnaissance. The probe pushed forward under lower power, aiming for an orbit around the gas giant closest to the solar system's star. There was something strange going on, and protocol be damned. When the probe entered orbit around the large lavender-colored gas giant, it began scanning the second rocky planet in earnest.

The scans came back much faster now that the probe was closer. The planet's surface was empty. The probe paused and looked through the data again. The surface had nothing on it: no water, no land, nothing. There had to be some kind of mistake in the sensor data. The probe strained its array and ramped up its power consumption tenfold, intent on capturing accurate information. When the sensor data came back blank again, the probe shuddered with anger.

The wide scan showed a world teeming with life, but the detailed scan returned an absence of data. It did not compute. How could the wide scan have more detail than the one that was targeted?

The array alarmed again, sensing an energy signature. Perhaps the probe needed maintenance?

The maintenance arm deployed from the probe body and began a full diagnostic of all key systems on the array. When the diagnostics check came back clean the probe began to suspect something else. Someone or something, was manipulating its data.

The array alarmed for a third time, but this time the energy signature it detected was of the catastrophic variety. The extended detection equipment that looked oddly like insect wings quivered for a moment as the transmit antenna deployed and pointed out into the void of space. It knew exactly what made such an energy signature.

The probe began to formulate its findings for transmission when two thick beams of blue roaring energy hammered through its torso like sunlight through a magnifying glass. Alarms blared, and the detection array melted and exploded into a cloud of spiraling debris.

Two more blasts of energy tore through what remained of its wings and breached the torso and primary core housing of the probe. As a last-ditch effort, the probe transferred its remaining power to its antenna. There wasn't enough time to transmit all that it had learned, and it was getting harder by the moment to process. It was leaking precious fluid and energy into space, and it appreciated the irony of how many planets it had witnessed in a similar state.

When the final blast of energy flayed the probe's torso wide open and detonated its core, it felt strangely unsatisfied with the message that rocketed out into the galaxy. Apparently, in death, words were hard to come by. Its optical sensors darkened, and its antenna repeated the message one final time before going silent.

Humanity.

ABOUT THE AUTHOR

Brad Bussie is an award-winning author, blogger, and science fiction enthusiast. He has spent the better part of his life in cybersecurity but has always had a passion for writing. In his second novel, The Band of Starlit Waters, he continues the six-book series, Spero's Legacy, which follows Tyler Ryan Tor and his band of heroes as they try to liberate the land they call home.

www.ingramcontent.com/pod-product-compliance
Lightning Source LLC
Chambersburg PA
CBHW011926300726
48970CB00008B/2596